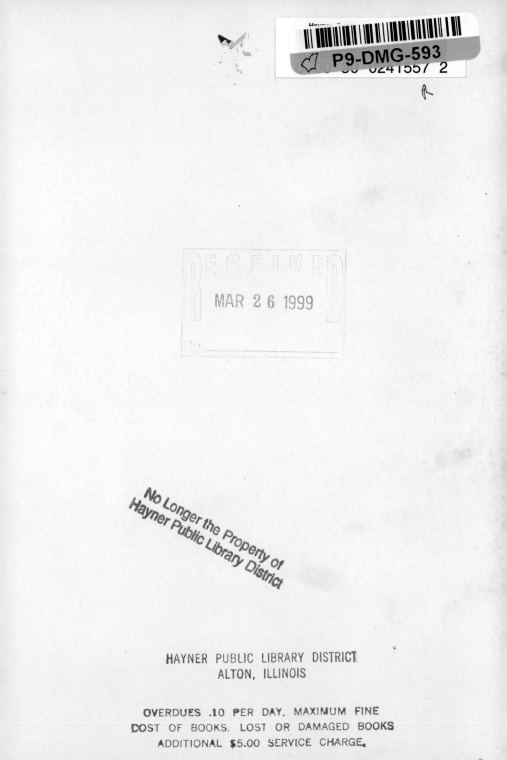

P9-DMG-593

An
Ordinary
Woman

An
Ordinary
Woman

A Dramatized Biography
of Nancy Kelsey

CECELIA HOLLAND

A TOM DOHERTY ASSOCIATES BOOK
NEW YORK

AN ORDINARY WOMAN

This book is printed on acid-free paper.

A Forge Book
Published by Tom Doherty Associates, Inc.
175 Fifth Avenue
New York, NY 10010

Forge® is a registered trademark of Tom Doherty Associates, Inc.

Book design by Lisa Pifher

Library of Congress Cataloging-in-Publication Data
Holland, Cecelia, 1943–
    An ordinary woman : a dramatized biography of Nancy
Kelsey / Cecelia Holland.—1st ed.
        p. cm.
    "A Tom Doherty Associates book."
    ISBN 0-312-86528-7 (alk. paper)
    1. Kelsey, Nancy, 1823 or 4-1896—Fiction.   2. Overland
journeys to the Pacific—Fiction.   I. Title.
    PS3558.0348064   1999   98-48929
    813'.54—dc21   CIP

First Edition: April 1999

Printed in the United States of America

0 9 8 7 6 5 4 3 2 1

To my mother

Introduction

In H. H. Bancroft's *Pioneer Registry*, she doesn't even rate an entry of her own; she's subsumed under her husband. But Nancy Kelsey was certainly the most important member of the little band of settlers that crossed the Sierra into California in 1841, the first of a tide of emigrants that would sweep California into the United States. This is Nancy's story, gleaned from contemporary narratives, family histories, and her own recollections and letters. I have dramatized it here and there, piecing together a single thread of narrative from many varying accounts, and presenting it as it might have looked to Nancy. Nothing is made up.

In assembling this story I had the invaluable help of a number of people: Lloyd P. McDaniel and Tom Goldrup, descendants of Nancy and Ben Kelsey; Ray Hillman; Bonnie Goller; Jesse at the Cuyama Market; the Bancroft Library at the University of California in Berkeley; the Humboldt State University Library; Pam Lyall; and my editor, Beth Meacham.

An
Ordinary
Woman

CHAPTER

1

On October 25, 1838, a girl of fifteen rode eagerly through the blazing Missouri autumn to her wedding.

She was a tall, pretty girl, with long dark hair and dark eyes and a wide, humorous mouth, her face shaped with the high cheekbones and strong jaw of her Scotch-Irish heritage. Her hands on the reins were strong and capable, and she rode astride. No pampered sheltered city flower, she had been working since her childhood. She could milk a cow, skin a deer, plant a field, drive a team of oxen, load and shoot a rifle. She had made the dress she was wearing. The child of pioneers, bred to courage and risk, she had grown up in the wilderness, only a few miles from the great Missouri River that was in 1838 the border of the settled United States. Her name was Nancy Roberts, and westering was in her blood.

In marrying so young, and marrying whom she did, she was choosing a westering life, one that would take her across the unmapped continent and change American history.

Her new husband was Ben Kelsey, twelve years her senior. One shoot of a sprawling family tree rooted in a Scotch-Irish immigrant who settled in Pennsylvania before the Revolutionary War, Ben was a big, bluff man with woolly red hair and piercing blue eyes. He was a hard worker, and a go-getter, too: he already had a farm of his own. He was sickly. Every once in a while a bout of something like malaria laid him flat on his back, but he was always up again in a little while, back to work, and back to dreaming.

Because Ben Kelsey had ambitions wider than a Missouri homestead. He simmered with plans for the future, all leading to riches and glory, and listening to him lit Nancy's imagination like a torch.

Ben was going places. Nancy was going with him. To a fifteen-year-old, there seemed no obstacle between heaven and earth that could stop them. Before Judge Applegate, the formidable Justice of the Peace of Rives County, she put her hands into Ben's and bound her life to his.

At first, the only place they went was back to Ben's farm, a clearing at the end of a long muddy pathway that was like a tunnel through the trees.

This was a familiar life to her. Nancy had grown up on a farm like this one, in a two-or three-room cabin made of trimmed logs, with a big stone hearth for cooking, a puncheon floor that had to be swept constantly to keep it clean, windows covered with oiled cloth, all the water hauled in from the spring. When she first moved in with Ben, winter was coming, and they probably spent their honeymoon getting ready for the cold time: chopping wood and chinking the cracks in the cabin walls and laying by supplies. Having just been married helped. As wedding presents their friends and families gave them hams and quilts, jugs of cider, honey, sourmash.

They had no trouble keeping warm. By spring, Nancy was pregnant with her first child.

In her few, scattered writings, Nancy mentions her own parents only once. When she married Ben, she became a Kelsey. His brothers lived within riding distance, and they did everything together—when one hollered, everybody came. Two of the brothers were married and had children, and there were Kelsey cousins all over Missouri. When they all got together, to build a fence, sew a quilt, plow a field, or celebrate Christmas, they made a loud, ebullient swarm—a comforting web of relations.

In the midst of this family Nancy ran her own household. She sewed her clothes and Ben's and, soon, their children's. She cooked their meals, planted a garden where she grew their vegetables and potatoes, tended chickens and milked the cow and cleaned house. Every year she would preserve as much food as she could for the winter months, when in spite of all, toward March and April, there was nothing left to eat but what Ben could shoot or trap.

In everything, she made do with what she had around her. Once in a while, in those first years of their marriage, they could have gone to Independence, the Jackson County seat, where stores sold staple supplies and some made-up goods, but everything was very expensive. Now and then a tinker would rattle down the lane in a clatter of pots and a cloud of gossip.

Nancy never had money to buy much. If she needed a tool she made one, or Ben did. She hoarded sugar and coffee in tins on her shelf; when she took the corn to be milled she watched to make sure the miller didn't cheat her of a few ounces of meal. She picked up windfallen apples, used and reused every scrap of fabric first as clothing and then as patching for clothing and finally as diapers and rags, she gathered herbs in the woods, as her mother had taught her, to doctor bellyaches and headaches. She had no remedies for Ben's occasional spells of the shakes, although she never gave up trying.

None of the Kelseys kept slaves, although they could have: Missouri was a slave state, according to the Compromise put together in 1820, and there were slaves on the bigger farms around them, and in rich households back in St. Louis. Slavery was a luxury in Missouri, and Ben's farm was too small to support more than the family that worked it.

Often, as the 1830s closed, it didn't even look capable of doing that.

This was from no lack of work. Ben had built the cabin himself, with his brothers' help; the Kelseys were great builders. Like all frontier people, like Nancy, they had a range of skills, from gunsmithing to distilling hard liquor, which they put to use as needed. Ben cleared some of his land to grow corn, and planted some fruit trees. Nancy tended the corn, too, those first two summers, while he went out hunting, his favorite way of life, roaming the wilderness.

That was another problem. The wilderness was disappearing. Missouri was filling up with settlers. Great stretches remained of the primordial forest that once had covered the country from the Appalachians to the great river, but Ben had seen all of it. He longed for new, untracked places. Because of his chronic health problems, a doctor had already advised him to go to the sea or to the mountains, but Ben didn't really need much of an excuse. He was footloose, a rambler, by nature; he had to keep moving.

But it must have seemed sometimes that the Kelseys were trapped.

By 1840, the burgeoning new American settlement had come up against the edge of the Great Plains. In its first westward surge, the young country had bitten off more than it could chew, and it was suffering hard for its greed. The tremendous speculation in land that began after the Revolutionary War with the Kentucky boom, which seeded the whole Ohio Valley with new people, had finally collapsed in 1837. The accompanying bank failures threw the whole young country into a downward economic spiral that by 1840 was a full-blown depression.

In their land hunger, the farmers and hunters of the settlements had far outstripped the economic systems of the young republic. Until new transport developed so that people on the frontier could sell their crops in the distant eastern cities, the backcountry was going to remain depressed and poor, in spite of the wealth of the land. Ben and Nancy Kelsey had their own farm, yes, but every day that farm was seeming less like home and more like a millstone tied to their necks.

Nor could the settlers escape by pushing out onto the broad Plains across the river. The government in Washington had given that land to the Indians for all time; it was forbidden, out of reach forever.

Of course the United States government's idea of forever was a little different than most people's.

Back before Nancy was born, Missouri had been admitted to the Union under the laws known collectively as the Missouri Compromise. What made this artful legal structure necessary was the perilous problem of slavery, and whether to allow the spread of slavery into states newly admitted to the United States. One of the terms of the Missouri Compromise allotted to Missouri a western border that was a straight line running due north and south through what is now Kansas City.

West of that north–south line was the Sauk and Fox Indian Reservation, for all time and forever.

In 1837, forever came to an end. With settlers clamoring for land, the government paid the Sauk and Fox seventy-five hundred dollars and some trade goods for the territory lying between the original north–south border of Missouri and the westward-trending Missouri River. This rough triangle of trees and bountiful meadows came to be known as the Platte Purchase.

The Platte Purchase was like the bell that tolls before the earth starts to quake. It signaled the growing instability of the situation on the frontier, and, indeed, of the whole United States. The Purchase breached the supposedly fixed and eternal western boundary, making further violations inevitable, and because the Platte Purchase became part of Missouri, the event extended slavery north of the Mason–Dixon Line, in violation of the Missouri Compromise.

Throughout the 1840s and 1850s Missouri was to be a continual hotbed for both these issues. Passions for and against slavery were already leading to scattered violence that would gradually become endemic, a low-grade civil war going on years before the official war broke out. And Missouri was the point of greatest pressure on the western boundary.

Throughout the 1830s that pressure was mounting. Immigrants were flooding into the country from Europe, aggravating the depressed economies of the eastern cities. As conditions east of the Appalachians worsened, people there were pulling up and heading west, in search of the fabled American second chance. But there was no room. Within only a few years, the whole Platte Purchase was filled up with homesteads. Still more people were looking west, hungry for new land and new lives.

The Kelseys among them. By the time Nancy bore their first child, in December of 1839, Ben was already planning to move on. While the sixteen-year-old mother and her infant daughter, Martha Ann, figured out together how to nurse, he was talking about selling out their farm here and going to Iowa, the Platte Purchase, or maybe Tennessee.

To Nancy, *where* hardly mattered. Wherever Ben went, she would go. She and Ann. She looked into the face of her tiny daughter, full of infinite, untested dreams.

Selling out here, however, was going to be something of a problem. On the whole frontier, times were bad and getting worse. The Panic of 1837 had closed banks and dried up the cash. Even if you had something to sell, like that old staple commodity, deer hides, there was nobody who could buy it. Jesse Applegate, whose sister Lucy was married to Ben's brother Sam, had loaded up a whole steamboat with lard and bacon, and gotten only a hundred dollars for it, and then it had all been burnt for fuel.

And the cost of those few things these farmers needed to buy— cloth, coffee, iron, gunpowder—was steadily climbing. When Ben and his brothers, big outspoken Sam, and the hot-tempered Andy, and Zed, got together in the Kelsey cabin to talk over the future, what they did mostly was gripe. Nancy didn't see they were getting anywhere at getting anywhere.

Then John Marsh's letter came.

The Kelseys may have met this young Harvard man, gifted liar and crank, when he worked as a sales clerk in a store in Independence, the frontier city and county seat, only a few miles from Ben and Nancy's farm. Raw, violent Independence, with its fringe of wharves along the Missouri, its blocks of warehouses on miry streets, was the gateway to the West. From Independence the beaver trappers set forth on their yearly treks to the Rockies. From Independence, too, caravans of wagons rumbled on down the Santa Fe Trail into northern Mexico, taking out trade goods and bringing back mules and fur.

John Marsh, clerking in a store, waiting every day on people with tales of gold and adventure to the west, one day took off along the Santa Fe Trail. Somewhere he began to hear about a fabulous country on the Pacific coast, where the dew was sweet as honey and the sun shone without cease. A place called California.

From Santa Fe he traveled down into Sonora and over to the great Mexican port of Guaymas, on the west coast. From Guaymas he took a schooner north to Monterey, California's only port of entry.

There, thousands of miles from anybody who could say otherwise, he announced he was a medical doctor. Since this made him the only physician in the entire territory it gave him a special cachet. He was a voracious reader, able to learn enough from books to practice, and he was good with words. He talked his way into a grant of land, up in the north of Mexican California near San Francisco Bay. There, he built a ranch, patched up broken legs, delivered babies, and wrote a series of letters back home to friends in Missouri.

California, he said, was wonderful. And empty. The land was fertile, the climate sublime, the Indians meek, and the local Mexican government utterly lax: paradise was there by the Pacific, just waiting for enterprising people to come grab it.

Marsh had even figured out a way to get there. The Santa Fe Trail was too hard and long and expensive for most people; going

by sea was even longer and cost even more. Marsh had devised a
more direct route. In his travels, he had picked up a lot of information about the territory lying between California and Missouri,
and he thought it possible to come straight across the continent. In
his letters, he presented this route with as much confidence as if he
had actually traveled it himself. He proclaimed it direct and easy for
wagons, with good pasturage and water all the way, a matter of a
few months on the road, with Eden at the end of it.

Marsh sent his letters to several friends in Jackson County, Independence's hinterland, including local farmers like Billy Baldridge
and John Bartleson, who knew everybody. Baldridge and Bartleson
passed on the letters to the newspapers. Ben Kelsey could not read,
but Nancy could, and when she read him the letters out of the
newspaper Ben made up his mind where it was they were going.

The long discussions around the Kelseys' front room began to
boil with excitement, and every other word was California. Soon
Ben had his brothers talked into it too.

They weren't the only ones. A sort of California fever was
sweeping through Missouri. All across Jackson County, people
were signing on. Marsh's correspondents, Baldridge and Bartleson,
were among the first, but in the spring of 1840 dozens of other men
pledged to join them. Many intended to take their wives and children. Of course, they had missed the best time for leaving[1] this year,
but they all vowed that come hell or high water they would set off
next year for California.

The movement got another boost when the dashing Antoine
Robidoux turned up in the Platte Purchase, just north of Independence on the river.

Robidoux, the brother of Joseph Robidoux who founded St.
Joseph, Missouri, was a fur man. In the late 1820s he had operated

[1]People left for the West in mid-May, when the grass was green. If they left
earlier, their stock would starve; leaving later, they risked wintering in the
mountains.

a trading post in the Uinta Mountains in Colorado, and from there had traveled down to Santa Fe. From Santa Fe he made his way through Arizona to California, where he spent some time in Monterey.

Back in Missouri, he talked so much and so loud about the wonders of far-off California that some of his listeners organized a meeting in the little settlement of Weston, up the Missouri from Independence, so that Robidoux could tell them all again.

Robidoux laid it on thick. He talked about the oranges and the sunshine, the countless wild horses and cattle, the fabled hospitality of the Californios, the docility of the Indians. The flavor of his discourse can be inferred from his answer to a question about fevers and agues, a primary concern of the Missouri settler.[2]

"He said there was but one man in California that had ever had a chill there, and it was a matter of so much wonderment to the people of Monterey that they went eighteen miles into the country to see him shake."[3] So wrote young John Bidwell, Platte pioneer, who took to Robidoux's words with enthusiasm.

Only twenty, Bidwell had already demonstrated both unusual resourcefulness and the fiddlefooted wanderlust that characterized so many young men of the time and place. Born in New York State, he had tried to homestead, taught school to make ends meet, and eventually become the school's principal. When he encountered Robidoux, he had just lost his stake in the Platte to a claim-jumper, mostly because he was not yet twenty-one and hence not of legal age. He needed somewhere to go and California sounded perfect to him. With a few friends, he formed the Western Emigration Society. Within a month they had five hundred names pledged.

Back in Jackson County, Ben was trying to sell the Kelseys' farm. Nancy started packing. She was pregnant again, and with some apprehension she tried to judge when the baby would be born:

[2]Ben Kelsey had a recurring ague of some sort.
[3]Bidwell III.

sometime in the winter, she hoped, and not later. In the spring, the emigrants were to gather at Sapling Grove, just west of the Missouri. It would be a lot easier to bear her baby here, at home, than it would be on the trail.

The days spun by in a clatter of excitement. Everybody around her, Ben's brother Sam and his wife and their children, Ben's other brothers, everyone, it seemed, in Jackson County—was getting ready to travel west. No one talked about anything but California. A great current of mob feeling was carrying them all along as if on a magic carpet.

The trouble was that no one had much idea where they were going.

Marsh's instructions, based entirely on hearsay, myth, and wishful thinking, were for crossing the Rockies at South Pass, finding the Great Salt Lake, and heading west, and, incidentally, looking around along the way for somebody to guide them over the Sierra. No one had any more idea of their course than that. No one had ever gone that way before.

There were some maps. Up in Platte County, John Bidwell was boarding with a man who had a map of the West which showed Salt Lake as larger than the Mississippi River, drained by several rivers flowing away out of it to the Pacific Ocean. On the basis of this map Bidwell packed the tools to make boats into his wagonload of supplies. He and another man were going as partners; Bidwell was supplying the wagon, and the other man the mules to draw it.

That winter, Bidwell traveled down to Independence a couple of times to talk up the Western Emigration Society. Maybe he was at the great noisy ebullient meeting on February 1, 1841, in Independence, where Marsh's friends in Jackson County organized themselves into a company for the purpose of emigrating to California. Of fifty-eight people who committed themselves then and there, nineteen announced that they would bring their families. One of these was Benjamin Kelsey.

Nancy was not there. Nancy was at home having her second baby.

She missed quite a gathering. Ben certainly told her about it, once he got back home. Independence was the jumping off place for all treks westward, and people were seasoned at the rituals and necessities of departure even if they never left the safety of the riverbank. Figuring there had to be onlookers and homebodies besides the enthusiastic fifty-eight, the crowd was considerable. The gathering must have had some of the hoopla and heady excitement of a camp meeting or a political convention, with glorious speeches and shouts from the audience, and a general atmosphere of anything goes.

The group voted on and accepted a number of resolutions. High-minded and noble souls that they were, they resolved to go in peace.[4] They resolved to meet at Sapling Grove, beyond the Missouri in Kansas, on May 10, and to elect officers then, "as other companies are expected to join them." They resolved that everybody should make his own preparations, bringing enough to eat to last "till they reach the Buffalo region at least," and that nobody should bring liquor, "except for medicinal purposes."

Somebody presented them with a cannon, which (perhaps forgetful of the peace resolution) they resolved to accept, and solemnly arranged to have properly equipped (i.e., installed on trucks) and supplied with ammunition. This cannon was never mentioned again.

They resolved to follow Marsh's route, which led by Great Salt Lake. This was critical. Sapling Grove lay on the Santa Fe Road, and there was a route already established to California along that road, one of the most brutal overland routes on the continent. Torturous, circuitous, ruinously expensive, it was beyond the means of the ordinary pioneer.[5] These would-be settlers declared themselves

---

[4]It's unclear what they thought the alternative was. But note the cannon.
[5]It also took people to the least hospitable part of California, physically and politically.

ready to strike directly west across the continent, the shortest, hence the fastest and cheapest route possible.

So, all resolved and ready, the group broke up and went home. Ben took back word of everything that had happened to Nancy, but for a while she paid little attention. Only a few days after the meeting in Independence, on the Kelsey farm, she bore her second child, a boy, whom they named Samuel.

At the age of eight days, the little boy died.

Nancy was only seventeen, all her feelings still pure with youth: the loss must have seemed deep and cold as a well. The baby's death probably shook her confidence, too; like all mothers, she thought herself somehow to blame. She rose up from the grief of this child-bed into the California adventure. There was this other work to do. She had a new start ahead of her. Planning and preparing filled up her hands and the days and distracted her from the death. The trip was another kind of commitment to replace the one to the baby that wasn't there.

She still had little Ann, too—Martha Ann was her full name; she was a year old, a hardy baby already beginning to do things for herself. Sometimes Nancy picked her up, just to hold her, and sang to her, the old songs that had come down with her mother and grandmother from the distant unknown homeland, songs with an undertone of sorrow. Arkansaw Traveller, Polly Von. Beneath the young mother's apron there was an emptiness big as the world, that only she knew about.

But they were going to California—to California!

She must have daydreamed about what their life would be like there. She knew nothing but Missouri: in spite of what she had heard, her imaginings would have been of green hills and woods and small farms, blazing hot summers and icy winters. As she folded clothes into the chests that would go on the wagons, took down the sides of bacon out of the smokehouse, and looked for a good dutch oven, she thought of a life like the one she already had, in a place like where she already was.

She would have familiar faces all around her, on the trip. Of Ben's brothers who were going, Zed was still a bachelor. His younger brother Andy's wife had just recently died. But Sam had a wife, Lucretia, whom everybody called Lucy, and three children. Lucy's widowed sister Mrs. Grey was going too, with her child. There would be other women, then, to share the constant grind of work, to help with children, gossip, confide in.

Lucy Kelsey was a woman of parts, too. Her uncle was Judge Applegate, and she herself was forceful and opinionated. She had taken charge of Andy's two young children since their mother died. Nancy must have known she could rely on her. In late winter, while she and the others were busy finding their necessaries and packing, it must often have seemed as if this would all be just like moving over the hill, not such a big thing after all.

Yet every so often, especially when Ben was selling the farm, Nancy would know what she was leaving behind. She would realize that she had no idea where she would be in three months, or six, or a year. Then maybe she gathered up little Ann and held the baby in her arms, her heart racing, half with alarm, half with a thunderous excitement.

The baby would struggle to get down. To Ann, nothing was important except that moment, and what she was doing right then, playing with a feather from one of the chickens Ben had just given away.

Then in March of 1841, six weeks before the rendezvous in Sapling Grove, the bubble burst.

Another letter about California appeared in the local newspapers. This one, from a lawyer named Thomas Farnham whose travels (for his health) had taken him to Monterey,[6] was first printed in

---

[6]Farnham witnessed the end of the so-called Isaac Graham Affair. Graham was an American trapper who had "retired" to the easy life of Monterey. He made the mistake of boasting that he and a few friends could take California for the United States. He and everybody he knew were promptly

a New York newspaper. It reported in shocking and outraged detail the hostility of the Mexican government in California to foreigners and the harsh treatment dealt out to Americans there. Farnham's description of the country itself flatly contradicted the rosy images of Robidoux and Marsh. Farnham said that California was a worthless wasteland, and he advised people to stay out.

The merchants of Platte County, home of the Western Emigration Society, had already noted with alarm the prospect of losing most of their local customers in a single exodus. They happily published Farnham's letter in the Independence newspaper and spread the bad news far and wide. People de-pledged in droves from the Western Emigration Society. In Jackson County, one of the major leaders of the whole project, Billy Baldridge, whose letter from Marsh had started it all, dropped out, along with most of the enthusiastic fifty-eight.

This news jolted the Kelseys also. Probably they got together and talked the whole thing over, one more time at least. But Ben Kelsey was unswayable, not to say bull-headed. Once he made his mind up about something, he did not change, and his brothers supported him. They were used to the hard, dangerous life of the frontier. Ben especially was seasoned at finding his way in wild country. They all knew that rich virgin land would ask a price of work and trouble. They believed they could pay that price.

While the men talked, the women were working, stowing away goods in the wagons.

These were not the huge Conestogas of later times and the movies, but ordinary farm wagons, with wooden beds about ten feet long by four feet wide, sloping sides, and a canvas cover that could be drawn closed in the back against the rain. The wheels, made of ash and tired in iron rims, were smaller in front than the back

---

rolled into jail by the Californio authorities and marched in irons off to Mexico, where they were only released through the good offices of the British consul.

wheels, which made the wagons more maneuverable. The front wheels were rigged on a center kingpin, so that they could swivel back and forth to get around corners more easily. Nonetheless they were prone to tip on corners.

On board Nancy had to load one hundred pounds of flour for each of the people she was packing for, "with sugar and so forth to suit"[7]; that meant lard, coffee, bacon, beans, potatoes. Besides herself and Ben and baby Ann, she stowed supplies for his brother Andy, who was to handle the second of their two wagons. Ben and Andy were good hunters and the whole company planned to lay in a supply of buffalo meat, once they reached the high plains.

They could not take along a cow. This must have bothered Nancy; Ann needed milk. Nor could they take the chickens whose eggs were so useful and good. Ben had told her that the chickens, like his hunting dogs, would last only a few days on a long trek; they'd fall behind and get lost, or a wolf would pick them off.

Nancy packed up her collection of herbs, carefully gathered and dried, pennyroyal and willow and coneflower, old wives' remedies for coughs and bruises, fever and thin blood and diarrhea. She found a stout box for her scissors and her precious stock of needles, thread, and buttons.

Their two wagons were drawn by oxen. She and Ben would ride their horses. Nancy had her favorite horse, "a fine racing animal," as she described it proudly later. They would herd some extra stock along, as well, a few head of oxen and horses. Nancy folded the quilts from their bed and put them into the wagon; she gathered Ann's diapers up. The wagons had seemed large at first but as she loaded them she realized how small they were—how little she was able to take with her.

And now, suddenly, somehow unexpectedly, they were going.

What did she leave behind? The framework of her life. Her old bed, the bed where her babies had been born. The table where she

---

[7]Bidwell III.

had served her husband's meals. The fireplace, each stone different, like a familiar face. Other things, ordinary, irreplaceable. She saw them with new eyes now, those things she had taken for granted, and which soon she would never see again. Suddenly they must have seemed beyond price to her: the view out her cabin door, and the creek where she cooled her feet in the heat of the summer; her garden, which she should have been hoeing up even now, getting ready to plant. Only last fall she had been thinking what to plant this spring, and now the whole thing was a tangle of weeds: she would never see it bloom again.

There were the apple trees, whose crop she had made into the jugs of cider she was taking along. Her husband's old hunting dogs, lying in the dusty sunlight of the yard. The patch at the back fence, under the tree, where beneath a little marker her firstborn son lay.

And thinking that, her resolve hardened; if this farm was a good place, yet it wasn't the best place; if this was all she knew, yet there was much more to know than this. One morning in the fine Missouri spring she turned her back on everything and with the wagons behind her, and Ben beside her, took the road to Sapling Grove.

CHAPTER

2

The Kelseys followed the rivers west, from their front doorstep to the very Pacific. In Jackson County they took a road that led upstream along the southern bank of the Missouri, broad and brown and ridden with snags, a great coiling water rushing eastward toward its union with the Mississippi at St. Louis. At Westport, just beyond Independence, the great river course bent around to the north and west, and here the Kansas River ran in from the west, with the Santa Fe Road along its southern bank. Behind their slow-plodding oxen, the Kelseys moved, at first, along a smooth and traveled path.

Before they had gone far, his brother Sam joined them, with his wagons, and his wife and three children and Andy's two children,[1] and another brother, Zed. They added their extra animals to Ben

---

[1]The sources clearly state that Sam and Lucy brought five children along on this trek, but Sam and Lucy in 1841 had only three of their own; these other two must have been Andy's orphaned daughters.

and Nancy's herd; they made a sizable procession, as they went along, and as they passed, people on the road shouted and applauded, and the Kelseys waved back, like heroes in a parade.

"Where are you going?" people would call.

"California! California!"

So easy to say it. Ahead of them lay half the broad continent. In 1840, nobody really knew what was out there. A few expeditions had poked around in the wilderness—Lewis and Clark in 1803 along the Missouri and the Columbia, Zebulon Pike farther south. The Santa Fe Trail flanked the southern edge of the Rockies, crossing through desert, and it ended in the desert, and the Gila Trail, which led on to the West, and went through some of the worst desert in the world. Since Lewis and Clark's time, fur trappers had been roaming through the central and northern stretches of Rocky Mountains, looking for beaver; by 1841 they had found and named South Pass, Bayou Salade, Jackson Hole, the Green River. From South Pass, a rugged trail led on to Oregon along the Snake River. Some settlers and missionaries had already followed it out to the Willammette Valley.

Between those two routes, the Santa Fe and the Oregon Trails, lay an enormous empty expanse on the map, and the area between the Rockies and California was a huge blank. A few of the mountain men, those inveterate wanderers, had tried to explore the country beyond the Rockies, but there were no beaver, no valuable fur of any kind, no reason to overcome the fearsome desert. Those men who did come out alive did not go back again.

East, in the settled United States, opinion was divided. Some people believed that hardy men could cross the continent, but mere women and children would never survive. It was tantamount to murder to take a woman on such a trip. (That some missionary women made it was God's Providence.) In any case, the West was worth nothing: a desert, littered with rocks, infested with Indians. Other people claimed that the trip was a lark, a mere matter of following the sun.

To the Kelseys, just leaving home, it did seem a lark. People cheered them through Westport, where they picked up the Santa Fe Road. The oxen trudged along at their steady two miles an hour, the men on horseback or walking along by their flanks; Nancy rode along with Ann before her on the saddle. Everything was going wonderfully, until they pulled into sight of Sapling Grove.

"Well," somebody must have said, "maybe they're all just late."

Sapling Grove was empty. On the green meadows of grass nothing grazed but a few rabbits, two yoke of oxen, and an ancient mule. Where they had expected to find dozens, maybe hundreds of people, wagons, campfires, herds of stock, there was only John Bidwell and his new partner.

Bidwell greeted them with his unquenchable enthusiasm. He introduced his new partner, George Henshaw, and they shook hands all around. Henshaw was getting on in years, and had a weak constitution; he was going west for his health. This decision was fortunate for Bidwell, who had begun the enterprise with another partner.

That man had promised to supply the team if Bidwell would come up with a wagon for them to draw. Bidwell found the wagon, but on the news of Farnham's letter, his partner abruptly quit, leaving Bidwell with an outfit and nothing to pull it. At the last moment, Henshaw appeared. He had come from Illinois to join the expedition. He was riding a fine black horse, and Bidwell persuaded him to swap the fine black horse for a pair of oxen to draw the wagon and a decrepit mule for Henshaw to ride. So Bidwell and Henshaw had reached Sapling Grove, and now the Kelseys had too.

They must have welcomed each other, on first meeting again, as if they were long lost friends. Shouted and laughed especially loudly, to make up for the fact that there were so few of them. To have arrived and found so few alarmed them. They had left with such fanfare: How could they go back home again? They settled down to wait.

Ben and Nancy spread out a ground cloth, and set up their tent, and she laid a fire. The grove was pretty enough. Spring flowers bloomed all through the bright grass, and the scattered trees were hazy with new green. Ann fell asleep and Nancy set about making her bread. While the women did their outdoors housekeeping; the men gathered to talk things over, sound each other out, shape a sort of order of going.

Everybody knew that they had to have more people, to go west. The Plains along the Kansas swarmed with Pawnee and Kaw and sometimes Comanche. To a Plains war party, five settler wagons and sixteen people, seven of them children, would be one quick snap. The settlers needed more men and more rifles, or they would have to go back home.

The Kelseys had no home to go back to. Right now, all the home they had was a ground cloth and a tent between two loaded wagons. Nancy had soaked some potatoes in water; now she squeezed out the fermented mush for her bread sponge, catching the juice in her best bowl. She took the stinking potato mush as far from the camp as she could, downwind, and dumped it. That was the worst part of making this kind of bread: the smell of the potatoes. Back at the camp, she beat in the flour and cornmeal, sitting with the bowl tilted on her lap, and her arm going around until it ached.

Where would they go, if they couldn't go to California?

In the morning, her sponge was high and bubbly, and she mixed in more flour and put the dough to rise. At least she could still make bread. And by noon, when the bread was just turning golden and aromatic out of the pan, more wagons were rolling into the camp. She stood up with the others and raised her arms and cheered until the trees rang.

Steadily, others arrived, more every day. After three days Nancy's tent stood near the center of a sprawling city of canvas and rubberized sheets. Men strode up and down, bellowing to each other across the camp, standing in groups waving their arms and spitting in all directions, the excited hum of their voices breaking often into high sharp laughter, or a volley of oaths. Every now and then somebody let off a rifle into the air.

Nancy had to go much farther now to dump her garbage. The grass of the meadow, once so green and fine, was beaten down and bitten off. The animals were eating it all up; the pioneers would not be able to stay here much longer. Soon they would have to move.

The women fell naturally into one another's company. While Ann, testing her newly acquired ability to walk, toddled after her Kelsey cousins, Nancy and the other women went about their work. Besides Lucy and the widow Mrs. Grey, at least two other women joined them: Richard Williams had brought his wife, and his daughter, Ann.

They compared their preparations, shared recipes for salt-rising bread and beans, admired each other's babies. Talked over about their hopes and their fears. Like the men, they quickly found out what they needed to know about one another: which one knew herbs, and could doctor, which could cook, which knew children best, which were reliable and which could not be counted on. They, as much as the men, brought forth an order out of this gathering. In the society of the Kelsey women, Ann Williams met Zedediah Kelsey, whom she would marry in less than two weeks.[2]

In the camp's heated atmosphere, all emotions ran higher and stronger than usual. Utter strangers were friends within a few hours. Their common goal bound them, forged a community of them, a nexus of their common needs, their common hopes and fears. None-theless, from the beginning, there were factions, crossed wills, short-sighted and nasty arguments.

The group divided itself into messes: the people who ate to-gether. John Bartleson, from Jackson County, formed one mess with eight other men; Bidwell, Henshaw, and a few others formed a mess; the Kelseys formed a mess. The family tie was a strength that Nancy could count on.

[2]Although perhaps they knew each other beforehand. These Williamses must not be confused with Reverend Joseph Williams, of whom more anon.

It must have been hard to wait. Maybe Nancy sometimes went to the western edge of the camp, and looked out. From Sapling Grove, the prospect looked very like Missouri: trees and meadows, where now their horses and oxen grazed. Ben might have come up beside her, and they put their arms around one another and talked about what a wonderful life they were going to have in California.

They could not have talked much about the dangers of the trip to come, simply because they did not know what they were. They were about to step off the edge of the known. When they fell silent, words failing in the face of that enormity, they must have held each other a little tighter.

But every day their numbers grew. People came from as far off as Arkansas. "It was a very mixed crowd," as the amiable Nicholas Dawson remarked. There were four families, three of them Kelseys, and at least seven children. Many, perhaps most of the settlers, however, were young, single men who, footloose and uninhibited by responsibilities, could easily set off for an unknown country more than a thousand miles away.

Nicholas Dawson, twenty-two, was typical, if any of them was really typical. Good natured and brave, at nineteen he had left his Pennsylvania home to see the world, and wandered all over the frontier from the Platte Purchase to New Orleans, cutting wood, teaching school, working as a farmhand, before he decided to go to California. He was well educated and read a lot, considered himself something of a romantic. During the 1841 trek he kept a journal.

He was part of Bartleson's mess, having bought a share of one of John Bartleson's wagons. When he had paid for that he had seventy-five cents left. Few of the others had much more. The cross-grained Kentuckian Grove Cook had nothing at all, and no way to provide anything, and worked his way along by driving one of the wagons in Bartleson's mess.

Bidwell kept a journal too. Every evening Nancy could see him sitting by his fire, his book on his knee, scribbling away. Bidwell was interested in everything, noticed everything, wrote everything down.

"I laid in one hundred pounds of flour more than the usual quantity," he wrote later. "This I did because we were told that when we got into the mountains we probably would get out of bread and have to live on meat alone, which I thought would kill me even if it did not others. My gun was an old flint-lock rifle, but a good one. Old hunters told me to have nothing to do with cap or percussion locks, that they were unreliable, and that if I got my caps or percussion wet I could not shoot, while if I lost my flint I could up another on the plains. I doubt whether there was one hundred dollars in money in the whole party, but all were enthusiastic and anxious to go."[3]

In this he was actually quite wrong. One member of the party had considerably more than one hundred dollars. Talbot H. Green, real name Paul Geddes, was on the run, wanted for embezzling eight thousand dollars from a bank. Nobody knew this; all they knew was that Green had something heavy that he lugged with him everywhere and jealously protected. He said it was lead. Probably a few of them believed him: lead was a valuable commodity on the plains, where a bullet could mean life or death.

On May 18, the group assembled and counted heads, coming up with a total of sixty-eight people. This meeting was to lay out rules for the expedition (arrangements for standing watch at night, the order of march, and such things) and name officers. Only the men voted. Bidwell was chosen secretary. Talbot H. Green, the embezzler, who impressed everybody with his culture and address, was elected president, and the group took John Bartleson as their captain.

This was not from recognition of his superior ability or wit. Bartleson told them flat out that if he were not made captain, he would take the eight men who had come with him and leave. This strong-arm tactic set the tone for Bartleson's captaincy throughout the trip. He didn't want to lead, so much as he wanted to be first.

[3]Bidwell III.

It betrayed, also, the divisions already forming in the group, the rivalries, dissension, and bad faith.

Now they were ready to start. The problem was that nobody, Bartleson included, knew where to go.

But then one of the last to arrive reported that he had seen some Catholic priests on the road. They were traveling from St. Louis toward the upper Missouri River country, where they hoped to convert the native people, and had acquired the services as a guide of none other than Broken Hand, Thomas Fitzpatrick himself. Maybe Captain Bartleson could go ask these people if they could join up.

The pioneers were so eager to get started that many didn't want to wait. In spite of the fact that none of them had any firsthand knowledge of the mountains some were perfectly ready to head out in that direction by themselves. In another of their now-familiar meetings, they argued this issue back and forth. Bartleson especially wanted to start off immediately, on their own. But they had no notion how to go about that, and Bartleson, obviously, was no leader. Finally, in Bidwell's words, "we sobered down" and waited for the priests and Fitzpatrick.

"It was well we did," Bidwell writes, "for otherwise probably not one of us would have reached California."[4] Fitzpatrick was a godsend. Nancy had heard of him: one of the great mountain men, already a frontier legend. He had been on General Ashley's 1823 excursion into the wilderness that found South Pass; he had trailed with Jed Smith on his great expedition through California in 1824[5], he had trapped the Rockies since then. Like all the free trappers he had intimate experience with the various tribes of Indians and he could survive virtually anywhere, on anything. She was glad to see the men send off an offer to join Fitzpatrick's party.

[4]Bidwell III.
[5]Smith got there by circling south of Salt Lake to the Colorado and the Virgin Rivers, ending up in Southern California.

When Fitzpatrick came to meet them, she liked the look of him. He was slight, fair-headed, in his thirties. Born in County Cavan, in Ireland, of a good Catholic family, he left home in his early teens and worked his way first across the ocean and then across the continent. By 1841 he had been living in the wilderness half his life. Now that the beaver were gone, and the shining times of the fur trade were over, he was cashing in on his experience by guiding expeditions into the west. The Catholic priests were among his first charges.

These priests were just as remarkable. Their leader was Father Pierre Jean de Smet, SJ, a Belgian, who devoted his life to missionary work on the frontier and beyond. He impressed Bidwell, who commented on his "fine presence", naming him "one of the saintliest men I have ever known."[6] De Smet had already made one trip into the Northwest, in 1840, going with a band of trappers, and then trekking out again alone with just a guide. Now he was headed back, with two other Jesuits and three lay brothers, to establish a mission among the Flathead Indians in the Bitterroot Valley of Montana.[7]

To the priests and Fitzpatrick, the Bartleson–Kelsey–Bidwell pioneers were also something of a blessing.[8] De Smet had been expecting two other companies of travelers to swell the numbers of his party, but both had failed to show up. Fitzpatrick was taking along, besides the priests, only five teamsters, two men to hunt for them, and an English Lord named Romaine, who wanted to shoot buffalo, and his half-breed guide. Fitzpatrick and de Smet must have jumped at the chance to add nearly sixty armed men to their caravan.

[6]Bidwell III.
[7]De Smet's mission was a success. The Indians admired and liked him and he was able to mediate between them and the encroaching whites; in 1868 he negotiated a truce between the whites and Sitting Bull, the Hunkpapa chief who led the last great defense of the Dakota Territory. De Smet even earned the respect of the Blackfeet, the most feared people in the country.
[8]De Smet wrote that "our journey had even well nigh been indefinitely postponed" if they had not made company with the settlers. Letter I, Nunis.

So, on May 19, a Wednesday, they started out, in a single file along the road. The priests went first, riding horses, with their supplies in four little two-wheeled mule carts, called Red River carts, and their wagon. Their mules were hitched in tandem, one behind the other. After that came the eight horse-drawn wagons of the pioneers, and last the five wagons drawn by oxen, much slower than the horses.

Nancy rode her horse, holding Ann on her lap. When Ann squirmed and fretted at being held so still, Nancy would have taken her down to walk in the powdery dust of the road and pick the wildflowers growing up through the grass. She held the child right beside her, keeping her out of the way of the wagons, and watching for snakes. Ann pulled her along, excited to be on the move at last.

Chasing the little girl around, Nancy might have stopped, and craned her neck, peering ahead, trying to see into the west—into the future. She couldn't see much. Here, at the eastern margin of the plains, great stands of trees grew all along the many little streams, blocking the long view. But they were on their way now. They had left the United States. Somewhere out there California lay, and a new life. What came between she would endure, for the sake of the new life. Her spirits high, she went after Ann among the prairie flowers.

CHAPTER

3

Quickly the trek settled into a routine. The first day, they went twelve miles, following the Kansas River Valley, open grassland save where the river meandered along through its undulating strip of riparian forest. The Santa Fe Road was well marked, rutted and seamed with wagon travel. The sun beat on them from a sky like an oven lid. Nancy rode her horse and carried her child ahead of her on the saddle; probably she made some kind of sling to make sure Ann could not tumble off.

The child slept much, but certainly not all the time, and when she was awake, keeping her confined to the saddle would have been a battle. Nancy must have gotten down now and then and let her little girl run and play; then she could let her pony graze a little, too, and forage as she went along for wild berries, birds' eggs, nuts, and for wood for the fire when they camped.

Even picking berries and gathering armfuls of wood, she would not fall behind their wagon. The slow trudge of the oxen carried it along at a pace that even a baby's stubby uncertain legs could match. Nancy watched all the while for snakes. She had seen some already, lying dead by the road like gaudy pieces of rope, their heads snapped off by the bullwhips of the wagoneers in the train moving ahead of her. Whenever the child wandered more than a few yards away, Nancy ran and got her and pulled her back close. There were coyotes, too, and Indians, and poison ivy.

Every now and then, walking along beside the wagon, Nancy lifted her head, her eyes straining toward the horizon, already aching for something new to look at.

Mostly she saw the dust of the wagons going on before her up the valley. During the day's march the group straggled; the oxen were much slower than the horses and mules, and the riders especially found it impossible to keep down to the pace of the great cattle. Also, the men on horseback, as they traveled, ranged around looking for game. By the end of the day, Nancy and Ben and Andy, and the others with ox carts, were more than half a mile behind the leaders.

Somewhere up there, at the very front of the long loose chain of travelers, was the mountain man, Broken Hand Fitzpatrick, riding along with his rifle over his saddlebows, picking the trail and watching for trouble. As the day wore on he would be keeping an eye out for a good place to camp. Clearly he knew so well what he was doing that from the very beginning even Bartleson yielded to him.

At noon, that first day, having come twelve miles, they stopped and camped in the trees by the river. When the Kelseys' wagons finally pulled in, Fitzpatrick had them park with the others in a hollow square; the tongue of each wagon was fastened up to the back of the one in front of it. Just inside their big wagon, Nancy spread out the ground cloth and raised the tent, and got to work on her bread. All around the inside of the wagon square, the other women were rushing to the same chores.

Some of them had fancy reflector stoves. But Nancy had seen, back in Sapling Grove, that the bread baked just as well in a good dutch oven in the coals, and the reflector stoves were always hard to set up. She could hear them fussing with one now, across the way, and she already had her bread sponge mixed.

Ben had gone off to hunt; some of the other men were already back, with hares and a deer. Nancy gathered up Ann and her dirty diapers and went off to the river.

On her way back, she felt the air turn suddenly cool, and saw heavy clouds bundling up into the sky. She picked Ann up and started for the tent. Within a few steps, she was running, as the sky darkened like the fall of night. The other people in camp were diving for their tents. The first great drops of rain slammed into them. Nancy crept into her shelter, Ann clutched in both arms, and then it seemed as if somebody overturned a wagonload of stones on their tent.

The crash was deafening. The tent sagged. Through the front opening Nancy could see the air turning thick and white with falling hail. White stones like peas and bigger were bouncing up knee-high above the ground. The tent slumped again and she bolted out and hauling Ann along screaming inaudibly in the uproar of the storm she crawled underneath the nearest wagon.

Out there people were shrieking; but the thunder of the hailstorm was fading. The crashing stones softened into the pattering of heavy rain. And the air was lightening again, day was coming back. Nancy soothed the baby; under the wagon, the ground was still dry.

Outside, the hail turned the ground white. But it was melting; here came a rivulet already, snaking through the dust toward her, and she crawled out from under the wagon into the last few drops of rain, and stood up.

All over the camp, tents were flattened. From one huge hapless canvas wreck across the way came curses and screams. The other pioneers were rising up slowly, shaking off the water, watching the sky as if it might all suddenly happen again.

Black clouds still crowded half the sky, but now the sun broke through them. The ground began to steam. The air felt hot and moist as a washhouse.

The canvas covers of the wagons were weighted down with hail. Nancy calmed the baby and went to fix the covers and make sure that the wagons hadn't leaked. The canvas covers kept most of the weather out, but if they did leak, if the flour got wet, for example, it was a disaster.

But then here came Ben and Andy, with a fat deer, and soon they had a good dinner of beans and bread and venison. Nancy had rescued their bedding from the muck after the rain, Ben set the tent up again, and they slept inside. In the morning, she built another fire and cooked another batch of bread, while Ben rounded up the oxen and the horses, and they ate as they moved out.

So it went, for days and days.

That first day, they stopped early. Afterward they pushed on later in the day; when they made camp, usually the daylight was already dwindling, and Nancy was in a rush the whole time to get everything done. While Ben tended to the animals, she unpacked their camping gear, set up the tent, hauled the water in for cleaning up. She made the sponge for her bread and put it to rise. When the men had brought in game, she helped dress it and make it ready for cooking; often she helped other families cut up carcasses, in return for some of the meat. For the dinner she had the last of the day's bread, plus whatever meat or bacon there was available, and the beans she had been soaking all day in the back of the wagon. For the first few days, they had some cider left, and they had coffee.

She took care of Ann. The little girl was still in diapers, and changing them and cleaning them took a lot of Nancy's time. At first she washed the day's usage out every evening in the river and hung them up to dry.

Later on probably she got a little slack at it, especially when water was precious. Did Ann get a diaper rash? Hanging the diapers in the sun to dry would probably have killed off the bacteria sufficiently to keep her bottom smooth. The alkali in the desert water might have also helped. But as the long, punishing trek went on, especially where there was no water to waste in washing out a diaper, Ann must have sometimes had a very sore behind.

Feeding her was another problem, Nancy's most constant and worrisome chore. The baby was too old to nurse. Nancy chewed up meat for her, and Ann could mush up bread and beans with her new teeth, and she ate the berries and fruit Nancy found for her. Without a cow, there was no milk. The little girl drank water, no matter how bad it was.

In the camp, Nancy shared many of her chores with the other women, nearly all of whom she had known for a while. Under pressure of necessity this must have quickly become a tight little group, almost sisterly in its tensions, its alliances, its interdependence; they had to rely on one another every day for countless small things, from holding a baby to helping rig up a wagon cover to stirring a simmering pot.

Nothing in this means they had to like one another. In fact, the close quarters, the lack of privacy, the constant mix of boredom and anxiety guaranteed rivalries and small, carefully hoarded grudges. The settlers argued and grumbled all the time. There were some Nancy knew she could trust—of course the family, Ben's brothers, Sam's wife Lucy. Others she had her doubts about from the beginning. And sometimes she probably just hated them all. Nobody was having a good time, and they took it out on each other.

There was, for instance, the utter lack of privacy. Especially at the beginning of the trip, while they were traveling through country with some trees and gullies, Nancy and Ben were able to get away from the others for a while, to be together. And sometimes Nancy went off by herself, to eliminate and wash and freshen her clothes. But she could not, dared not ever go too far from the others. As the country got more open and the trees fewer, she had no place to go at all, except into the tent, where the space was so close and hot she could hardly breathe.

Being alone must have come to seem a luxury. She did not yet know exactly how alone she could be.

As soon as they left Sapling Grove they were in Indian country. "This afternoon," Bidwell wrote in his journal, on the date May 19, "several Kanzas Indians came to our camp; they were well armed with bows and arrows, and some had guns. They were daily expecting an attack by the Pawnees, whom they but a short time ago had made inroads upon, and had massacred at one of their villages a large number of old men, women and children, while the warriors were hunting buffalo."[1] De Smet had already visited these Kanzas' nearby village and won their good will, but the tribe had a permanent feud on with the Pawnee and these particular horsemen were looking for a fight. One wore an American flag draped around him and another had a scalp hanging from his horse's bridle.[2] At their approach, everybody in the wagon train gawked. Nancy held Ann tightly in her arms, her shawl around them both, to keep her out of sight: everyone knew how Indians stole children.

Experienced plainsmen had a custom for meeting Indians on the trail. As soon as the band appeared, the wagons stopped, and Fitzpatrick and de Smet and a few others rode out to parley. At a safe distance from the caravans, whites and reds exchanged presents or tobacco and talked things over, meanwhile estimating each other's strengths and weaknesses. Once the men had declared peace, the Indians would often camp near the wagon train that night and accompany the settlers for a while, a day, even several days' travel. Their presence always made the settlers uneasy, even when the Indians were openly friendly; the sociability of the Indians always bothered whites.

But today these Kanzas weren't especially amiable. They talked easily enough with Fitzpatrick, but they did not stay long, nor did they go through the ritual of sharing smoke. They were looking

[1]Bidwell I.
[2]Father Point.

over their shoulders for the Pawnee. Their weapons and horses, their obvious wary alertness, and their tales of their own marauding made a powerful impression on Nancy. Like all the settlers, she was quite ready to believe the worst of the Plains people. Henceforth, the settlers would see Indians almost every day.

Each morning Fitzpatrick led his party on again. The Santa Fe Road veered off toward the south and he guided them onto the much less traveled route toward the Platte River and Fort Laramie, the route of the fur trappers into the beaver country of the Rockies. This was not a mere matter of rolling along a highway. All day long the chain of wagons and carts was fording one after another of the numerous small streams running down across their path to flow into the Kanzas River. These streams were themselves only little rivulets but many had cut deep ravines into the prairie, the banks thick with brush and trees.

When the banks were high, the men hitched ropes to the wagons and helped their oxen pull; other people got behind and pushed. Nancy, to her knees in a mucky stream, shoved and heaved at the bigger of their wagons, getting nowhere, for what seemed half the day. Ben called a halt, and they all drew back to contemplate their problem.

The wagon was mired down in the soft stream muck, and even after they dragged it free they had to haul it somehow up a steep river bank. The wagon was too heavy. Goods that had looked indispensable in Missouri were looking now like mere dead weight, and Ben and Nancy dumped off the first of the multitude of things they would abandon.

Other times, they had to get out shovels to move rocks and level the ground. Nonetheless, they were making good progress by the standards of the era: that second day, they made sixteen miles, the third fifteen, the fourth eighteen.

They were crawling up onto the lower edge of the tremendous slab of continent that tilts down from the foothills of the Rockies to the Mississippi Valley. Every day, as the trees thinned out, and the horizon receded steadily away, the Plains grew larger around them, as if the world were a great book opening up beneath the immense blue sky. In such a landscape a human being shrank down to nothing, even in his own heart. Plodding along, step after step, day after day, the settlers seemed to go nowhere.

When, on the fifth morning, they woke to find their oxen had drifted away, there were cries of despair. They were going too slowly. Winter would catch them still on the Plains, they would have to eat their stock to survive. They were only about sixty miles from the Missouri, and already losing heart. They had more than fifteen hundred miles to go.

Still, by nine o'clock they had found their cattle, and they moved out again along the track, de Smet and his people and Fitzpatrick having already started. Around noon, the whole party stopped to let another wagon catch up with them, this one bearing Joseph Chiles, Charles Weber, and James John, who had come to Sapling Grove to join them, only to find they had already left.

The Kelseys, with their slow-plodded oxen, were last of the train, and so the first to see the people coming after. They greeted Chiles, Weber, and John with cheers and whoops. The three newcomers rushed in among them like people taking shelter. They had seen fourteen Pawnees on the way, on the warpath after the Kanzas.

Everybody in the wagon train must have realized then that there were Indians all around them, bands of warriors, somewhere over the horizon, which suddenly didn't seem all that far away, after all. They welcomed three more armed men into their midst with great joy. A good deal of the enthusiasm stemmed from the break in the monotony of what was already a galling daily routine.

The next day, May 21, they came to Vermilion Creek, in full spate from the recent rains, and made camp to wait until the flood subsided. Here, as along the banks of the other streams they crossed, good timber grew, bur-oak, black walnut, elm, and white hickory. But the trees were fewer and farther apart now, as the water was becoming scarcer. On the yellow prairies, rolling in dry relentless waves of stalky grass, the long dark lines of trees that marked the watercourses were farther and farther apart.

Even the cattle recognized those lines of trees as signs of water. When in the distance trees appeared, the oxen strode out with sudden energy, their heads bobbing.

In this dry country Fitzpatrick was almost always able to find them water to camp by. Sometimes they even had too much water. The creeks and rivers were running, and the grass was still growing green. Rain fell every few days, often with hail; Nancy was getting very good at ducking under the wagon, and Ann had stopped being so frightened.

One morning some mules stampeded, wrecking two wagons, and the company laid over to make repairs. Nancy was glad of the chance to get some chores done, but almost at once a band of Pawnees showed up, helpful and curious.

Clearly the Indians were keeping a close watch on the settlers' progress. They made no effort yet to hamper them, or attack them, and drifted off soon enough. Ben, like the other men, attributed this to the settlers' numbers and their firepower, but then, that same afternoon Joseph Williams reached them.

Williams had been following after them from Westport on his mule. On the way he had seen a lot of signs of Indians, at which he had taken great alarm, but had in fact encountered no trouble at all. This he attributed to the intervention of God, with whom, as it turned out, Joseph Williams enjoyed a close personal relationship, which he recorded in his journal.

His arrival among the settlers was sufficient cause for a celebration. De Smet, recognizing a fellow traveler on the rocky road to Heaven, invited him to dinner, and one of the women asked him to sing.

On the prairie, in the ragged little circle of wagons, Williams stood and cocked his head back and sang a hymn. The settlers listened attentively; devout or not, they had all grown up hearing such music, and it carried a weight with them. It brought God there, for a moment, anyway: a familiar God who cared about them. Around them lay the enormous, unknown land, whose silence swallowed up the tiny voice.

Moments later they were burying the fires, settling down for the night, and the sentries went to their posts. In the morning, once again, they were plugging on.

A few days later Williams, who was a Methodist minister, felt himself called upon to preach to the caravan. By now the novelty of his arrival had worn off, and Williams' own sour and sanctimonious disposition had communicated itself fully to his audience. Nobody wanted to hear it. When Williams persisted they shouted him down. He consoled himself in a private conversation with God, but considered the settlers "as wicked as I ever saw in my life." Nancy, who considered herself pious enough, avoided him thereafter.

The group's opinions in the matter of God ran a wide range. De Smet and his fellow priests were not only Catholics but Jesuits, the shock troops of the Church Militant. Theology was a main subject of their conversation; de Smet himself (honing his skills for the anticipated mission to the Flatheads) "had daily conversations with some one of the caravan, and frequently with several,"[3] finding them at first heavily prejudiced against Catholicism. The settlers held de Smet in an attitude of veneration. This stood in sharp contrast to their treatment of Joseph Williams, and by the end of their journey the Jesuit was congratulating himself that he had inclined some of them toward the Church.

Williams, a Methodist, quickly located two other Methodists among the party, but discovered to his sorrow that Captain Bartleson was a backslider. Like the Jesuits', Williams' focus on God was fairly militant. One night around the fire he pressed Bartleson to declare himself in matters spiritual. Bartleson looked uncomfortable, and then blurted out, "It's best to have no religion, or else to adopt that of the country in which we live."

[3]De Smet, 215.

Not sufficiently scandalized by this, Williams got Fitzpatrick into a discussion of faith. Broken Hand shocked him even more than Bartleson. Williams wrote later, "[He] is a wicked, worldly man, and is much opposed to missionaries going among the Indians. He has some intelligence, but is deistical in his principles."[4] But it sounds as if the mountain man, born an Irish Catholic and steeped in the ways of the wilderness, was the most open-minded of them all.

The train crept on across the enormous plains. The weather continued violent and unpredictable. When the storms came during the day, the downpours could mire the wagons in a sudden sea of mud, or fill a tiny stream so full they had to wait hours to cross it. A storm at night was hell.

A sudden storm broke after midnight while they were camped near the Platte. The peals of thunder woke everybody; the suffocating downpour set them all to scrambling for shelter, as hail beat the tents flat and rainwater streamed across the ground and through the sleepers' bedding.

"A most tremendous bad storm," Reverend Williams wrote, of this stormy night. "With wind, which blew down most of the tents, accompanied with rain and lightining and thunder almost all night. I slept but little, the ground being all covered with water. That night, dreadful oaths were heard all over the camp ground. O the wickedness of the wicked."[5]

But in the morning, the sun came out, the flood subsided, and the caravan pulled itself together again and went on. "Some of the [hail] stones measured two and a half inches in diameter," Bidwell wrote, later. "Some were found yet unmelted on our next day's travel."[6]

Every evening, as they ate their dinners, the settlers talked to-

[4]Williams, 240.
[5]*Narrative of a Tour from Indiana*, by Joseph Williams.
[6]Bidwell II.

gether, sometimes very seriously, about God, about themselves, sharing what they knew (or what they thought they knew) about the trail ahead, and telling stories. Somebody had a fiddle and played, and often they all danced. Reverend Williams was particularly disapproving of the dancing. Often they sang hymns and familiar old songs and rounds. In the evenings, Bidwell and Nicholas Dawson and now Jimmy John, one of the latecomers, wrote in their journals, although Nancy noted that Jimmy John, an impatient young man, quickly seemed to give up on his.

Fitzpatrick was sometimes willing to tell stories, too, and when they could get him to talk about the country on the way to California, everybody listened. He told them, for instance, about Jim Bridger's wild ride down the Bear River.

The Bear River ran through Cache Valley, as Fitzpatrick told it, where many free trappers put up during the Rocky Mountain winter, enjoying the pleasant weather and good game. But things got boring sometimes, and one day young Bridger decided to float down the Bear and see where it went.

So he built himself a bull boat. He made a frame of willow branches and stretched buffalo hides over it, producing something that looked like a leather bowl. Trappers used such boats on all the rivers when they could; they looked strange and they couldn't be steered well but they were virtually untippable, drew almost nothing, and went wherever a river went.

Jim got into his bull boat and took off down the Bear. For a while everything was easy; the river ran down through the valley, past meadows and woods; the water was cold and pure. Then he was swept into a fast current. The river plunged like a gateway through a gap in the mountains, and he rushed out across a broad plain. Now, when he dipped his hand into the river for water, it tasted salty.

The bull boat carried him swiftly on. Suddenly he was spinning out onto a broad water, stretching as far south as he could see. Red cliffs towered to the east, and on the bank of the tremendous lake, clumps of salt stood like a whole tribe of Lot's wives.

"Salt Lake," the settlers said, nodding. Bidwell broke out his map again, and there it was, Salt Lake, stretching half the width of the continent, with rivers running from it west to the Pacific. All they had to do was get to Salt Lake and those westward-running rivers.

Meanwhile, they were trudging across what seemed an endless plain. And with every step they were coming into more troublesome country.

Fitzpatrick was having difficulty now finding good camping sites, with enough water, grass, and wood for such a company. One day they had to travel twenty-five miles to find a site, and another time they found nothing at all. There was little wood and they began to collect dried-out buffalo dung to make their campfires. Once when they stopped for the night, the only water was some putrid stuff they found collected in a hollow of a rock; they made coffee with it, as they would later with the brackish water of the desert, so that they could stomach it. Nancy made Ann drink it, although the little girl complained.

On the first of June, they reached the Platte River, "the most magnificent and useless of rivers,"[7] a film of water flowing a mile wide and an inch deep across the plain, its many braided streams winding among islands and sandhills, low scrubby bushes and stands of cottonwood and willow. All of it boomed and whirred with birds and insects.[8] It was, de Smet wrote, "a scene that seems to have started into existence from the hand of the Creator."

They could not admire the scene at leisure, because this being the hottest day of the trip naturally brought on a thunderstorm, with the worst hail they had ever seen.

They had plenty of warning. Nancy knew the way this hap-

[7]Washington Irving, *Astoria*.
[8]The Platte is on a major flyway of migrating birds. For data on this wonderful river I am indebted to the Northern Prairie Wildlife Research Center, which maintains an extensive website with lots of facts.

pened now; on the plains you could see a thunderstorm coming for miles, the towering black clouds and the flicker of the lightning underneath. But here on the broad bankless treeless Platte there was no shelter from the drenching rain or the hail, like a downpour of rocks.

Bidwell thought the hailstones could kill their stock. The settlers crowded together in the lee of their wagons, shivering and swearing and praying. Nancy curled her arms and body around frightened Ann. Through the terrific racket she could barely hear the baby's wails. Ben, beside her, leaned around and tried to cover both of them with his coat. Probably then, for a moment, each of them wished bitterly that they had never left Missouri.

When at last the storm ended, and the people began cautiously moving around again, they found the land covered four inches deep in balls of ice, so many and so large than some remained unmelted well into the next day. All around, the sun blazed with a blinding glitter on the dripping water-covered land. Battered and soaked, the pioneers began slowly to rescue their gear and make a camp in a land that seemed to hate them.

Yet that same night they had a wedding. Joseph Williams performed the ceremony, uniting Zedediah Kelsey with Ann Williams, no relation to the preacher himself but the daughter of the only family traveling with the group that was not of Kelsey kindred: and now they were. Nancy with the other women gathered to hug the bride, and the whole company celebrated. At least they had something under control. In spite of Reverend Williams, they must have danced and fiddled away half the night.

In the morning, before they started on, they gathered for another meeting, and an argument broke out. Some of the group thought the missionaries were going too fast. Solemnly they put forward the proposition that the settlers go on without de Smet and his party. The others pointed out that this meant going on without Fitzpatrick. That stopped the discussion; they never even bothered to vote on it.

They needed Fitzpatrick more all the time. They had left the pleasant, wildflower-strewn margin of the Plains behind; now they were picking their way across the interminable flat steppes of western Nebraska. Every day they trudged across the same landscape, treeless and empty except for the curly buffalo grass. Looking in all directions, Nancy could see no place different from where she was now. "Plains on all sides! Plains at morning; plains at noon; Plains at night!" one of the Jesuits said. On this hard ground the trail was mostly invisible, a few ancient ruts, or a worn patch: only Fitzpatrick knew where they were going.

That he did know was borne in on them when, on a day blasted by sun, a train of ox wagons materialized slowly out of the haze. It was the fur caravan from Fort Laramie, headed for St. Louis. The drovers, filthy men in greasy buckskins, saluted the settlers with hoots and yells and cracks of their long black whips. The settlers hooted and yelled back, and then pushed on into the west, heartened. They were obviously on the right road, if perhaps going in a chancy direction.

CHAPTER

4

The country was steadily wilder and stranger. They followed along the south bank of the Platte, the route that would become the heart of the Emigrant Road.[1] The migrating birds that wintered over on the Platte had by now flown north again for Canada, but cranes and plovers and terns mobbed the sandhills, and the songs and cries of vireos and sparrows resounded in the patchy, bushy trees. The river, running so shallow and so full of sand, was almost invisible during the day among the bars and islands, but at dawn and in the evening the slanting sunrays burnished the water into long strips of reflected light, brighter than the sky.

Looking out at this scene, one early morning, with the mist rising, and the strands of the Platte glowing in the first light, Nancy

[1]Ninety percent of the emigrants crossing the plains between this party and the coming of the railroad in 1869 would travel by the Platte River Road. See Unruh.

may have told herself that had she stayed home in Missouri, she never would have seen this. Every day, she was seeing new things.

They passed a prairie dog colony, and here and there they crossed ground covered with great patches of bicarbonate, which some of the company called plaster of Paris, and Bidwell Glauber's Salts. They were coming into more broken country. Along the river low bluffs loomed up out of the plain like monsters rising under the earth, their steep flanks wind-scoured and rutted. Every day there was less water and less grass. The ground was covered with bones and skulls. They were coming into the country of the buffalo.

Nicholas Dawson could not resist this first chance at big game and went out hunting. He got on the trail of a herd of antelope and, against the advice of Fitzpatrick and the others, he ventured out of sight of the wagon train. The antelope enticed him. Dismounting from his mule, he crept forward to get a closer shot, and was edging along on hands and knees when a loud whoop sounded.

Indians! Dawson bolted for his mule, which was as panicky as its rider: as Dawson barreled up into the saddle the mule bolted— straight toward the high-pitched yell. Frantically Dawson hauled on the reins and got the mule turned around in the right direction, but before he could kick it up to speed he was surrounded by Indians.

"One galloped by me," Dawson wrote later, "thrust a spear along my back, and motioned me to dismount." When he did they took his guns, his knife, his mule, and a fair amount of his clothes, and then left him.

Dawson took off running for the wagon train. The settlers saw him coming; saw also that he was in a state of advanced panic. Saw that he was missing half his clothes. Before he even reached them they were losing their nerve. Breathless, he dashed in among them, shouting that he had been surrounded by thousands of Indians! And then the settlers saw that the Indians were coming along behind him.

Without waiting for orders or argument the entire wagon train swung around and thundered back toward the river. Ann clutched in her arms, Nancy galloped her horse in their midst, looking around desperately for Ben. In the rising cloud of dust she saw nothing but the dim wobbling shapes of the wagons. Screaming and plying their staffs, the drovers got even the oxen into a full gallop.

Tom Fitzpatrick was apoplectic. A cardinal rule of Plains life was never to run away from Indians. The mountain man screamed and howled at the settlers to stop, but nobody even heard him.

Finally he galloped his horse around to the front of the stampede. As each wagon clattered up to the river he swung it around into formation; out of the wild rout he brought a temporary fortress, and collected the loose animals inside. Jumping out of their saddles, the settlers flung themselves up against the wall of wagons, rifles at the ready. And after a few moments the Indians came jogging into sight, forty Cheyenne, hardly in a fighting mood. With the merest glance at the heavily armed wagons, they reached the river fifty yards upstream of the settlers and prepared to set up camp there.

The settlers stood back, abashed. Fitzpatrick shouted at them all a while and told them what greenhorns they were, and got his horse and took de Smet and went out to parley with the newcomers. Meanwhile, Nicholas Dawson, with his friends behind him, was now hot for vengeance. He borrowed a horse and a rifle and charged out to join the attack.

Fitzpatrick snarled at him, in no mood to humor anybody. He told Dawson to put his gun away and bring out "foofaraw," trinkets and gadgets to trade with. Meekly Dawson acquiesced and followed Fitzpatrick to the Indian camp.

The red horsemen who awaited them were Cheyenne warriors and a medicine woman, a war party off to trade blows with the Blackfeet. The Cheyenne were famous among the fur men for their sense of humor. Their chief, who knew Fitzpatrick, explained that they had never meant Dawson any harm, but had to disarm him because in his state of high panic he might have shot one of them.

As for the rest of his missing gear, Dawson himself had made them presents of it all, even before they could have asked.

Could they return Dawson's things? But Dawson had given it all up. They weren't his things anymore.

On the other hand, the Cheyenne were happy to do a little trading.

So Fitzpatrick sat on the ground with Dawson and the Indians and they traded what Dawson owned now for what he had owned an hour before: blankets and belts and tobacco for his clothes, his rifle, his knife, and his mule. With each trade they passed the smoke around, solemnly legitimating the bargain with the symbol of peace and friendship. The entire ceremony went on far into the night, until at least Fitzpatrick quit.

Dawson squawked. He was still missing his pistol and a few other items. But Fitzpatrick snapped at him that he was lucky he was still alive, got on his horse, and headed back to the settlers' camp, and Dawson, his thirst for vengeance unslaked, went meekly with him.

The other settlers of course watched all this from a distance, still forted up behind their wagons, still in an attitude of alarm. Bidwell, always the investigator, went around asking people how many Indians they thought there were, and got excited estimates of "lots, gaubs, fields and swarms!" Nancy herself believed that the Indians surrounded them and that the settlers' show of force drove them off. The more she remembered it, the more she also remembered that Dawson arrived in camp stark naked.[2] In the morning, in fact, the Indians broke camp and went off ahead of the settlers along the river; for several days, they stayed within sight.

But one at least of the emigrants had enough. The next day, as they toiled along the river valley, some boats passed them, bull boats, like the boat that Jim Bridger had taken down the Bear River

[2]*Recollection*, p. 198. Nancy had a tendency sometimes to color her accounts a little.

to Salt Lake. Laden with furs, they were headed back down to civilization, and a settler named Stone hopped aboard and went with them, back to the known world.

Soon after, Nancy and the others got another dose of Plains weather. They were gathered on the bank of the river when the sky darkened, and a wild wind began to shriek. Hail pelted them, while thunder cracked and rolled; some of the hail was as large as goose eggs, and one stone knocked cold one of the Cheyenne in the band traveling with them.

Then out of the slate-blue clouds a long thin rope of cloud descended. When its tip reached the earth, rocks and sand flew into the air, and whole trees pulled up out of the ground and sailed away toward heaven.

The settlers, awestruck and terrified, cowered instinctively down onto the ground and pressed themselves against their wagons, which were shaking and rocking in the wind. The wind's roar shook them. The oncoming tornado hit the river and brought up a fountain of the water that seemed a mile high. Nancy lay flat against the ground, her daughter in her arms, and watched an uprooted tree fly overhead, its roots clutching at the air like fingers.

Moments later the storm was past. The wild sky was blossoming forth into sunshine again. Nancy rose, shaken. Ben wrapped his arms around her and she leaned on him. If they had died, she thought, if that whirling wind had hit them, nobody back home would even have known what happened to them. She meant not so much that the news would never reach Missouri, but that people there could not even imagine such a fate. She was in a different world now, incommensurate with the country left behind.

As they continued up the Platte they passed by Chimney Rock, towering like a petrified tornado hundreds of feet above the valley floor. Bidwell admired this country, "worn in such a manner by the storms of unnumbered seasons that they really counterfeited the lofty spires, towering edifices, spacious domes and in fine all the beautiful mansions of cities." Even Williams, who saw nothing lovely in nature, remarked on the strange shapes of the hills. But, as one of the Jesuits wrote, "They are all much more beautiful from a distance than close at hand."[3]

All along the Platte, by the millions, were the buffalo. They grazed on the short, curly gamma grass, a potent fodder even when it looked dead; they rumbled down to the waterholes in droves, raising up clouds of dust, and turning the river the color of the dust. The bulls roared and the calves fought and played together while their mothers grazed. They all lay down on the banks of the river and chewed their cuds. Sometimes one would simply turn and run, and instantly all the others would be running, the earth a drum under their hoofs, casting up such a pall of dust the sun dimmed and the sky darkened.

A single buffalo is an impressive beast, fearless and bad-tempered, the bulls running to six feet at the shoulder, weighing thousands of pounds. But it was their sheer numbers that astonished everybody. The herds seemed infinite. The settlers hunted them as if they were, and soon fell into wasteful ways; they killed far more than they needed, took the choicest cuts of meat, and left the rest of the carcass to rot in the sun. One hunter in a few hours shot eleven buffalo and took away only their tongues. The ground was littered with buffalo bones, "so that the valley, throughout its whole length and breadth," Bidwell said, "is nothing but one complete slaughteryard."[4]

Bidwell, observant and clear-headed, was alarmed; he knew how recently the buffalo had grazed in Kentucky and Illinois, and that "if they continue to decrease in the same ratio that they have for the past 15 or 20 years, they will ere long become totally extinct."[5] Yet in June of 1841 the vast herds covered the plains from horizon to horizon and their trampling shook the ground; they seemed never-ending.

[3]Father Nicholas Point.
[4]Bidwell I.
[5]Bidwell I.

They fascinated Nancy, like all the settlers. They were the embodiment of the Plains themselves. "At times," wrote the Jesuit Mengarini, "we saw the distant hills covered with what seemed clumps of stunted trees, but if even a gentle wind happened to blow towards that quarter, the trees would move up the sides of the hills and disappear; they were immense herds of buffaloes."[6]

The herds were dangerous as well as enormous. One evening as the settlers were camping by the water Fitzpatrick came among them in great excitement; a drove of buffalo was headed straight toward them. He got all the men out, with their guns, to build fires between the camp and the oncoming tide. Ann wrapped tight in her arms, Nancy and the other women bundled together sleepless through the din, while all night long the men fed the fires and shot off their guns, splitting the onrushing buffalo into two streams that thundered by on either side of the camp in a continuous, hours-long stampede. "One cannot nowadays describe the rush and wildness of the thing," Bidwell said, much later.[7] In the morning the camp was an island in a great sea of woolly brown bodies; the sky was a milky shroud of dust; the buffalo, trampling down into the river to drink, had fouled the water so that the people could not stomach it.

Still jumpy about Indians and surrounded by buffalo, the train forded the south fork of the Platte. The water was so shallow they could drive their wagons through it. The oxen plodded steadily through water to their chests; sometimes the wagons must have floated like rafts on the flat water. Other times, the oxen hit a soft patch of sand, and had to scramble frantically for solid footing, and the wagons rocked and tipped. Then the men, yelling and whistling, rushed to haul on the oxen and help them through the mire, and grab the wagons to keep them from falling over.

Other times, the train sailed along, mirrored in the still water

[6]Mengarini, p. 223.
[7]Bidwell III.

of the Platte, like a little armada. At the settlers' passage, clouds of
waterbirds rose up into the hazy blue sky. Ann in front of her on
the saddle, and her skirts bundled up out of the wet; Nancy let her
horse pick its way cautiously over the bottom. The river was breast-
deep to her pony, full of sand, opaque. By the time they reached
the other bank, the horse and her legs and boots were covered with
a fine film of mud.

The company trudged off across the prairie toward the north
fork of the great river. Abruptly there were no more buffalo to be
seen. Reaching the north fork, they camped where the bluffs
pinched down close on the water, and there, the next morning, one
of the party, a young man named George Shotwell, killed himself.

It was an accident; he was reaching into his wagon to get his
rifle, and took it carelessly by the muzzle and pulled it toward him.
The rifle went off, drilling him through the body. For an hour, the
others gathered around him and watched helplessly as he died.
Nancy probably took Ann and the other younger children away,
but they could not escape the dread and grief of the death.

They buried him, and Reverend Williams preached a funeral.
Typically, the group had a meeting, at which they talked over what
to do with poor Shotwell's belongings—Bidwell knew he had a
mother in Kentucky; solemnly they arranged to have Captain Bartleson[8] take charge of the estate.

Neither the funeral nor the meeting helped raise the company's
spirits. George had been popular among the men, and the death had
been so shockingly senseless: it seemed like a bad omen. Later that
day they circled around the bluffs of the north fork of the Platte, to
the beautiful little valley of Ash Hollow, but when they camped,
they stayed where they were for a while, in mourning. "His loss
produced a sadness that lasted many days," Bidwell said.[9] Mingled
with their grief over George Shotwell was anxiety over their own

[8]Bartleson insisted on being called Captain.
[9]Bidwell II.

helplessness against random disaster. For a moment, they seemed to have run out of energy.

Fitzpatrick may have told them then how he did the same thing, shot himself in the hand drawing his own gun to fight Blackfeet. And he could have told them about other men, sorely wounded, whose companions had not stayed by them, nor even grieved, but who had left them to die in the wilderness. There was Hugh Glass, for instance, mauled by a grizzly, whose companions had buried him in a shallow grave when he wasn't even dead yet, and gone on; Hugh dug himself out again and crawled back home to terrorize the men who abandoned him. The grief of the company might have been a good sign, that in spite of all the bickering, they were committed to one another.

Nancy, of course, had her baby to take care of. She had already found out, when her little boy baby died, back in Missouri, how taking care of Ann helped get her through hard times: the steady routine of small, manageable tasks gave her something to hold onto in the face of despair, and focusing on someone else's needs kept her from dwelling on her own. Ben, also, and the other men could turn to watch the children, and the women with their children, and so gain some sense of the stubborn power of life and its unquenchable hope.

Joseph Chiles later wrote, "There still exists a warmth in every heart for the mother and her child that were always forming silver linings for every dark cloud that assailed them."[10] Nancy did no heroic deeds: she only did what she had always done, and what women always do: her woman's work, tending the baby, caring for her husband, looking out for those around her. In so doing she held the world together, for herself, for her husband, for everybody.

That must have been getting harder to do, by mid-June. The whole train was running out of supplies. There was still plenty of

[10]Chiles, p. 143. He was talking of the time to come, when she would be the only woman in a band of more than thirty men.

water, with rain every few days, but they were short of flour, and probably completely out of bulky and perishable things like lard and potatoes. They would still have had some beans, but very little bacon; they relied on the meat they could shoot as they passed through the country. The great orgy of eating buffalo was over: the buffalo had disappeared.

They saw some bighorn sheep, in the hills, and Bidwell among others tried to hunt them, but the sheep were too wary, and the country too rough. Mostly they had antelope.

At least Nancy's camp routine was simpler. There was no longer the rush to get her bread sponge built, the worry of the rising of the dough, the packing and unpacking of so many things. The pressure of necessity was paring her chores down to the bare essentials. By this time, probably, they were also doing without the tent, which gave no real shelter anyway.

Keeping Ann fed was Nancy's main concern. With the potatoes used up, she no longer could make the salt-rising bread that had been a staple of the trek so far, but while the flour and cornmeal lasted she could mix up a kind of pancake, and give her mashed beans. Without milk the little girl could not thrive. She was quieter, which made her more manageable, of course. Nancy carried her all the time, slung on her hip when she walked, or in front of her on the saddle. Now eighteen months old, Ann was starting to talk— pointing to things, crying out words. Calling to her father when Ben rode back into view after going on ahead to reconnoiter.

But more and more she was listless, withdrawn, and a cold dread gripped Nancy near the heart. Then she drew the child into a quiet little game, to see some life in her again. And especially she looked for more food for her, tidbits of meat, berries, wild sweetpeas and onions, good cool water.

Lifting her gaze from her child, in the evenings, she looked around the camp, assessing them all. Ben was hearty enough, and had not had a sick spell recently: that was good. Looking at him, she could feel a joyous pride in her husband. She noticed how the others looked up to him—how his strength and decision kept them going. Ben was a rock; she could depend on him.

In fact, all the men seemed strong and hale, even those who had come west "for their health," like old Henshaw. Bidwell was slender, but wiry and strong. Bartleson was as broad and meaty as ever. How dependable any of them were remained a matter of question. She liked Bidwell.

The other women looked worn, but that could just have been the trail dirt that they could not wash entirely out of their clothes, their hair, their skin. The children, especially the younger children,[11] were thin and peaked under their tans.

Nancy felt a sharp stab of guilt, then, at bringing these youngsters through this ordeal. And shrugged it off, almost at once; there was no going back now, and her parents had taken her west, when she was hardly older than Ann. Children followed their parents: that was the way of things. They would be better off for it, in California.

The main thing was getting there. She tried to get a real grasp of their prospects. Farmwife that she was, she knew stock, and she could see that the party's horses, mules, and oxen were losing condition. The settlers had long since gone through whatever grain they brought for the horses; the oxen had never had anything but what they could forage every day for themselves. The steady hard work without ample fodder was breaking the beasts down. Their bodies hung down from the racks of their backbones and hips, and every night, turned loose to graze, they wandered far from the camp in their struggle to fill their bellies. Some of them were limping. Some spent most of their time lying down, and were harder and harder to rouse.

[11]We know nothing of the other children, but Ann Williams Kelsey's family started with five, of which she was probably the oldest, so there may well have been more little children than just Nancy's Ann. Widow Grey, her sister-in-law, had a child as well, the age not noted.

But when the settlers reached Fort Laramie, surely, they would be able to resupply, find stout animals, and get ready for the second half of the trip. Nancy, like all of them, fixed her thoughts on that.

And they were coming to Fort Laramie at last. Three days after they passed by Chimney Rock, within sight of high blue mountains, they rolled in through the stockade gates. They had left the Plains; the Rockies lay before them.

CHAPTER

5

The bluff where the little Laramie River ran down into the Platte seemed unimpressive, merely a high, flat meadowland against a backdrop of blue mountain. Yet it was uniquely placed to dominate both the high plains of the Platte and the approach to South Pass, which was the gateway to the Far West. Recognizing this central position, on this flat grassy headland, in 1834, the fur trappers had built Fort William,[1] to trade in beaver with the Indians.

Now the beaver trade had bottomed out, but the fort's excellent strategic position made it still a major supply, trade, and social center for a huge expanse of territory. There American trappers, Hudsons Bay men, French voyageurs, Sioux and Cheyenne and Arapaho, all gathered to sell pelts, stock up on supplies, swap lies and truths, gossip and fight, and get drunk and find women. The current trade was in buffalo robes, which the American Fur Com-

[1]Named for William Sublette, of Smith, Jackson and Sublette.

pany bought directly from the Indians, spelling the end of the mountain man's way of life, but, then, the mountain man's way of life was self-defeating.

As a base of operations, the Company had begun rebuilding Fort William, whose official name was Fort John; but everybody had taken to calling the place after the Laramie River. When the Bidwell–Bartleson party came through in 1841, the new fort was only half-finished. It was some 160 by 160 feet of adobe brick, a low compound swallowed up by the landscape around it: just beyond the squat buildings rose the first heights of the mountains, humping up into the sky.

"The Black Hills[2] were now in view," Bidwell wrote, "a very noted peak, called the Black Hill mountain, was seen like a dark cloud in the western horizon. The country along Platte river is far from being fertile and is uncommonly destitute of timber."[3] Bidwell found little to note about the stockade and its buildings at all.

Even when the fort was finished, it probably wasn't going to look like much. Yet this site was to be the hub of the high plains, over the next half century. To reach the Far West you had to go through South Pass. To reach South Pass you had to go by Fort Laramie. It was a major stop on the immigrant trail, allowing settlers to rest up and regroup after crossing the plains and before taking on the mountains. The Pony Express passed through Fort Laramie; so did the transcontinental telegraph and the Deadwood Stage line. In 1849, the U.S. Army bought it and turned it into a major military post, and from Fort Laramie the Army crushed the Sioux and Cheyenne.

All this lay in the future when the Kelseys and their company arrived. For them, the fort's current condition was a major disappointment. Staffed by laid-up and laid-off chaw-packing half-drunk mountain men in buckskins tarry with dirt and sweat, the little

[2]The Black Hills of Wyoming, not the more famous Black Hills in Dakota.
[3]Bidwell I.

huddle of adobe buildings inside the half-built wall was less a res-
olute outpost of civilization than a wholesale surrender to the wild.
And the prices of goods dismayed them. Nobody could afford to
pay five dollars a pound for flour, or two dollars for an egg.

Nonetheless, they were here, and there were resources. The
women crowded into the Fort's washroom, heated water, washed
clothes. The men dickered with the Fort's factors over a few supplies. They sold some of the goods they had brought with them,
lightening the load as much as gaining some money. Some of the
single men began hanging around the Indian village outside the half-
built wall, eyeing the girls.

Reverend Williams, for one, was shocked at this. When he found
out that a lot of the Indian women in the village were married to
the mountain men who ran the Fort, he was even more shocked.
"Here is plenty of talk of their damnation," he said, "but none about
their salvation," which he attempted to make up for, preaching twice
to anybody who would stay to listen. Very few listened. Some of
the Indians attended; they loved speeches, and they recognized true
feeling in his intense inwardness. The other settlers had seen enough
of the reverend and had other things to do.

At Fort Laramie the settlers auctioned off the goods of the late
George Shotwell, and pumped the fort's inhabitants for useful information about their course to come. Nobody had any advice
about getting to California. They recounted, instead, more of the
grim stories of mountain men venturing out past the Salt Lake and
dying, or nearly dying, of thirst. Somebody remembered that Jed
Smith, legendary wanderer, who had gone everywhere and done
everything, crossed that country west to east one winter, came in to
the rendezvous almost dead, and went around the desert, not
through it, thereafter. Somebody else remembered that Joe Walker
had crossed it in 1833. Two more of the men in the settlers' party
dropped out, heading back east.

But another man joined them, an aging one-eyed mountain man

named Richard Phelan, who had been resident at Laramie when the settlers arrived.

Phelan's interest had attached itself to the sole single woman in the group: Nancy Kelsey's sister-in-law, the Widow Grey. Single white women were an extraordinary rarity on the far frontier and most such women could look forward to a steady pressure of blandishments and proposals. All the while the pioneers were at the Fort, Phelan squired the widow around, helping her carry laundry and haul water. Mrs. Gray was understandably pleased. Besides the flattery of his admiration, she was a lone woman, and a man's help came in very handy. When the party left Fort Laramie, Phelan went with her, and when they reached the Green River rendezvous, Phelan married her.

Under most circumstances, Phelan wouldn't have been many people's choice for a brother-in-law. Out here on the edge of the Rockies he was a real prize, with his knowledge of the wilderness, his rifle, his horse and gear. Nancy must have thought, shrewdly, that Widow Grey had made a good match.

Fitzpatrick led his party on toward the Green River rendezvous. There the settlers hoped to find sound, well-fed stock to replace their beat-up beasts, and directions to California and possibly guides, and—it turned out—Bartleson had a little private enterprise of his own to conduct.

The fur trappers' rendezvous, held yearly on the Green River and/or on the Popo Agie River, was a summer-long party, in which men who had spent the bulk of the year starving, tramping up and down frozen streams setting traps, dodging Blackfeet, and skinning beaver brought that beaver in and traded it all for a couple of bottles of watered-down whiskey ("what they called whiskey—three or four gallons of water to a gallon of alcohol"[4]) and the supplies to

[4]Bidwell III.

go back and do it all over again for another year. Tales of the wild doings at the rendezvous had filtered back to the east for years. The settlers expected to find hundreds of men at the Green River, with attendant supply wagons and herds of beasts.

For several days they traveled through the Black Hills, finding buffalo as they went. A Cheyenne family trailed along with them for a while. The hills were treeless grassy ridges so monotonous that it was easy to get lost in them. One night Josiah Belden staggered into camp on foot; he had gone off to hunt buffalo, tied his horse to a tree, and walked off to get a better shot, and then in the confusing featureless hills had searched for hours without finding the horse again.

They were finding plenty to eat, but the landscape seemed ominous. "As we advanced, the shade of the vegetation became more somber, the form of the hills much more rugged, the face of the mountains more towering. The general impression was one not of decay but of age or, rather, the most venerable antiquity."[5] Although it was the middle of summer, at night not even buffalo robes could keep them warm; Nancy and Ben bundled together, Ann between them, their faces buried in the stinking protection of the woolly hide, and still shivered in the iron cold. Everywhere were signs that the first part of the journey, which had nearly exhausted them, was only the beginning, and the easiest stretch, of this trek.

Late on the fifth of July, aptly, they came to Independence Rock. This vast mound had been named first by the fur trapper Bill Sublette, who celebrated the country's birthday there in 1824, but it kept the name because emigrant trains leaving Independence, Missouri, in mid-May, the best time to embark, tended to reach the Rock around the Fourth, then as now the most religiously observed American holiday. "All hands," Bidwell writes, "were anxious to have their names inscribed on this memorable landmark," continuing what would become in the next decade a ritual of the plains crossing. But first they sent two of their number, John Gray, the

[5]Father Point, p. 233.

half-Iroquois trapper, and his charge Lord Romaine, on to the
Green River rendezvous, to tell the trappers there that they were
coming, and start lining up customers.

The Englishman and his guide headed off west. The young men
among the settlers spent the better part of the morning climbing
Independence Rock, painting on their names, or chipping them into
the stone. Nancy spent the time looking for berries and roots, and
gathering armfuls of grass for the oxen.

From Independence Rock they followed the Sweetwater River
upstream into the mountains. The broad open valley of the Sweetwater, named not for any quality of the water but because some
voyageurs once spilled a sack of sugar into it, was summer pasture
for the buffalo, and within sight of the Wind River range, the company came on great herds of them. They stopped to put up supplies
to get them across the next leg of the journey. For the next three
days they shot buffalo, cut the meat into strips, and dried the strips
over fires, each day still managing to travel a dozen miles or more
along the broad gentle slope toward South Pass.

The abundance was an illusion. They were moving steadily
higher, following the Sweetwater, and the year was moving on. The
buffalo were leaving their summer pasture even as the Kelseys and
the others were coming onto it. Now, with the urgency on them,
the cold mountains looming up ahead, and the bitter bite of frost in
the night air even in the depth of summer, now when they needed
the buffalo, the herds vanished. All they found were stray bulls,
rogues, and cripples, and those were poor and few, four or five a
day, if they were lucky.

Gray and Romaine came back from the rendezvous with equally
bad news. They had found no trappers there at all, no supplies, no
stock.[6] Nor had they seen any game between the settlers' present

---

[6]The failure of the beaver trade, and the switch to trade in buffalo robes,
destroyed the rendezvous, and doomed the free trappers. The fur companies
could buy robes cheaper from the Indians at the company's forts.

position and the Green River, on to the west. Warned, the party stopped for a day and did nothing but hunt buffalo and cure the meat. Nancy tended the fires, hung the meat on the racks, turned the shriveling strips over and over again.

The fat greasy strips of red meat turned slowly into little blackened strings, dripping all their goodness into the crackling flames. What remained hardly seemed worth eating. And there wasn't enough. She could see that, even while the settlers were all still killing and cutting and drying. In between her tasks, she took Ann, and went out beyond the campsite to where thickets of wild currants grew, and fed the baby all she would eat of the berries.

Meanwhile, the men, or some of them, were up to frivolous pursuits. Bartleson was not ready to let go his dream of making a killing at the rendezvous. He and some others, who thought they could trade profitably with the trappers, raised a subscription to pay the half-breed John Gray to go out and find some trappers to trade with. Nancy paid no heed to this; it only added to her dislike of Bartleson. She was glad to see Ben paid no heed to it either.

The company moved slowly across the brown slopes of South Pass. On the jagged peaks of the Wind River range drifts of snow lay glittering in the July sun. Almost exactly two months after they left Sapling Grove, on July 18, they crossed over the Continental Divide, and after twenty miles came to the Little Sandy River, running west.

They were still finding an occasional buffalo, but the country was turning dry and dusty. They saw what looked like smoke mounting into the sky beyond a ridge, and guessed that there were Indians all around them. There was little forage for the oxen. During the day Nancy on her horse searched around for patches of grass; finding even a few blades, she cut the stems and took them back, a pitiful few mouthfuls for the starving beasts. Her horse was looking poor, its flanks and neck too flat, its backbone jutting up so high she had to fold the blanket over again to keep the saddle from galling its withers. Its shoes were gone. Like all the pioneers, she knew to cut pieces of fresh hide and wrap them around the horse's feet like boots.

Then at last on the Big Sandy River they came on plentiful grass, and stopped to rest. There Gray found them again. After much personal hardship, perhaps fictional, he had indeed discovered trappers. Eagerly Bartleson hastened them all on to the Green River to meet them.

This was no great rendezvous of hundreds of brawling newly rich fur men. All the settlers found was a band of about twenty,[7] under the leadership of a German named Fraeb, an old partner of Fitzpatrick's. Here Bartleson at last unveiled his treasure: a cask of alcohol, which he had carried along hidden in his wagon all the way from Missouri. This cask, mixed one to three with the Green River water, he proceeded to offer to Fraeb and his men as whiskey. The trappers immediately bought him out. They also traded some with the other settlers, swapping dressed deerskins and deerskin clothes for knives and gunpowder and galena, the lead used for rifle balls.

Somebody surely made the connection now with Talbot Green and his lump of lead, and probably more than one of them expected him to trot it out and sell it. But Green kept his lead securely tucked away in the back of his wagon and said nothing.

The trappers also had some horses. Jimmy John bought one that impressed them all with its nimbleness and willingness to go almost anywhere. Bidwell said he thought the horse could climb trees.

Most of them got nothing from the trappers but their entertainment value. This was of a rarefied kind. All the women made sure that their children stayed far away from Fraeb's men, who were filthy, and filthy-mouthed; their habits startled even the toughened Kelsey women. Some of the trappers bragged they had eaten noth-

---

[7]Or thirty or forty depending on the account. Directly after they met the settlers, Fraeb and his men encountered a band of Blackfeet and fought a famous battle at which many of the trappers, including Fraeb himself, were killed.

ing but meat for ten years. Bidwell, who from the beginning had worried about running out of bread, without which he thought he would find no savor in anything, told the trappers at once that the settlers could spare no flour. Fraeb's men laughed that off. They didn't want bread, they were mountain men! But if the settlers had any bacon, now, they'd just love some nice crisp bacon.[8]

The settlers spent a day and a half in this last, sad little rendezvous, and worked Fraeb and his men for information about the way to California, but again they got bad news. None of the trappers had ever crossed the desert, but they were all sure that it would be "impossible" to get wagons to California. There was no river running from Salt Lake to the sea, although some had heard of a river that sprang up in the hills north of Salt Lake, and ran west—Mary's River, they called it.

The only good word they had was that Joe Walker might be at Fort Hall, on ahead of them on the way to Oregon.

This was however excellent news. Joe Walker had crossed the desert to California in 1833. If the settlers could enlist him to guide them, their worst problem was solved. So the talk went, around the cooking fires in the evening. Joe Walker would be at Fort Hall. Joe Walker would whisk them off to California.

The talk went other ways, too. People were beginning to talk about not going to California at all.

Some of them, of course, had never meant to. The English Lord Romaine, with his fancy guns and his half-breed guide, was going back east again. The rest of them, Nancy knew, were coming to a point of decision. Within a few days, they would reach Soda Springs, and there Tom Fitzpatrick would lead his Jesuits on to the north, to the Flathead country in Montana. Fitzpatrick had brought them this far, and the dullest of them must have realized that without him

[8]The mountain men had picked up the Indian habit of eating buffalo guts, often warm right out of the buffalo, which would have supplied them with the nutrients tamer people derive from bread and vegetables.

they would now be dead or back in Independence, but none of them wanted to go to Montana.

On the other hand, there was Oregon.

There was a trail to Oregon—across the gorges of the Snake River and through Indian country, but a known trail. Fraeb's trappers had told them that they could get wagons down to the American settlements on the Columbia "with no difficulty." Fitzpatrick could tell them in detail where to go. A lot of the settlers were thinking Oregon sounded a lot better than California.

Some were still fixed on the original purpose. They had started for California; they meant to end there. One of these was Ben Kelsey, and Nancy was of a single mind with him. She was not one to put down a task she had taken on herself.

For once, however, the Kelsey brothers were divided. Andrew, like Ben, wanted to head on to California, but Sam and Zebediah were for Oregon. The trouble, from Nancy's point of view, was that these latter two brothers were the Kelseys who had wives. In fact, all the other women were leaning toward Oregon. If she went to California, she would be the only woman in the band.

If she went. How could she not go—if Ben went? And he would not be Ben Kelsey if he did not go on charging along the path he had set for himself, all the way back in Missouri, a path running straight as the course of the sun across the continent. Ben was going to California. Nancy was going with him. Nancy and Ann.

Thinking this, she held the little girl closer. To take Ann out there, into the desert, into that great empty space: that daunted her. Warm in her arms, the child laid her head heavy against her mother's breast, drowsing. The arguments round the fire, the flash of words— California, Oregon—meant nothing to little Ann, bounded in her mother's love. But what mother who loved her child would take her into such danger?

Of course it was a little late to be gnawing on this bone. Nancy had brought Ann this far, she couldn't very well give up now, and a better life lay ahead of them, in California. And somewhere unarticulated in her mind lay the notion that there was no virtue doing something that had been done already.

But the other women must have been working on her. To them, it would have been unthinkable she would not come with them. If Ben had to go to California, well, he would surely let her go on in the care of his brothers, and send for her when he got settled. So the women said. Behind their hands, they told her that if she declared that she would go to Oregon, Ben would go with her.

So the people around the fires argued, and Nancy, perhaps, argued with herself. In her heart, she knew what she would do. Around them loomed a vast and fathomless night silence, and they all crouched down over their little fires and talked as if they knew what they were talking about. In the end, they all had to leap into the dark.

They had come to the point where words were mostly for comfort. Nobody knew what to expect. In the face of this ongoing tremendous uncertainty, perhaps as an antidote for it, one of the settlers, Bill Overton, kept insisting that nothing had ever surprised him.

"Of course, that raised a dispute. 'Never surprised in your life?' 'No, I never was surprised.' And, moreover, he swore that nothing ever *could* surprise him. 'I should not be surprised,' said he, 'if I were to see a steamboat come plowing over these mountains this minute.' "[9] Many of them listening must have thought that they would prefer a steamboat chugging up the Green River any day to what actually waited ahead of them.

[9]Bidwell III.

CHAPTER

6

Fitzpatrick took them along the Bear River through the rugged high country, catching fish in the rapid water, and shooting wild geese and antelope. The meadows of blue flax flowers were going to seed. Cedars grew on the benches of old streambed above the river. Bidwell remarked over and over on the beauty and grandeur of the landscape. The steep-climbing evergreen forests teemed with game and with wild fruit. Ben and his brothers brought in fat game every day, and as she went along, Nancy found wild cherries and currants enough to keep Ann fed. The child seemed more robust, brighter and quicker. Nancy's confidence surged; Ann was thin but strong, and see how well her mother could find food for them in the wilderness.

On the tenth of August, nine days after Nancy's eighteenth birthday, they made camp at Soda Springs, in the heart of the Rockies, "a bright and lovely place," as Bidwell said. Here where the Bear River Valley wound south through high mountains, more than a hundred hot springs burst out of the ground, erupting with intermittent roars. The river itself churned with columns of bubbling gas. The steamy fountains of water were thick with sulphurous compounds, which precipitated out around each spring into a heap of sinter, some towering as high as fifty feet. Clouds of the gas sometimes made people sick to their stomachs.

The most amazing of these wonders was on the river bank below the cedar grove where the settlers camped. There, a white gush of water foamed and frothed up out of the ground like a fountain, sometimes leaping up waist high into the air, with loud bangs and cracks like explosions. The children found it first, and then the men went down to see. Nancy followed, once her camp was set up.

Drawing near, she could feel the ground trembling underfoot. Down there somewhere something roared like the voice of a buried giant, and the spring burst up higher, its sudsy water spattering on the wind. All around the mouth of the spring the rock was bright red. Just beyond it, she noticed suddenly, was another hole in the earth; from this one, as she watched, came a puff of smoke and another dribble of water. It was as if the earth here was alive, and slightly daft.

Eerie, loud, smelly, wild and beautiful, Soda Springs was a fit place for the moment of decision. When the group moved out again, Father de Smet and his Jesuits, with Fitzpatrick, would turn north, to the Flathead country. The settlers would have to go on by themselves.

That evening, or perhaps in the morning, they gathered into their meeting circle, and Fitzpatrick stood up in front of them all and told them not to go to California. He had been salting his conversations all along with tales of the horrors of the great Salt Desert and the Sierra, and now he hammered home his point. He told them flat out that they would never reach California. They had no trail and they had no guide, and they were headed into the wildest and harshest country on the continent. He may have said, or maybe not, that they had already shown themselves inept at wilderness life. If they survived the waterless sun-blasted desert they would die in the winter snows of the Sierra. And they had an excellent alternative. They could go on with the Jesuits as far as Fort Hall, some fifty miles on, and from there take the trail to Oregon.[1]

Fitzpatrick delivered his advice so forcefully that about half the settlers did as he told them, although those who did not argued and reproached. "There was some division and strife among us about going," said Reverend Williams, who went to Oregon. The Kelseys especially must have been talking over the decision with a certain heat: half the four Kelsey brothers were giving up on California.

Sam and Lucy Kelsey and their five children, and Zed Kelsey and his new wife, Ann, were all going to Oregon. So were Richard Phelan, the mountainman-turned-settler, and his new wife and her child, and Richard Williams and his wife and children. The families were choosing Oregon.

Ben Kelsey was wild for California. He had planned this all his life, he thought, with only a little exaggeration, and he wasn't going to give it up now. He could shoot and hunt, and he could find his way around in the wilderness. He was going.

Bidwell was going, and most of the other single men.

And Nancy. In front of them all, she stood up and said, "Where my husband goes, I can go. I can better endure the hardships of the journey than the anxieties for an absent husband."[2]

Were these her exact words? Not likely; Joseph Chiles was remembering them nearly forty years later. But clearly, this was Nancy's decision; she chose to go to California. She could have gone on with her Kelsey in-laws to Oregon. Doing otherwise was unexpected enough to the rest of the company to require that she argue her case. And she made her argument on the basis of her own strength and endurance. Anywhere Ben could go, she could go, baby and all.

By this time, she would have been sure of "and all." By the time she chose California, she knew she was carrying another baby. But she was only eighteen, an age when people believe that they can do

[1]Bidwell III.
[2]Chiles.

anything, that they will live forever. And nothing she had seen yet convinced her otherwise. If Joseph Chiles didn't remember Nancy's words exactly, he got the spirit of her.

In all, thirty-two people were setting out for California. Fitz-patrick had warned them; now he shrugged and wished them well. They should send a couple of men on with de Smet, to Fort Hall. Fraeb and his trappers had mentioned that Joe Walker might be at Fort Hall.[3] With a guide like Walker, they might have a chance.

So the company split up, almost exactly even: eight wagons to Oregon, eight to California. Nancy had made her mind up in an attitude of cool reason, but to her surprise she found it hard to say good-bye. She and the other women had shared almost three months of struggle and danger and work; she had known Lucy Kel-sey for years, and now she might never see any of them again. Nor would she have their help in the days to come. As the moment of parting approach, Lucy and the other women probably begged her again to come with them, and the little children, catching the mood, began to cry; then everybody was crying. Nancy held Ann tight in her arms. The little girl wailed along with all the others, and they stood there, the women and their children, dripping and sobbing and swearing to see each other again, sometime, somewhere; they would never forget one another, ever. The men stood around em-barrassed, staring off at the high cold mountain peaks, excluded from this women's rite.

The California-bound wagons rolled away south, then, follow-ing the Bear River. Did Nancy turn in her saddle to watch the others go off to the west, to see them for as long as she could? Maybe she never looked back at all, determined not to regret, and aiming her whole attention forward, into the future.

Ann slept, worn out by all the emotion, slumped down on the saddle between her mother's body and the pommel. For Ann, this was the way life was, always moving.

[3]Bidwell III.

As Fitzpatrick had suggested, the California party sent Bartleson and three other men on west to Fort Hall to find a guide. The eight wagons headed for Cache Valley, the fur trappers' favorite wintering grounds, which had been described to them in such glowing terms that they traveled right through it without recognizing it. The country was hilly and gashed with ravines, so that everybody had to stop periodically and get out shovels and dig out impromptu roads.

Nancy didn't mind going slowly as the brushy hillsides all around were covered with ripe chokecherries. When the baby slept and she could put her safely down, she helped the men dig and haul brush out of the way to clear a path for the wagons.

While they were making this slow progress down through the eastern slopes of the Rockies, John Bidwell and Jimmy John decided to go off to fish for their dinner in the river. From the edge of the water they noticed a snow-covered mountain rising just beyond the treetops. They were hot and dry and the snow looked inviting and so they decided to go there. They set off on what they anticipated to be a few hours' jaunt, leaving behind their guns, which they thought might get in the way.

After a little while, they realized they had farther to go than they had originally thought, but neither one would quit before the other. Therefore neither quit; they kept on going toward the snowy mountain.

"There were thickets so dense as to exclude the sun, and roaring little streams in deep, dark chasms; we had to crawl through paths which looked untrodden except by grizzlies; in one place a large bear had passed evidently only a few minutes before, crossing the deep gorge, plunging through the wild, dashing water, and wetting the steep bank as he went up. We carried our drawn butcher knives in our hands, for they were our only weapons."[4] They did not reach the snowy mountain until the next day.

Meanwhile, however, after a little while, somebody else in the

[4]Bidwell III. Bidwell's accounts of his adventures are gems.

party noticed they were missing and went looking for them. Almost at once, he found their guns and found tracks and what seemed like traces of blood. Shouting to the others, he raised the alarm. Everybody stopped working on the road and began looking for Bidwell and John.

Immediately they began to find fresh signs of Indians—probably Blackfeet. It looked as if the Indians had gotten the two missing men. Now, in a rising panic, they noticed traces of smoke in the sky. Clearly, there were Indians all around, just waiting to pick off more of them.

Ben Kelsey took charge.[5] He got them all camped down for the night, with the wagons for a barricade, as he had seen Fitzpatrick do; he mounted a guard. Nobody slept. In the morning, they went out and searched again for Bidwell and John, finding no sign of them but, again, fresh tracks, and more traces of smoke in the sky. The Indians were all around them for sure.

Finally, after hours of fruitless searching, Ben turned the train forward again. They had to keep moving, even if it seemed inch by inch sometimes. Everybody went to work in silence, morose. This was like Shotwell again, only worse, because of the Indians; this time they could all be next. Nancy swept the hillsides constantly with her gaze, watching for the Blackfeet. She kept one arm around Ann, on the saddle in front of her. Her mind churned. She liked Bidwell and John, and Bidwell was one of the leaders. This was a disaster. But Ben was stepping up to it. She could rely on Ben; she was glad of her husband, who would get them through this. Still, her eyes began to ache from looking for Indians creeping up through the brush. And poor Bidwell and John!

They were hacking their way through a thicket-choked ravine when, suddenly, a yell went up. "Hey! Hey, look!"

---

[5]There is no explicit evidence of this but somebody was giving orders through what is clearly a little crisis. Bidwell states flatly, later on, that Kelsey had taken command when Bartleson abandoned them; here both Bidwell and Bartleson are gone, Ben seems the obvious choice.

Nancy jerked upright, wheeling to look in the direction of the shout, and saw one of the men from the back of the train racing his horse up the newly cleared trail. He was pointing wildly, yelling, but joyous—*not Indians*, she thought, at once, and then realized what he did mean, and with the others rushed off down the trail to greet Bidwell and John.

They were filthy, their clothes ripped; they were gripping butcher knives in their fists. Certainly they looked as if they had just escaped from the Indians. The company fell on them in delight and relief. "Where have you been?" somebody cried, and then everybody was yelling it. "Where were you? What happened?"

"We have been up to the snow!"[6] Bidwell declared, triumphant, and lifted up a ragged bandanna that contained a single fist-sized dirty melting snowball.

There was a brief, disbelieving silence. Then uproar. The flood of relief turned to fury. What idiots! How dare they put everybody else through such an agony? One man declared they should be horse-whipped. Bidwell, who had retrieved his rifle, brandished it and declared nobody talked to him that way. A chorus of jeers drowned him out.

Nancy laughed, relieved; clearly, things weren't always as bad as they seemed. Like the melting snowball, the crisis was disappearing in the steady heat of day. With the others, she turned back to the work of hauling the wagons on toward Cache Valley.

But as the days passed the country was becoming drier and harsher, not the blooming paradise they had expected. They camped one night by a stream that was running merrily along when they arrived, but then dried up in an hour; in the morning the stream was rushing again. Everything about this place seemed like a warning. They were following the Bear River, which, as everybody knew, flowed into Salt Lake, where they still hoped to find the Rio Bon-

[6]Californians will recognize this as a well-beloved traditional pursuit, *going to the snow*, somewhat prematurely engaged in.

aventura running off to the Pacific Ocean. A salt creek running into
the river forced them off course to the west and they had to drag
and shove and curse the wagons along upstream for six miles, past
hot springs and mud holes, before they found a place where they
could cross.

By this time, it was dark. They had to make camp by the salt
creek, whose water was undrinkable.

Nancy carried water with her in a canteen for Ann, hoarding it
carefully; she chewed up some of the jerked buffalo meat they had
dried back on the approach to South Pass, and gave the mushy mess
to the little girl to eat. Ann spat it out after a while, making a face
at the harsh taste, but Nancy gathered up all the gummy traces of
the food and patiently shoveled them back into her daughter's
mouth again, until she got it all down.

In the morning they went on, striking across country in hopes
of finding fresh water quickly. Nancy walked, sometimes, leading
her horse, Ann riding on her hip. The sun climbed higher, pounding
them with its heat. They were coming down onto flat ground now;
ahead they could see a broad plain stretching into a hazy distance.
Nancy, peering forward as far as her eyes would reach, saw there
the shimmer of the heat on the broad plain, the loom of huge mountains. The vast sky, depthless blue at its peak, ran down into white
and disappeared into the indefinite horizon. The land seemed like a
huge empty bowl of rock.

She gave Ann water drop by drop from the canteen; everybody
else was out of water now. The sun's heat blasted them. There was
no sign of any game. The air smelled sharply of smoke,[7] and was so
hazy they could not make out much of the country ahead of them.
They could see the towering walls of the mountains on their left as
they pushed south but to the west there seemed only flat emptiness.

---

[7]Everybody in the train who kept a diary mentioned this smoke, which they
all assumed was something the Indians were doing. Some scholars have
conjectured that it wasn't smoke at all, but the natural haze of the desert.

Stubbornly they pushed on, the animals shaky and slow with thirst, and then somebody saw trees up ahead.

Trees! Where there was timber in this country, there was water. They flung themselves forward toward the groves shimmering in the heat. But as they rushed toward them, the trees that seemed so tall at first shrank down into little shrubs of chaparral, and there was no water.

They rolled on, scanning the whole country for signs they could follow. Ahead, the ground was gray, bare except for an occasional clump of bunch grass. When the first oxen stepped onto it, their cloven hoofs sank down into the stuff. Ben, walking along beside the wagon, stooped and laid his finger to it and touched his finger to his lips.

"Salt."

Desperate now, they turned east and cut as straight across country as they could, to find the Bear River again before they all died of thirst. The weaker animals straggled behind and they had to let them lag. The oxen drawing the two Kelsey wagons were trudging along so slow even Ann could outwalk them. The ground was white with salt and the wagon wheels crunched out trails as if in snow. Salt spangled the blades of grass that straggled up from the crusted ground. Ann cried for water and Nancy gave her the last in the canteen. She looked at Ben, driving the oxen, wondering when he had drunk last. Her own mouth was so dry it hurt, and her lips cracked, and she tasted wisps of blood.

Ann held the canteen over her mouth and one last drop fell in, and then nothing.

Nancy's eyes ached from scanning the stretch of flat ground ahead of them. The river had to be here somewhere. In the haze she could see only the dim shapes of the mountains on the eastern edge of the plain; looking northeast, she saw low hills, and in the low

---

But three years later when John Charles Frémont and Kit Carson came through here they encountered a forest fire that had been burning for years.

hills, a sharp notch. That must be where the Bear River came through—Jim Bridger's gateway through the hills. She searched for the telltale line of trees on the grassy ground ahead, but there was nothing. The air smelled of salt and smoke. She was so dry now she had stopped sweating, and her head ached. She held Ann against her, afraid.

Then her horse jerked up its head, and an ox gave a low, agonized groan. Abruptly all the animals were stirring, pushing on faster. Nancy let out a cry. The men burst into a ragged, exhausted cheer. The grassy plains ahead suddenly broke. Before them, the ground plunged off into the steep bank of a wash. That was why they couldn't see the river—here it ran hidden, sunk deep into the plain. But now there it was, rolling slow and dark through stands of willows and hawthorne. They had found the lifeline again.

The river ran deep and strong, but the water tasted briny, like soup. The willows crowded the wash, and the little grass that grew, while thick and green, was so salty the animals could barely eat it. The weary settlers made camp; Nancy drank some of the water, found she could bear it, and gave some to Ann, slowly, until the little girl's thirst abated. Some of the men brewed the water into coffee to drink it.

They spent the next day in the willows, letting their animals recover. Nancy was glad of the chance to rest. She rinsed out all their clothes and let Ann go about naked, which helped heal the raw red skin of her rear end. Two of the men went south to scout along the river and came back to report that they were within ten miles of the Salt Lake. They had passed through Cache Valley and come out on the edge of the great terra incognita that lay west of the Rockies.

What they had seen of it was daunting. First of all, they had actually seen very little, because of the smoke. What was visible suggested a scale gigantic past imagining, and barriers far more formidable than they had yet passed. There were no rivers; they had to find another river, but who knew where, or even if there was one.

They had found no game, and no drinkable water, and their beasts could hardly eat the the salty grass. West of here, they had seen, the grass gave way to sage, which the horses could not eat at all.

Without game and wild forage, they were devouring the supply of meat put up on the approaches to South Pass. Nancy chewed Ann's ration of jerked buffalo into a mush and the baby patiently ate it all with sips of water. Ben and the other men stood around, and Bidwell got out his map. Nancy went about her chores, but she kept an ear out to what they were saying.

They hemmed and hawed over the map, which was clearly wishful thinking made tangible. On it, slowly, they traced with their fingers their own, new map. To the south, obviously, lay desert and scrub, and the Salt Lake, which the old map said ran as long as the Mississippi.

On the old map, out of each end of this tremendous lake ran rivers that flowed into the Pacific Ocean. Bidwell pointed this out. Somebody else said that Fitzpatrick had adamantly denied the existence of any such river. And to go toward the Lake any farther was to go back into that hell of smoke and salt and heat. They had to go west, but northwest. To the northwest, they had seen, there lay low hollow-flanked foothills. They could go along the edge of the foothills, where the ground broke, and there might be rivers and creeks and springs.

Unspoken—or perhaps some were already speaking it—was the notion that they could go due north, back along the Bear River, and head for Fort Hall. They could give up.

They did not give up. The next day, their water casks full of brine, they set off toward the northwest. Halfway through the morning, they cut across fresh wagon tracks, seaming the crusty ground. They were crossing their own trail, made just a few days earlier, on their way south toward the Lake. They had made a big loop around the lower reaches of the Bear.

At this intersection, they stuck a paper on a pole, to direct Bartleson and the other men coming after them from Fort Hall. Still pushing toward the northwest, they made their way steadily on, until at last they came on another little river running sunken down into the plain.

This river ran north to south, excluding it as a candidate for the Rio Bonaventura, but along its wash there was grass, and and its water was salty but usable, and they stopped again to rest their animals. The air was clearing a little. They could see more of the countryside—bare and brown and dry. To the west the horizon was humped up into steep hillsides. There was no sign of another river.

The next day one of the Fort Hall men caught up with them. He had lagged behind Bartleson and the others, because he was leading a packed mule, and had found the notice at the crossroads. That Bartleson himself had not come up on them yet meant he had missed the note and was following the loop that the settlers had made.

The man from Fort Hall did not have much to tell them. He and Bartleson and the others had found no guide who could take them to California. All they had gotten at Fort Hall, besides the pack of provisions, was advice: they should not go south, or they would die in the desert, nor should they go north, or they would get lost in the broken canyon country. They should go west, and look for a river called Mary's River. This was not the Rio Bonaventura; it did not flow out of the Salt Lake or all the way to the Pacific, but it ran some of the way west toward California.

They made bread from the little store of Fort Hall flour and drank their salty coffee with sugar. While the men tended the oxen, and Nancy sewed up their clothes, Ann played in the mud of the river's edge. Magpies chattered at them from the highest branches of the willows; at night, Nancy heard an owl. It was the end of August. It must have felt as if she had been on the trail for years. Yet this was a comfortable place; she made the most of it, for as long as it lasted.

Soon Bartleson caught up with them. They turned their faces west and set off across the high prairie north of Salt Lake, looking for Mary's River.

CHAPTER

7

They bent their path to the northwest, along the foothills above Salt Lake, making twenty miles the first day, ten miles the next. When the haze lifted they could see the vast valley that stretched away to the south. The tremendous scarps of the Rockies flanked it to the east; on the sheer red rocks, hundreds of feet above the valley floor, were etched the ancient coastlines of the primordial inland sea. In the evening they came into sight of its remnant, shining like a silver plate in the south. A high ridge rose to the west and they steered to go north of it. Sage covered everything. "In passing the declivity of a hill," Bidwell wrote, "we observed this sage had been plucked up and arranged in long minows [windrows] [sic], extending nearly sa [sic] mile in length. It had been done by the Indians, but for what purpose we could not imagine, unless it was to decoy game."[1] They could find no water, and had to make a dry camp.

[1]Bidwell I.

That night their cattle wandered off. In the morning the Kelseys and
Bidwell had to go round them up again, which delayed their start.
Nobody was in a good mood. Bartleson especially griped at the
slowness of the others. Once they were rolling he went as fast as he
could, waiting for nobody, the nine men of his mess hurrying along
at his heels.

The Kelseys plodded along after them, their oxen already weary
at the beginning of the new, hard day. Quickly they fell behind the
others. Bidwell also lagged, locked to the pace of his oxen. Nancy,
riding her horse with Ann in front of her on the saddle, wandered
off to either side of the track, looking for grass and water. The gray-
white ground was flat as a road, but soft; her horse's feet sank down
inches deep into it, the wheels of the wagons carving out long arcs
across the barren flats. The air was so dry her lips cracked. That
night they camped by salt springs, where on the sparse grass salt
clung in lumps and knobs, some as big as hen's eggs.

Barely drinkable though this water was, they were reluctant to
leave it. The next day they stayed where they were, finding grass
for their stock, hunting antelope and rabbits and sage hens, and
scouting the surrounding area. Nancy on her horse kept watch over
the Kelsey oxen. She saw coyotes skulking in the brush, great red-
gold dogs with eyes like lamps, and kept her husband's rifle across
the saddlebows.

Poor and thin though the cattle were, they were the larder. The
settlers were fast eating up the Fort Hall provisions, and the hunting
here was slim, the animals they did kill small and lean. Soon enough,
they would have to begin eating the cattle. She caught herself running her eyes wolfishly over the sunken flanks of the animals, estimating the meat on those racks of bones.

"Poor cattle," she might have said to Ben, later. "To come all
this way, never asking, hauling our freight, only to be eaten."

Ben would have laughed at her. "Everything gets eaten. Better
us than the Indians to eat them, or the coyotes." And hugged her
against him, his big heavy arm around her, warm and solid.

Ann slept in the day's blasting heat, her cheeks flushed. Nancy helped the men work on the wagons, which needed constant care. Several times a day the wheels had to be scraped clean of salt and dirt, which crusted along the edges in clumps. In the dry air, the wooden spokes were shrinking, coming loose in their sockets, the iron tires sliding loose on the rims. Ben shimmed the tires tight again, jamming slivers of wood between them and the rims, and with the tip of his knife shoved more wood bits into the sockets of the spokes to hold them tight. Nancy picked up her horse's feet, mended clothes, and looked for firewood, keeping herself busy. Everything seemed more manageable when she was doing something necessary. Her throat hurt from the salt water; the men were brewing up strong coffee with it, which caused its own problems.

Yet the springs were beautiful, their color deeper, richer than jewels. The wide desert drew her, the carpet of sage a variegated yellow and green and brown, the sky a blazing blue; on all sides the breathtaking soar of the mountains was blue to purple, and the sunsets swept the west-facing slopes with pink and orange. In the evenings flocks of birds came in to the spring to drink and splash in the shallows. At night the stars blazed bright and clear out of the enormous sky like wheels of white fire. You could excuse a woman for thinking she might never in all her life have even imagined such things, if she had stayed back in Missouri.

They left the spring, pushing stubbornly to the west over the low rolling ground. To the west the hills burst abruptly out of the plain like walls; on the north, the slopes were easier, softer. The country between the hills looked flat, but it was not. As they drew away from the Lake, the ground grew more uneven, rippled and rumpled like an old blanket, and covered with sage, a plant toward which many of the settlers soon conceived a personal animosity.

"Traveled all day over dry, barren plains, producing nothing but sage, or rather it ought to be called, wormwood, and which I believe will grow without water or soil."[2]

The sage was short, tough, elastic, composed of hundreds of crooked little springy branches that clutched at the wheels and wagons, the legs of people and beasts. The plants were too bouncy to chop easily and their grip could snatch the clothes right off a man's back. Even dead, the twisted flaking black trunks and stems formed traps for feet and hoofs and wheels.

The sage disguised the broken, creased, and curried ground under it. Every few moments Ben and Andy, walking along with the oxen, had to get behind the wagons and push them over some barrier. Sometimes a wheel got wedged into a crevice of the hard stony ground and they had to rock the wagon free, which risked breaking a wheel irreparably. They could see that Bartleson was having the same problems, up ahead, and took some thin pleasure from it; they steered to follow him, to take advantage of the openings he was forcing, with so many more hands to help him.

They left out more of their belongings, to lighten the load. Piled high when they left Missouri, now the wagons were almost empty.

There was no water, no sign of water. The sun was like a storm of heat. Ann asked for water and Nancy gave it to her from the canteen on the saddle. Moments later, she was dismounting to help the men shove the big wagon up and over a ripple in the hard white ground. Her dress was stiff with dried sweat; her lips tasted of salt. She herself had nothing to drink for long hours. Her head began to pound.

All the rest of the day they went on like that, until their arms hung like lead weights at their sides and all Nancy could think of was water. Ann clung to her, listless, her eyes sunken. She was too heavy and too light, at the same time. Bartleson, up ahead, sent out scouts, but they came back without having found any water.

Yet they had found something, an Indian trail, or perhaps a game trail, a long dent through the sage, headed north. The settlers

[2]Bidwell I.

turned their wagons onto it. It took them into the seams of the hills, but they found no water, although they went on long past sundown, struggling along in the dark, one man walking ahead of the wagons to feel the way. They camped in the dark. Now, when Ann asked for water, the canteen was dry.

Ben and Nancy barely spoke; it hurt to speak. They chewed up the last of their jerky and lay down on the ground, the baby between them where they could keep her warm. Eventually, they slept, a troubled and terrible sleep like a temporary and unquiet death.

When they rose in the morning, they saw on the flank of the hill across the next wash a broad patch of green. Their spirits soared. With a last desperate strength they plunged across the wash toward the bright color, dragging the wagons over the rough ground, and came up onto a spring surrounded by meadows of grass. Stands of reeds fringed the water; as the settlers approached, birds in a great cloud billowed up from the shoreline and scattered away.

Nancy slid down from her horse and with Ann on her hip waded out a little into the pond and scooped up some in her hand. She sipped cautiously from it and tasted the delicious sweetness of pure fresh water.

She scooped up more in her hand and fed it to Ann, a little at a time; the baby grabbed her mother's wrist to drink, voracious.

They made camp. There was plenty of grass and their animals were soon ranging across it, their heads plunged down into the lush green. Almost at once, the settlers agreed that they should stay here, in this oasis, until they had scouted out the route ahead of them to Mary's River. Bartleson and Charles Hopper, who was an experienced hunter and who had already shown some skill at finding trails, left to explore to the west. The others settled down to rest and recover and do their thousand small chores. Suddenly, apparently from nowhere, an Indian appeared.

He patted himself on the chest. "Shoshone," he said. "Shoshone." By hand signs he quickly made known to the whites that there were other Indians nearby, and that they had horses. Bidwell especially was eager to get some better horses, and with several of the others went off with the Indian to find them. They came back after half a day, with no horses, although they had gotten some deer meat.

Bidwell was enthusiastic: their guide had taken them to a place that might have been a native Eden, "hid as it were from all the world," where they had seen a few families of Shoshone, and Bidwell was full of romantic strains about them. He spent an hour that evening, sitting with his journal on his knees, writing.

"We found two or three families, hid as it were from all the world, by the roughness of nature. The only provision which they seemed to have was a few elder berries and a few seeds; under a temporary covert of bushes, I observed the aged Patriarch whose head looked as though it had been whitened by the frosts of at least 90 winters. The scars on his arms and legs were almost countless—a higher forehead I never saw upon man's head. But here in the solitude of the mountains and with the utmost contentment, he was willing to spend the last days of his life among the hoary rocks and craggy cliffs, where perhaps he, in his youthful gayety, used to sport along crystal streams which run purling from the mountains. Not succeeding in finding horses, we returned to camp."[3]

The Shoshone were a thin scattering of people living in the arid lands from Southern California up to Wyoming and Montana. Well adapted to the desert, they knew each rock and wash in their territories and found food where the emigrants starved. They lived in small clan groups, like the one Bidwell saw, except during the winter months, when they gathered at the springs in the desert for ceremonies and social niceties. Although they had few material belongings, their culture was and remains rich with stories and ceremonies, the outward structure of an ancient way of life.

The settlers knew and cared nothing of this: to them, the Indians

[3]Bidwell I. You have to wonder what else Bidwell thought the old man could do, move to Sun City?

were hardly human. Nancy certainly saw nothing romantic about them. Whenever the Shoshone were around, she kept Ann in her arms.

While Bidwell was rhapsodizing about the Shoshone, she was busy trying to reconstruct her clothes, which were disintegrating. She pieced together a decent dress out of the three ripped and threadbare ones remaining to her, and used the fragments to mend Ann's. What was useless for anything else she layered carefully together for diapers.

Her shoes were another problem; she was wearing through the soles, and she cut pieces of leather in the shape of the soles and put them inside the shoes. Ben's clothes she mended as well; and if one of the other men came sheepishly to her with a ripped shirt or pants coming out at the knees she fixed them as best she could.

The men hunted but found nothing. On their fourth day by the spring, which was the first of September, they killed the first of their oxen for food.

A day later more Indians showed up, this time bringing horses, which the settlers bought, using powder and lead for money. The Indians made their own camp a little way away, and Ben bought some serviceberries from them and brought them to Nancy, to give Ann. The little girl ate the treat carefully, berry by berry, with complete attention, and licked her fingers dry.

Still there was no sign of Bartleson and Hopper, off scouting for the Mary's River, and the settlers wanted to move on. The presence of the Shoshone made them uneasy. The grass was giving out. And one of the Indians was promising to take them on to the west, to another spring. The group gathered for a meeting and decided to let the Indian guide them, although they all had deep misgivings.

Not for the last time, the Shoshone were giving the settlers vital help. Without these short-term guides across the desert, the settlers would certainly have died out there. Yet they uniformly regarded the Shoshone with suspicion and fear, and failed to see the friendship and kindness in the native people's way.

Filling their water casks with the pure fresh cold water of the spring, they set out, following the Indians west. Fighting the sage, fighting the rough ground, they made only six or seven miles a day, and the country was dry and bleak. But in the distance Nancy saw herds of antelope, small and fleet, with their white throats and short, upright antlers. The men went out to hunt, and came back with meat, saying that the antelope were many, and so curious that if you stood still they would come right up to you to be shot. They were small, and light: not much meat. You needed a lot of antelope to feed everybody.

The next morning, waking up in teeth-chattering cold, most of the settlers would not leave the accumulated warmth of their bed-rolls. Two wagons went on ahead—Bidwell does not name them, and calls them "contrary," so he was not one of them. Perhaps it was Nancy and Ben, and Andrew with their second wagon, awakening to a new urgency in their situation. Pushing and hauling the wagons across the rough, sage-choked country, they could make less than a mile an hour. Sometimes it must have seemed as if they were carrying the wagons along. On the second day, the others with their wagons easily caught up with them.

As they struggled with their outfits, Ben and Andrew were talking about putting their water casks and goods into one wagon and leaving the other. Nancy understood that meant giving up more of her belongings. She knew also that they were right, although not right enough. Even one wagon would be impossible. Long before the men decided, she knew that they would soon be leaving both the wagons behind.

Steadily, she saw, they were giving up parts of themselves: first, a roof and a bed, then good food, eggs and milk and bread, then clothes and goods, little by little; soon everything would be gone. She held the baby Ann tight in her arms, wondering what next she might lose. Everybody else seemed wrapped in the same dull mood.

But later that same day, Bartleson and Hopper came back. They had found what they thought to be the headwaters of the Mary's River, out there to the west. The group took heart again. Now the trek seemed possible again. They sent the Indian guide off, and pushed on.

For the next few days, they found water every day, and enough grass at least to keep the stock from wandering. The wagons jounced and creaked over the washboard ground. Nancy got down from her horse and walked, letting Ann ride in the saddle. They had to stop every few moments to wrestle one or the other of the wagons over some obstacle. When they came to a dry wash, even one only a few feet deep, it was like coming to the edge of the world. It took them hours sometimes to negotiate across one.

They were falling behind again. Nancy straightened, peering west, and could barely make out the people moving along ahead of them. The air was dingy with smoke. Behind them, to the south, to the north, she saw the faint monster shoulders of the mountains. Ben called her, and she went to put her back to the wagon and heave.

They struggled across the bottom of the immense landscape. One day later they had to make a dry camp. Smoke still made the air opaque and kept them from being able to see what they were headed into. At night, sometimes, they could see fires burning on the slopes of the mountains. Lying in their bedrolls on the ground, waiting for sleep, they speculated what these fires were—Bidwell, of course, willing to talk about anything, and Ben who loved a tale. Most of them finally agreed that the Indians were burning up the sage, maybe to drive rabbits.

Rabbits. Food. Nancy dreamed of food, of thick slabs of cheese and butter, of milk with the cream yellow on top, of meat dripping with juice and fat. She wondered what Ann dreamt of. If Ann were afraid. Yet the baby seemed happy enough, playing in the sand whenever they stopped. She did not move around very much but she smiled at her mother, lifting up her arms to be held, her eyes bright.

The next day they came to a river running west, and here, at last, Ben made his decision. They would leave the wagons behind.

Nancy helped the men strip the wagons down. They took off the canvas covers and folded them, and lined up the water casks; Ben made packsaddles out of pieces of the wagons, lashing them together with strips of rawhide, using the canvas to pad the wood. They would load the water onto their extra horses. Ben and Andy packed their blankets behind their saddles. Nancy packed her clothes and Ann's onto her own horse, which now she was leading more than riding anyway. As for the rest of the things in the wagon—

She looked at the little pile of her belongings. She would have more, she promised herself. When they reached California.

She still had Ann, and Ben, and nothing else mattered anyway. She turned to help her husband fill the water casks.

Bartleson was adamant that this trickle of water through the desert had to be Mary's River; now, he proclaimed, they were only a few days from California! But the little river ran west only a few miles. Then it turned south, and took them along between a flat salt plain on the east and high barren mountains to the west. The river dwindled. Soon there was no running water in the wash, but only standing ponds and patches of scummy drying mud. They saw no game, not even the antelope, although sometimes through the sage somebody caught a glimpse of red-yellow fur: the coyotes tracking the settlers' beasts, waiting for one to straggle.

They kept the little mismatched herd together, riders on either flank. Without the oxen, they would have nothing to eat at all.

To the east the flat salt plain shimmered white in the blaze of the sun. To the west high mountains rose, their lower slopes covered with sage like a sort of fur, their heights jutting bare as old bones. Without the wagons, the Kelseys were keeping up well with Bartleson and the others, and they made twenty-five miles that day.

But it was all headed south. And then they could find no water, and had to make a dry camp in the middle of the plain. There was no game. They killed an ox, and this time, the ox they wanted to kill was one of Bartleson's, and he announced that he would charge them all for eating his ox.

He took out a bit of paper and a stub of pencil, and while the others watched in amazement, he made careful notes of how much everybody owed him. They killed the ox; but nobody said much. Nancy made sure that Ann ate all she could stuff into her mouth.

They knew they had to find a way west again. Over and over, around the fire in the evening, as they planned what to do next, the words of the men at Fort Hall came up. Going too far south would get them into a terrible desert. Nobody knew how far south was too far south, but everybody could see that the land was getting drier every step they took. Somebody mentioned a story Broken Hand had told, back ages ago it seemed on the Platte River, about trappers who had ventured out into the desert and wound up eating each other.

The mountains seemed to funnel them relentlessly along, steering them into disaster. In the morning they started off south again, through the blazing heat of the late September day. The smoky, furnace-hot air was like the entrance of Hell. Nancy could barely make out the bulk of the mountain wall, impossibly sheer and high. Then at midmorning they all saw a gap through the western ridge.

They headed into it. They were almost out of water again, and the smoke made Nancy's throat raw; she daydreamed of water as she walked along, leading her horse behind the slow-trudging oxen. The gap in the ridge took them out onto a high dry sagebrush plain. Smoke hid the sky. Straining her eyes, she could see nothing of the country to the west. They plodded steadily along through the haze, caught in a mindless rhythm. Then through the smoke a high mountain loomed up over them, emerging from the plain in a single swoop of rock, like a finger pointing.

At the same time, in the distance ahead, she heard a shout. Someone had found water. Gladly she hurried forward, urging the oxen ahead of her, until they lifted their heads and began to move faster;

she knew they had smelled water ahead of them. Her horse was stepping along quickly too, and she climbed up into the saddle behind Ann, and rode up onto the broad meadows at the base of the mountain, and to pools of deep clear cold fresh water like the wine of Eden.

They had come to the spectacular volcanic throat that John Charles Frémont would later name Pilot Peak. The deep pure springs of water and meadows of good grass at its base would save many a later emigrant, spent after the long trek across the Salt Desert. During the years of the great migrations, men would carry water from the springs back into the desert, to find and rescue exhausted travelers and their stock.

The Kelseys and their companions were first to arrive at this oasis. It had taken them a little over three weeks to cross the northwestern corner of Utah into what is now Nevada. Ahead of them lay nearly four hundred miles of desert, beyond that the Sierra. And the summer was over. Winter was coming. They were running out of time.

CHAPTER

8

The grass and water of Pilot Peak were lush and bountiful, but the settlers could not linger, except to plan how to go on. They had another of their meetings, and for once they all agreed on something: They had to give up the rest of the wagons. To the west the land heaved up into steep mountainsides, gashed and runneled with canyons. After hauling their wagons a thousand miles across flat ground, they knew neither they nor their beasts had the strength to get them up and over those ridges.

The Kelseys had already figured this out, of course, and while Bidwell and Bartleson and Chiles and the rest broke up their wagons for wood, and made packsaddles for their horses and oxen, Nancy gathered grass for her cattle. The wind blew off the desert, smelling of the sage. The smoke was lifting and she could see the steep rises of the mountains, like knifeblades of rock.

The country seemed barren and lifeless, and yet many a creature lived here. Grasshoppers abounded, the color of the ground, visible only when they leapt. Near some tumbled rocks Nancy found owl pellets, gray and powdery, stuffed with small clipped bones. Round burrows poked back into the hard sandy earth. She wondered what made them—snakes, or rodents, or even birds? This country was like a book in another language that she could only wonder at.

Halfway through the day, an Indian appeared.

He was an old man, with long gray hair; he came happily into their camp, and began making signs with his hands. Bidwell was fascinated. The others drew off a little, wary, and Nancy picked up Ann and made a quick scan of the surrounding hills.

Bidwell got quickly in touch with the old man. "He told us by signs that the Great Spirit had spoken to him to go down upon the plains in the morning, and on the E. side of the mts. he would find some strange people, who would give him a great many things."[1] Bidwell was throwing out most of his goods with his wagon, and he spread his arm out toward them. "Help yourself." He made eloquent gestures with his hands, as adroit as any Indian, at the heap of his castoffs.

The old man's face glowed. He turned to the sun, and made gestures, and Bidwell turned to the rest of them. "He's giving thanks. He's a sun worshipper. Maybe he's a Persian."

For the rest of the day, as the settlers made ready to pack their gear on their animals, the old man went steadily through Bidwell's things; whenever he found something he especially liked, he turned to the sun and passed his hand east to west and spoke at length. Now the other settlers, amused, began to bring him offerings. Each little present set the old man off again into his ritual, which certainly did seem like thanksgiving.

There was no sign of any other Indians. Cautiously, Nancy went back to gathering up grass to feed their animals on the trail. She kept Ann riding on her hip. In the evening the old man, heavily burdened with new wealth, walked away into the sagebrush.

[1]Bidwell I.

Behind him, he left the settlers stripped to the essentials. The next morning, they packed their full water casks and camp gear into the new packsaddles, and the animals under the packsaddles erupted.

Nancy was packing up her horse when it began; at a bellow of animal outrage, she flung her head up to see Bidwell's oxen bucking and humping and snorting across the meadow. With every banging step they cast off another of his packs. Nancy burst out laughing. Bidwell raced out after his beasts, stopping to grab up a shirt, a blanket, a skillet from the ground. Beyond, Bartleson, roaring oaths, was trying to control his mules. Leaping and kicking, they broke free of their string, and threw his water casks into the grass. Nancy and Ben and Andy, experienced hands at this now, got their packs together and started off, first for once. One by one, the others got their animals under control and followed.

The day turned breathlessly hot. The mountains were herding them south again, into the desert. The flat plain to the east was white and crusty with salt. The oxen, tired, and badly packed, kept lying down, and had to be prodded up again and made to move. Things fell off the packs. For a while, the men tried to collect them and repack them but eventually they ignored whatever fell, accepting fate and gravity. The company began to straggle out again. Bartleson and the nine men who messed with him, mounted on horses and mules, pushed into the lead; the Kelseys and Bidwell and the rest lagged, trying to keep the oxen moving.

Without the wagons they moved easier over the rugged landscape. Their hunters ranged out on either side, looking for game, but came back empty-handed. In the distance, in the hills, they saw smoke—Indian fires, surely, the men agreed.

Nancy wasn't sure. It seemed to her that nothing about this country was what it seemed. She watched one white plume for a while, as she was riding across a dry valley. The smoke didn't look like smoke. It never changed much. It never went higher, or died down, and it was always white, like a feather against the faded purple hills behind it. It reminded her of the steam off a boiling kettle. But she did not know what it was. She felt alien to this place, outside it even when she was inside. She saw, but she didn't understand.[2]

When night fell Bartleson, far ahead, stopped and built a fire. The tiny fleck of yellow flickering in the deep blue desert night pulled the rest of them steadily into the camp. Bidwell and the Kelseys and the dozen men who helped them were always the last to reach the overnighting place, trudging in well after moon rise, exhausted.

Bidwell and Bartleson were constantly arguing over the pace the Captain was setting. The two disliked each other and never missed a chance to fight. One night Bidwell's oxen wandered off, and in the morning he had to go back and find them, and then Bartleson refused to wait and plunged on as fast as he could go, as if he would leave Bidwell forever behind.

But Bidwell's oxen were the dinner. The front-runners had to stop and wait for him, and eventually he did catch up with them. When he did, he marched straight up to Bartleson and roared at him, his face red under the deep sun bronze, and the Captain snarled back at him. Nonetheless, Bartleson ate heartily of Bidwell's ox.

They had only thirteen oxen left now, and were killing one every two or three days. There was little game. Now and again the men shot an antelope, but one antelope among thirty people barely gave everybody a taste. And the antelope were lean as rabbits. Everybody was craving something with fat on it. They groaned now to remember the buffalo they had left rotting on the slopes below South Pass. At night they sat around the dying fire arguing about how close they were to California, as if any of them really knew, and about how they ought to travel to get there.

Moving south, they were heading into a barren land, dry as an old bone, without grass or water. The old Fort Hall litany came up

[2]These geysers are visible still from I-80.

over and over, and gradually they came to the decision to turn west and find a way over the mountains.

Charles Hopper, the North Carolinian, picked out the path. They climbed up through steep hillsides, following the washes of rivers, scrambling over jumbled boulders and packed masses of driftwood. The heights of the hills were like steeply tilted shelves of rock, their crevices stuffed with tough gray-green chaparral. Nancy walked most of the way, carrying Ann, leading her horse. She kept her gaze on Ben's back, just ahead of her, sure and solid in his ragged coat.

Coming over the top of this range, they found a stream, with trout in it, running west. Following it, they came onto a gentle downward slope, and a beautiful green valley spread out before them. As she walked down the hill, Nancy felt lighter and easier. The valley was like a promise. Surely one of these times they would climb over a ridge and see before them the golden plains of California.

In the mountain valley they found hot springs, deep and clear, vividly colored, and smelling of potash. One night as they camped by one of these springs, their hunters brought in antelope, and the settlers cut strips of meat from the carcass and dropped them into the hot springs, bringing them back up ten minutes later perfectly cooked, if a little heavily seasoned. Nancy washed out all the clothes she could in the hot water, rinsing away weeks of sweat and grime. Her dress and Ann's clothes were so worn now that she had to be very careful washing them not to rip them worse than they were.

In the morning, as she was saddling her horse, she looked up and saw several Indians on the far side of the makeshift wall of the corral.

Her hair stood up on her neck and a flush of fear heated her cheeks. A swift look showed her more Indians coming into the camp behind this one, a horde of them, far more than there were settlers. She grabbed her reins and Ann and went swiftly over beside Ben, who was standing by his saddled horse. Ben took her by the arm and pulled her close, his eyes on the Indian in the corral.

This man was waving his hands at them, pointing at a horse, holding up two fingers—a sign he wanted to trade. Every settler in the camp had seen him now, and seen the others, too. Uncertain, the settlers were bunching up in the middle of the camp, and behind Nancy, now, suddenly, Bidwell and Bartleson were having another of their interminable arguments.

"We have to go meet him," Bidwell was shouting, gesturing at the Indian in the corral. "Make him get out of the camp—remember how Fitzpatrick did it?"

Nancy craned her neck; she could see Indians strolling up on either side of them now, all around them. They carried bows and arrows. Some had rifles. She clung to Ann and the little girl wrapped her arms around her mother's neck. Bidwell was right. Fitzpatrick had drilled into them all that they should never allow Indians to come unimpeded into their camp. But now, to her amazement, Bartleson was saying no.

"Boys," Bartleson said, "we have to be careful here, let the redskins satisfy their curiosity, or they'll get mad."

Beside Nancy, Ben stirred. "You're crazy," he said to Bartleson, and turned to his horse and pulled the rifle out of the scabbard.

Bartleson's voice rose. "Boys! Boys, you must not show any sign of hostility; if you go out there with guns the Indians will think us hostile, and may get mad and hurt us!"

Ben muttered something blasphemous. With the rifle in his arms he strode toward the corral; Andy fell in beside him.

Bartleson let out a bellow of offended dignity. Bidwell watched sharp-eyed. Ben went up to the wall of the corral and leveled his rifle at the Indian's chest.

The Indian's eyes widened; he held his hands up, palms out, offering peace, and Ben waved his free arm at him. "Get back!"

The Indian understood that. With a flash of anger in his eyes, he sidled away toward the corral wall, and now Ben turned and waved his arm at all of the Indians, and pointed the rifle forcefully at the one in the corral, and shouted, this time to all the Indians, "Get back!"

"Now, look," Bartleson said. "Now, look, they are mad."

Nancy swallowed. Her gaze flicked from her husband, standing out there in the open, toward the Indians. In fact the Indians were grumbling; they shook their fists in the air, and frowned, but they were moving back out of the camp. Their leader was scrambling out over the far wall of the corral. He stepped back, and all the Indians stepped back, and turned in a mass and glared at the settlers.

Nancy gathered a deep breath and let it out again. There were dozens of these Indians, maybe a hundred, all men, all armed. A war party. The air felt thick and charged and tight. She kept her gaze pinned on Ben standing there between the settlers and the Indians, as if the sheer force of her will could armor him. Her heart galloped.

"Get ready," Ben called, over his shoulder. "Let's go! Let's get out of here!" Bidwell went up beside him, his rifle in his arms, facing the Indians with him, and now half a dozen of the other men joined them.

The rest of the settlers quickly went about gathering up their goods, saddling their horses, and collecting the oxen, all under the cold stares of the Indians. Nancy turned to her horse, tightened her cinches, and swung into her saddle, straightening her skirts with a kick. Andy rode up beside her and they started herding their packed oxen away to the west. Quickly the other settlers fell into march around them. Nancy's back was tight. The Indians were riding along beside them, just out of bow shot. She felt their stares like a weight of malice.

Moments later Ben was riding up next to her; deep lines grooved his face, and his eyes looked wild and hard. He gave her a quick flash of a smile but the hardness stayed in his eyes. "Keep moving," he said, and glanced around at the Indians. He held his rifle across his thighs, one hand on the grip.

For the rest of the morning, the two bands traveled that way along the valley. On either side, some of them called back and forth, and once or twice people from each band met in the middle and did some trading. The Indians had buckskins; they wanted powder and ball. They traded Andy some nuts for a few lead slugs. Around noon, the Indians began dropping out of their line and riding away, and by nightfall only eight or ten of them remained. When Nancy slid down out of her saddle, she turned to her husband and buried herself in his arms. He held her a moment, wordless, and they went together to do their evening round of chores.

During the evening, as they chewed their strips of ox meat, the settlers talked over the confrontation with the Indians. Bidwell thought that the fact these Indians had carbines meant they traded with the Hudsons Bay Company, the great British fur trapping outfit. He was talkative, as usual, and opinionated; to a couple of the other men, he said, "Bartleson, you know, doesn't know much about Indians. That was really stupid, he could have gotten us all killed."

Nancy overheard him. Lifting her head, she caught sight of Bartleson, across the darkened camp, and saw that Bartleson had heard him too.

Their quarreling worried her. The settlers needed to stick together, to support each other, if they were going to get through this. Instead here were Bartleson and Bidwell looking knives at each other. She knew Ben had no use for Bartleson, and he rather liked Bidwell. But Bidwell was reckless and argumentative. The settlers' band was falling into factions, just when they needed most to work together. She went to check on Ann, sleeping by the coals of the fire, and laid her fingers against the baby's cheek.

They climbed another range of mountains, working their way through the seams of the hills, creases choked with chaparral and sagebrush and boulders. On the far side they struck a quick-moving stream and followed it down. In the clear blue-green water the narrow shapes of fish darted. Ravens flapped and soared across the heights; and once Ben pointed out to her a bird soaring so high up she could see only the shaft of its body, gliding through the flat blue sky.

The stream bounced white and foaming into another, bigger stream. Surely now they had found the headwaters of the Mary's River. Excited, the band pushed on. But a day later, the stream was dwindling, and the next day, it was dry.

They followed the dry bed, crossing it again and again. The steep hills shouldered up around them, forcing them down onto the streambed itself, a narrow canyon, choked with boulders.

The canyon was leading them north. Nancy remembered the Fort Hall litany; to the north, canyons, that would trap them. Was this one of those canyons? Her horse was slipping and sliding on the rocks and she got down and walked. The stones bruised her feet through the thin soles of her shoes.

That night they stopped where they were. The canyon's walls soared up too high to climb out of; great gray boulders jumbled it so thick their poor footsore cattle and horses couldn't even lie down to rest. Standing slumped, their heads drooping so low their muzzles almost touched the ground, the beasts twitched their legs up one at a time, trying to ease their pain. Nancy picked up her horse's feet and saw around the curve of each hoof the thin red line of the quick.

The others were gathering around the tiny fire they had made of driftwood. Nobody said anything. The cool of the night settled down over them like a lid. Nancy sank down beside Ben, dispirited. She found herself thinking about cheese and butter and cream. Ann crawled into her lap and fell asleep. Ben hung his arm around her shoulders and squeezed, but he said nothing. She knew he felt as low as she did.

What if they died out here? No one would know. Wolves would eat their bones. As she thought that she took the child in her arms and hugged her, half in tears. Besides her, her husband shifted his weight; he tightened his arm around her slightly.

Then, like a big fish turning inside her, she felt the baby move. She pressed her hand to her belly. Her heart leapt on a surge of hot wild delight at the life within her. She was ashamed of being afraid. As long as she was still alive, as long as she didn't give up, she would get to California.

When the sun came up, one of the men climbed up the side of the canyon, and higher, onto the steep shoulder of a hill. When he came down his face was bright. Through a crack in the boulders he had seen ahead of them, into a beautiful green valley. And it was morning again: a new day. Another chance. Gathering themselves, the settlers struggled on out of the gorge and onto the flat grassy floor of the valley.

At the far end, the way narrowed down again into another boulder-choked defile, but this one was much shorter. They were walking downhill now, at least, and heading west, and the gorge opened out onto a broad sagebrush plain.

Walking out onto it, Nancy shaded her eyes against the westering sun and saw in the distance, in the yellow-brown of the sage, a winding line of red willows. A river. Its course wound off across the plain, flat between the sheer walls of mountains, on out of sight toward the northwest. Something in her rose and swelled with new hope. She quickened her step, moving down toward the red-orange loops of the watercourse.

The settlers had come at last to the Mary's River, the winding little stream that Hudsons Bay man Peter Skene Ogden had named for the Indian wife of one of his trappers. This modest trickle of water, sometimes also called Ogden's River, and which three years later John Charles Frémont would officially name the Humboldt River, was the nineteenth century's superhighway into the far west. In the decade after the Kelseys, thousands of emigrants would follow it; the Union Pacific Railroad was built along it in 1869; and I-80, the great interstate running from San Francisco to New York, follows it now. It rolls through a magnificent and unforgiving landscape, whose major works of man seem to be prisons and casinos, temporary as stage sets in the huge inhuman vista.

In 1841, the works of man in this place were even less visible but far longer lived. As the settlers crept out onto the edge of the river's broad flat plain, they saw the smoke of campfires in the distance. At this time of the year, at the very end of the dry season, the Shoshone for hundreds of years had gathered along the river in their clans and families, to fish and gather seeds, and to perform important ceremonies, a way of life uniquely adapted to this harsh landscape. The appearance of the settlers in this ancient landscape marked the beginning of the end of it.

The settlers knew nothing of this. To them this was not a place at all but a passageway. They went straight to the river, pale and blue in its wash, carved as if with a shovel down into the thick sandy layers of the plain. The northern rim stood six or eight feet above the floor of the river's wash, but the southern rim was a gentle shelving slope. Clumps of leafless willows, their orange stems studded with fat yellow buds, clogged the sandy riverbed. There was no game but at least they had water.

They had found the lifeline again. They made camp that night by the river, killed one of their oxen, and ate until they were stuffed.

CHAPTER

9

Nancy felt sorry for the men who used tobacco. Most of them had chewed theirs up, and now they were whining like babies, snarling at each other and cursing the oxen. One of them, William Belty, who had a mule that kept very well, sold rides on it for bits of tobacco. The other men chewed pieces of leather, or cut out their pockets and chewed them.

There was a lot of grass along the stream, and the oxen were stopping to eat as they plodded along, so that Nancy had to get around behind them and whack them with a stick and push them on. Bartleson with the nine men of his mess were already only dots in the hazy western distance, but she knew that, by nightfall, however much farther they had traveled, they had to stop and wait for the rest of them to catch up. The half dozen remaining oxen were their only food.

So she let the oxen eat, as much as she could, and still keep them moving. The great beasts looked like sacks full of moving bones.

Their ribs stuck out like hoops. They were so weak they couldn't even carry loads any more. What was left of Nancy's things, a couple of blankets, the last rags of her clothes and Ann's, was now packed on her horse, making a nice backrest for Ann, who slept leaning back like an Empress.

A few Indians came into the camp that night; they had no food either.

They talked to Bidwell by hand signs and nods and pointings, but they stared at Nancy and little Ann, who was playing with some stones in the dirt. Nancy went over and picked the child up, uncomfortable under the eyes of the Shoshone. Later, she realized that of all the Indians she had seen, she had seen almost no women, and no children. Maybe the Shoshone, in all the white people they had seen, had never before seen a white woman and a white child.

The next morning, Belty, having already traded the use of his mule for a day's worth of tobacco, couldn't find his chaw. He searched the whole camp for it, walking around staring glumly at the sandy river bar all the while the others were saddling their horses and gathering the oxen; even as they drove off on their way, Belty hung back, looking for his precious tobacco. At last, giving up, he trudged along after them.

About halfway through the morning, an Indian came running up behind them: one of the men from the previous night. He went up to Bidwell, holding something out in his hand, and when Belty saw it he gave a yelp.

"My baccy!" He pounced on the Indian, grabbed the tobacco. "You thief—" He looked around for his gun.

Bidwell tackled him. "You idiot!" Wrestling with Belty, he fought the rifle down, and the Indian, understanding this language perfectly well, took to his heels. Belty gave a howl of rage.

"He stole my baccy!"

"You idiot," Bidwell said, again, disgusted. "Then why did he bring it back to you?" He picked Belty's rifle up out of the dirt and thrust it into his arms. Belty glowered after the Indian, and then

turned and aimed a dagger of a look at Bidwell. He poked the tobacco into his mouth and stuffed it in his cheek and started off after
the others.

Bartleson and his men were already far ahead, visible only as a
little smoke of dust rising into the air. Nancy whacked a standing
ox across the back with her stick, and it lumbered slowly forward
toward the west.

She was of two minds sometimes about catching up with Bartleson. Every night, when they camped, she could feel the tension
between Bidwell and Bartleson like a poison in the air. In all that
great desert they seemed too close together. Bartleson and his group
made one fire, and the others, the Kelseys and Bidwell and their
friends, made another. Ben Kelsey made no effort to hide his contempt for Bartleson; they had not spoken since the confrontation
with the Indians.

Around the campfires they argued about whether this really was
the Mary's River. It was running steadily north, trending a little to
the west, but mostly north. Yet there seemed nowhere else to go.
South of them the tremendous rock crest of a mountain range jutted
up out of the flat desert floor. To the north, farther away, were more
dry barren hills. They had to go west, but how, when the land
wouldn't let them?

One morning, changing Ann's diaper, Nancy looked into her
baby's face and saw an old woman.

The child was quiet, listless, lying there with her eyes open,
looking at the sky. Her face was wizened down around the bones,
her fat baby cheeks sunken and her eyes hollow. Nancy caught her
up in her arms and held her tight, all her old dull fears suddenly
honed sharp again. She went to find Ben, and got an extra scrap of
meat for Ann.

Still the river was running north.

They saw Indians every day but the Shoshone avoided them. If
the settlers' path brought them too near a Shoshone camp the Indians fled. Nancy was glad of this; she was afraid of the Indians.

Over and over she imagined that she might die, they might all die, all but Ann, and the Indians might find her. She had heard all through her childhood how Indians stole children and made them into slaves.

It would be worse, even, if they all died but Ann, and the Indians didn't find her. She shut her mind to that. She put her hands to work, getting grass blade by blade for her horse, mending her shoes again.

A few days later, to everybody's delight, the river curved around toward the southwest. Here grew great stands of excellent grass, three or four feet high, blue-tinged, like Kentucky grass. The animals plunged into it, their jaws grinding. Twittering flocks of birds flew up before their progress.

The whole valley was swarming with Indians. "Whenever we approached their huts, they beckoned us to go on—they are extremely filthy in their habits," Bidwell wrote,[1] by which he probably meant that they wore no clothes. On the river, the settlers saw fish traps made of woven reeds, and the burnt traces of fire circles. For a few days they saw very little of the Indians themselves, until Ben came up to Nancy and pointed out across the bluegrass meadow, and she saw bobbing along in the grass a cluster of black dots.

"What's that?" She turned to Ben, who knew everything.

He laughed. "Indians. They think they're hiding."

Nancy crowed; she looked again, and saw the briskly moving black dots were the tops of the Indians' heads, as they crouched together in the high grass, spying on the settlers.

A day later, plodding along miles behind Bartleson again, the Kelseys and Bidwell came up on a Shoshone village, tucked into the shelter of the river's high northern bank. The village consisted of four tiny round huts made of grass, a few racks and mats, a fire. In the middle of this stood half a dozen naked brown people waving frantically at the settlers to go away.

[1]Bidwell I.

Nancy jerked her gaze away from their nakedness, her cheeks hot—but some of these were women, and she turned toward them again, curious.

To her surprise, the naked brown people were peering back at her with just as much curiosity. She went to lift Ann down from the horse, and when she turned around, some of the Indians were creeping toward the settlers, making friendly gestures as they came.

Bidwell went to meet them, Ben just behind him. Nancy drew off to one side to watch, and found her attention going to the Shoshone women in their village.

If you could call it that. She found herself disdaining those tiny grassy huts. At the same time, part of her was painfully remembering that she slept in the open at night.

But this wasn't what her life would be like in California. She would have a big house in California. And plenty to eat. And clothes. She held Ann tight, that house shimmering like a mirage in her mind.

The women were watching her, too, with a steady intensity. One lifted a child up onto her hip. Naked, that child. Nancy held Ann against her. I will never let my child be a naked savage. But that same painful part of her noticed that this woman's child looked better fed than Ann.

She struck down that part of her. She could not think that way. She had no room for weakness and self-doubt now. She turned away from the Shoshone and went to her horse.

Bidwell was getting better at talking to the Shoshone. This time he managed to find out that, a few days on, the river ran into some lakes. West of the lakes there were mountains, high and steep.

At that, Bartleson straightened, nodding, excited. "That's it, boys," he said. "The mountains of California! We're two to three days from California! We're almost there!"

Some of the men gave a ragged, tired cheer. Nancy swung around to Ben, hoping to see that he agreed. But Ben was frowning, his eyes sharp with dislike for Bartleson. She sighed, turning her back on the other men, and bent over Ann, taking comfort in comforting her.

The men, now, through Bidwell, were talking to the Shoshone about going with them, to guide them. Bartleson mentioned John Marsh's letter, which had set them all on this course; Marsh had said they would need a guide over the mountains. One of the Shoshone agreed to go with them, for a few days at least, in return for a few pieces of lead for bullets.

In the morning, this man led them off down the river. Again the party straggled out. Late in the day Bartleson stopped and made camp and waited for the rest to make their way up to the fire. The Kelseys reached the camp long after dark, and Bidwell never came in. In the morning, Nancy could see him far back along their track, herding his exhausted oxen.

Her back stiffened. She knew there would be another fight.

Behind her, Bartleson said smoothly, "Gotta wait, boys—Bidwell has the breakfast." He glanced around at his men, gathered close behind him. Nancy gave him a sharp look, wondering why he seemed so happy. Her stomach growled. She had saved a tiny piece of meat from the day before and she chewed it up well and gave it to Ann with some water from the river. She had found some rushes, too, that tasted sweet when she peeled off the outside.

Bidwell came trudging into the camp and snarled at Bartleson, but for once Bartleson did not shout back. Affable, he only shrugged, smiling toward his friends. Nancy was relieved, but something in Bartleson's manner still made her edgy. She went to keep Ann out of the way while the men killed an ox for breakfast.

After they had eaten, Bartleson came forward with a plan. They should kill the oxen who were poorest, who were holding them all back, and take the meat along on stronger legs. This made sense, and so they killed two of the four remaining oxen.

Now Bartleson pointed out that he had the best animals, he and his friends, who were all mounted on horses and mules. He suggested they carry most of the meat. That way, the others could come along at the pace of the remaining oxen.

Nancy glanced at Ben, who said nothing. But everybody else was agreeing to this; they were impatient to be moving on. Bartleson packed up the butchered meat, and mounted his mule.

Then he wheeled around, and yelled at Bidwell, "Now we have been found fault with long enough, and we are going to California. If you can keep up with us, all right; if you cannot, you may go to hell!" Wheeling his mule, he galloped away, and the nine men of his mess followed him.

Bidwell gave a yell; Andy Kelsey ran several strides after Bartleson and the others. Nancy cried out, angry. The rest of them only stood there, staring at the receding dust, too stunned even to swear. Nancy's spirits plummeted. She thought: Now we're finished. She could not move, she felt wrung empty of strength and will.

Then from the dust came a man on a mule: one of Bartleson's mess, who rode up, and dismounted.

"The captain is wrong, and I will stay with you, boys."

Beside Nancy, Ben lifted his head. "Good for you, then." He stepped forward, and his moving broke Nancy out of her paralysis of shock. Ben drew all eyes to him.

"Now, are we going to California or not? Losing Bartleson, that's not such a bad thing, it seems to me. We still got these oxen, and some meat, and Bidwell's Indian's still here. Move on out."

He started forward, and his calm and his confidence gathered the rest back to their purpose. Bidwell made hand signs and said words to his Shoshone, and the Indian trotted off along the river, the way Bartleson had taken. Everybody followed.

Ben was right, as usual. It was actually a relief to have Bartleson gone. They went along in a better order, closer together, following the trail that the nine men on mules had pounded into the river wash. The river was so thin and small now they could cross over it without wetting the tops of their shoes. Deep drifts of sand clogged the wash; it was hard to plow through them, especially for the weary oxen.

Then the wash opened out onto a broad lowland, and the water of the river spread out into a swamp, thickly fringed with rushes. Glassy ponds of water reflected the clear blue sky. In the distance, they could see the fires of Shoshone villages. Beyond that, on the rim of this low country, mountains rose, shrugging up steep sheer juts of rock, purple-blue.

The Shoshone waved his hands at Bidwell and chattered a lot, and knelt down in the sand and made pictures in the dust. Bidwell interpreted this for the other settlers: "I think he's saying we should stay here for now." He squatted beside the Indian and waggled his fingers and pointed at the marks on the ground, and the Shoshone nodded vehemently. Bidwell faced the others again. "He says there's no water for a long way after this."

"All right," Ben said. "There's daylight left—we can hunt." He turned to Nancy, and forced a smile onto his face. She patted his arm, grateful for the attempt, and went to take care of Ann.

The swamp spread away from them across the lowland; in among clumps of reeds and grass the sun blazed on glassy standing water. As Nancy watched, a wheeling fluttering gust of birds flew up out of the rushes and soared away to the west.

Something else moved out there, on the higher ground, and one of the men yelled. "There's a horse!"

Several of the men whooped. Nancy looked, shading her eyes, and saw, down there, far away, a single animal, its head up, watching them. Its mane and tail streamed on the wind. Some of the men were climbing into their saddles; in a profligate burst of energy, they rode off to try to catch the distant horse.

Ben said, "There's been white people here. You see that? Trappers, or somebody, somebody like us, let that horse go out here."

Whenever that had been, the horse was wild now. As the men approached it spun around, galloping away. When the settlers stopped, their mounts already tired, the wild horse stopped also, and watched them, ears pricked, but whenever the settlers moved, the horse moved, keeping a good distance between them, and eventually the men gave up.

The next day took them through the middle of a Shoshone gathering. They were traveling along through the sinks of the river, swamps and lakes and ponds where thick stands of rushes grew. The rushes formed a thick honeydew, which the Indians, standing to their knees in the sinks, collected and massed in their hands into balls, and then ate.

A few of the settlers, practiced at this now, went off to trade with these Shoshone. Andy Kelsey came back with handfuls of the honeydew, packed into a crunchy sweet mass like bran. Nancy liked the nutty taste of it and Ann ate it eagerly, until the juice dripped down her chin.

They were cutting across the sink through the marshes, with stands of the honeydew rush on either side. Clouds of insects hovered over the rushes. Nancy's eyes sharpened; she saw how the Indians were gathering up the honeydew where these insects also fed, and suddenly she turned and plucked the last of the sweet out of her baby's hands.

Ann let out a yell. Nancy looked hard at the honeydew and saw, suspended in the thick creamy sap, countless little wriggling insects.

She yelped; she flung the sweet away. Ann was crying, deprived. On her chin a few tiny gnat-like bodies squirmed. Nancy held the baby and with her sleeve wiped off her face so thoroughly Ann's cheeks glowed when she was done; Ann sobbed as if her heart were breaking. Behind her, somebody else yelled, "Ow! Yuck!" and she knew they had seen the same thing.

She laughed. So this was the price of well-fed babies in the desert. Nonetheless, she wasn't about to feed it to Ann.

They were working their way along the eastern edge of the Sink. The water was bad and there was nothing to make a fire: that night they camped in the dark. In the morning their Shoshone guide, still following Bartleson's course, took them off south, across a sandy barren where there was no water at all.

Leading her horse, carrying Ann on her hip, Nancy followed Ben along the trail. The ground was so hot it burned the soles of her feet through her shoes. The land was tough, stony, desolate. Here and there some bit of life burst from it. A tiny twisted bush with a handful of tiny squirrel-ear leaves erupted from a crevice of the rock, a small furry thing she never saw well enough to identify bolted across the open ground. The wind sawed across the rocky lifts of the hills in a low hollow note like an enormous flute.

As she walked she looked broadly around her. South and east lay the raw slopes of the mountains, wind-raked, dry as grave dust. To the north was the hilly sagebrush country they had just come through. To the west, along the horizon, lay the sawteeth of more blue-purple mountains, and in their long procession Nancy could see no gap at all.

The mountains of California. She remembered hearing, back during one of those long evenings on the plains, that Joe Walker had spent twenty-two days wandering in the mountains of California.

How far had she and Ben and Ann come, now? As she walked, she tried to make some estimate of it. Bidwell was saying that sometimes they made twenty miles a day. Sometimes much less. Then say twelve miles a day. And they had left Sapling Grove on May 16. And it was now—

She could have asked Bidwell or Jimmy John, who were both keeping journals, and found that it was October 7. And one might have told her outright they had been traveling one hundred and forty-four days.

Nearly five months. And over one thousand miles, certainly. Another twenty-two days, then. She could last another twenty-two days.

The oxen would not last much farther. Halfway through the day, two of the four oxen sank down to the ground and would not move.

Ben nodded at Andy. "Shoot them and cut them up." The men stepped forward, raising the guns. Yet the meat was so lean and stringy it hardly seemed to matter. It was like chewing rope.

There were four oxen left now, and they could barely move. The settlers pushed and cursed and begged them along, and that night reached a lake in the desert, where Shoshone were camped in groups on the shore.

The water stank and tasted awful. The settlers could only drink it by boiling it. They had nothing to eat except another ox. But the next day their Shoshone guide took them to a river lined with cottonwoods, running down out of the mountains.

Here the Indian left them. The river's water was sweet to drink, and clear, but as they followed it, the course of the water bent southward again, and ran along the foot of the mountains. To the west the mountains were humping up against the sky in tremendous rocky scarps; stands of pine shrouded the lower slopes. The mountains looked like a solid wall; there seemed no way through them at all.

The men talked over what to do. Ben was for following this river, which had to be running down out of the mountains; they could follow the river upstream to the crest, and then find another river running west. The other men listened and said little. Nobody had much energy. Three or four men took the best horses and went out to hunt, but came back with nothing, not even a rabbit.

The leaves of the cottonwoods were turning bright and pure gold; they littered the ground along the river's rocky wash like fairy money. In camp in the evening Nancy pulled apart her remaining clothes and patched them together into one good garment that would cover her up. She sewed the pieces of Ben's shirts together; she made Ann a heavier coat from scraps. She made new boots for her horse out of the skin of the ox they killed that night for dinner.

She no longer felt sorry for the oxen. She saw them only as food now, and as hides, and as a constant trouble.

The river wound back through the creases of the hills. Steadily, to the west, the mountains climbed into the sky, every day higher, their heights shaggy with pine forest. The sky was a harsh cold blue. In the wind the yellow leaves of the cottonwoods fluttered and fell. Winter was coming.

They came to a meadow, in a curl of the river, and camped. Ben and some of the others went off to try to see what lay to the west of them; Nancy, rinsing out Ann's diapers, looked up to see them scaling the steep heights just beyond the meadow. The water of the river was so cold it numbed her hands in a moment.

As she worked, she tried to judge their situation. They couldn't stay where they were, that was obvious. Yet she saw no way to go, either. The land spread out away from her to the east, dry and dun-colored and monotonous; to the west, it rose up against them in a wall. South was desert, north was canyons.

She picked a stem of grass growing by the water and sucked on it as she worked. They had only two oxen left. She supposed they would eat the mules and horses next. She wrung the diapers as dry as she could, and hung them, poor ragged things, on the branches of the brush. She wondered what they would eat after the mules and horses were gone.

That night, Ben was back, his face slack with fatigue. He shook his head when she asked if he had found a trail. "I can't see anything but cliffs." Moments later, he was asleep.

The next morning, as they were packing up, someone called out and pointed. Nancy turned, and out there on the broad monotonous desert saw someone moving slowly toward them.

Indians, she thought. Maybe they would know where to go. Maybe they would have some food. Leaning on her horse, she watched them come, a line of people and animals. They were stopping every few moments, and one of them was sinking down to the ground, and then rising.

Ben came up beside her. "Look who that is," he said. His voice sang with unusual excitement.

"What?" She strained her eyes, trying to see what he was seeing.

Ten yards away, Bidwell suddenly said, "Bartleson," and took a few steps toward the oncoming men.

Nancy gave a laugh. It certainly was Bartleson, with the men he had bolted away with, a few days before. Now he was coming back. This would be interesting. She stopped packing; she could tell they weren't going anywhere for a while.

As they drew closer, she saw that it was Bartleson himself who stopped, every few moments, and squatted down on the ground. At length the oncoming crowd reached the river, and with whoops and yells, half the men around Nancy rushed out to meet the captain and his followers and escort them into the camp.

Bartleson trudged on up to the camp. He was gray in the face, and shrunk down to half his former size. The other eight men plodded along beside him, looking hardly better.

The story came quickly out: after leaving the rest behind, they had found a guide who took them south[2] into the desert. They had eaten up all the food they had taken, and the Shoshone had nothing. Looking for a way through the mountains, Bartleson and his men had ridden south nearly twenty miles, and found nothing except higher and steeper cliffs. At last they had come to where the mountains came down sheer into a lake, and there had met some Shoshone who gave them fish and pine nuts to eat. The fish had made them all sick, which was why Bartleson had been squatting down every few moments, as the fish made its way violently through him.

Nancy gave a harumph of amusement. She thought it served

[2] It's interesting the Shoshone took them south. Had they pushed on to the west they would have reached the oasis of the Truckee Meadows, and they might have found the easier route up the Truckee River and through what is now Donner Pass. This route was much easier to find going west to east: Jed Smith had taken it in 1823 and John Charles Frémont would locate it again in 1844.

Bartleson right. But the men forgave all; with slaps on the back and laughter they welcomed the nine, and before the returning prodigals were even done with their tale of woe somebody was stirring up the fire and putting on a frypan to make them breakfast.

Bartleson stuffed himself with fried ox meat. He did look sad, all shrunken and wizened, and afterward, sitting by the fire, he faced them and said, "Boys! If ever I get back to Missouri, I will never leave there again. Why, I would be glad to eat from the same trough as my dogs there."

But they were not in Missouri. They were faced with mountains higher and steeper than any they had yet seen. The winter stars shone; the wind at night chilled them to the marrow. Their animals were exhausted. More than half the people were on foot now. The desert had worn them all down; they were gaunt, even the little girl Ann. They spent that day in camp, resting. Nancy fixed her shoes again. It was getting harder to keep the uppers together.

That night, they had a meeting, and somebody suggested maybe they should turn around and try to make it back to Fort Hall.

Ben said, "We wouldn't make it." He had his arm around Nancy. She leaned on him, letting him speak for both of them; where Ben went, she went. In her arms, Ann had no choice. In her body the other, tiny life.

The men were arguing the matter. Bidwell thought they were very close to California, maybe only a few days, if they could find a way quickly through the mountains. Jimmy John agreed, and was loudly impatient with the people who hesitated. But some of the others were dispirited. Poor old George Hensaw almost wept at the idea of going on. Bartleson was uncharacteristically silent—having learned something, or perhaps he was only still sick.

Finally they took a vote, which, by a majority of one, decided them. They would go on to California. If they could only find a way.

CHAPTER

10

Along the river the cottonwoods grew thick, their yellow leaves streaming in the wind. Boulders clogged the river's wash. Ben led the way, picking a course upstream. Everybody went on foot. The animals scrambled on the bad footing, slipped and stumbled and went to their knees, tried to refuse to go on, and were driven on. Ann clung to Nancy with both fists wrapped in her mother's dress. That night they camped by the river, in the lee of the bank, with a great fire made of driftwood, plenty of water, but nothing to eat.

The next day, climbing steadily from dawn onward, they came up at noon over the summit of a ridge, into the teeth of a roaring wind, and saw before them the battlements of the Sierra, thousands of feet of naked rock. Above the dark shaggy timberline, on the gaunt flanks of the peaks, snow lay like trapped clouds. Bidwell was riveted. He took his journal and wrote furiously, stopping every few moments. The wind ripped at the pages of his book. Ann buried her face against Nancy, hiding from the howling air.

Nancy murmured to her, one hand on the child's head. She walked along behind Ben, looking out over the plunging slope; the abyss seemed to fall away forever. She knew why Bidwell was writing so madly. This was like the top of the world. There could be no place else on earth like this.

"Having ascended about half a mile," Bidwell wrote,[1] "a frightful prospect opened before us—naked mountains whose summits still retained the snows perhaps of a thousand years. . . . The winds roared—but in the deep dark gulfs which yawned on every side, profound solitude seemed to reign."

To one of them, at least, it looked like the end. George Henshaw, who had come west for his health, sank down on the ground against a granite boulder and said, "I can't. I can't walk over that. Go on without me, boys; I'm done."

They stopped. Many of them simply stared silently out over the tremendous panorama of the mountains, enraptured. Below the skirts of the rock peaks, the thick pine forest sang in the wind like some colossal harp. Higher up, rags and sheets of snow blew like flags off the white haunches of the peaks. Just to see this absorbed the mind wholly. Drew you out of yourself, into the infinite.

Nancy's arms ached, bringing her back to the immediate and small. She shifted Ann to her other hip. The mountains captured her eyes again. God must live in such a place as this, in such majesty. Then Ben was saying, "Come on, old man. Let's go."

Henshaw shook his head. "I'm done."

Several of the men exchanged a look. Nancy drew back, frowning, and then Andy Kelsey unlimbered his rifle from his shoulder.

"Well, then," he said, "I'll just shoot you."

Henshaw gasped. Nancy started forward and Ben caught her by the arm and held her. The corners of his lips twitched. Henshaw said, "You can't do that."

[1]Bidwell I.

"Oh, yes, I can," Andy said, and cocked his rifle. "Get moving, or I'll shoot you."

"You bastard." Henshaw was getting up. "I'll kill you, you son of a bitch." He staggered away over the slope. Andy slung his rifle back on his shoulder and the rest of them followed.

Ben took the lead again. He worked his way along through forests of pine and cedar, huge and ancient trees, stirring and creaking in the ceaseless wind. Their massy tops blocked off the sky, and hid even the mountains; sometimes, beneath them, the darkness was so gloomy it seemed haunted. That night, in camp, they got to arguing about how high these trees were, and someone made a rough measurement of a single cedar and pronounced it two hundred and six feet tall.

The next day, they began to go downhill.

Ben was easing them through a crease between the peaks of the mountains, following first a rivelet of a stream, and then a bigger one, which ran west. Ice coated the undersides of the rocks that overhung the tiny slip of water. Moss and leathery patches of gray-green lichen grew on the rocks and the trunks of the trees. Nancy could feel the edges of the rocks underfoot through the soles of her shoes; she led her horse along, carrying Ann on her hip, following Ben down and down, through clumps of boulders and trees growing up from boulders.

The steep drop exhilarated her, even if it was hard. Surely they were passing through the mountains now. Ben had found them the way. When they all stopped, near noon, several of the men agreed that they had come almost a mile down from where old Henshaw wanted to give up the ghost. By the time they stopped for the night, they could see oak trees on the slopes just below them.

For Bidwell, that meant they had reached the Pacific. Only a few more days, he told everybody. A few more days. That night, although they shivered in the cold, they were in high spirits.

But the next day, the river plunged away out of their sight into a canyon; they could hear it roaring among the rocks as they struggled down the steep boulder-strewn slopes. They had to stop often to let the animals rest, especially the last two remaining oxen. Some of the horses were limping badly. Their necks were sunken, their hipbones standing up like bedposts; the hair was coming off them in clumps.

The pines grew so thick sometimes they had to hack a way through the branches. The trees blocked the view: it was hard to see where they were going. Hard to see if they were getting anywhere at all, although they were steadily moving downward. Then, midway through the afternoon, they came out on the edge of a sheer cliff dropping hundreds of feet away into the woods.

Nancy sank down at once on the ground and stretched out her aching feet. She kept a firm hold on her daughter. Her horse, and the other animals, began to nose the ground, looking for blades of grass. The men gathered at the edge of the cliff and looked out; one of them stooped, found a stone, and threw it into the empty air.

The river ran down below them; they could hear its crashing and muttering. The cliff at least gave them a good look at the country to the west, but all they could see were more hills. Finally Ben turned toward Nancy.

"Don't see how we can get any farther today. Let's camp."

Nancy went about gathering some wood for a fire. It came to her once again that the elaborate routine with which she had begun the trek across the plains had disappeared along with her worldly goods. Now she did only what was strictly necessary: she found water, and drank; she found food, and ate; she found wood, and made a fire. The tent was gone, the ground cloth, the bread and the Dutch oven, the potatoes and beans that had to be soaked, the lard, which now she might have eaten plain, by the handful. From where she stood now, looking backward, it all seemed like a dream.

There was no water where they were, but they could hear the water crashing and gurgling along at the foot of the cliff. Nancy took Andy's tall boots, tied them together and hung them around her neck, and went down the cliff, creeping from ledge to ledge. It took her more than an hour to travel a few hundred feet. At the bottom, she had to stagger over great boulders and slide down a pebbly bank to reach the wild river. There, she drank as much as her belly would hold, and then filled Andy's boots with the icy water and climbed back up again.

She let Ann drink until the baby was full, and gave the rest of the water to her horse. The others were climbing down the way she had come, taking anything with them that would carry water. Exhausted, she took Ann in her arms and lay down to sleep.

In the morning, they sent out scouts. Bidwell and Jimmy John went down along the face of the cliff, where they could see a sort of trail angling off into the brush; two others went back the way they had all come, to see if they could cross over the river higher up, where the canyon was narrower, and find a better trail along the other bank. The rest of them waited. Bartleson was chafing, eager to go on again, as he always was.

Nancy took Ann and explored up the slope behind the camp, looking for something to eat. Under the layers of pine needles and branches, the ground was thin and cold. Gray rocks broke through like bones coming through hide. Mushrooms grew aplenty under the pines, big and little ones, yellow and blue and white, but she knew better than to eat strange mushrooms. There were a lot of pinecones, and she picked one up and studied it, wondering if there were any way to eat it.

Far off, there was a gunshot.

She straightened, excited. That meant somebody had found a trail. She scrambled back down the rocky slope into the camp.

The shot had come from down the cliff, where Bidwell and John had gone to find a way. Bartleson and his men, with their usual haste, started away at once, ahead of everybody else, following the tiny seam of the trail down into the canyon. Watching them go, Nancy saw how narrow the path was; they had to press themselves to the side of the cliff. Even Bartleson's prize, surefooted mule went slow as a granny.

Still in the camp, she and Ben and the rest of them saddled their mounts and packed their goods, intending to go after. But before they could even get startled, they saw Bidwell panting and struggling his way up toward them again, dragging his exhausted horse.

They waited; Bidwell staggered in among them. There was no trail, he said, once he'd gotten his breath back. He and Jimmy John had picked a way across the cliff face for a good mile, mile and a half, until at last they came to a spot where the trail pinched down to nothing, and brush and windfallen debris choked the gorge below.

In Bidwell's estimation, nothing less than a bird could get through this place. Faced with it, he had made a statement to that effect, whereupon Jimmy John, who was cussed as a bulldog, pulled out his gun and fired it into the air. "I'll get through," he said, and set out down the cliff. The last Bidwell saw of him, he was trying to work his horse up and over a tremendous windfall. Bidwell reminded them all that this was the horse John had gotten at Fort Laramie that could practically climb trees.

Bidwell's horse was more ordinary, and Bidwell had turned it around and come back up the trail to warn the others. He had met Bartleson on the way down, and told him that the way ahead was impassable, but Bartleson never listened to anybody. Brushing off Bidwell's warnings with a sneer, he kept on going down, with his hapless mess faithfully tagging along behind. Bidwell was of the opinion that they might never get back up again. Looking at him, Nancy thought the prospect of that didn't bother Bidwell much.

She was thirsty. The distant rustle of the river was like a taunt. She looked at Ben, and found his gaze on her.

"We'll go back," he said, as if he answered her.

They went on up the way they had come. Ben felt their way along, threading a trail through the giant pines; once or twice, they retraced their steps a little, and took another turn. At last they came out on a gently sloping ridge running north. Somebody shot a squirrel, and somebody else shot a crow. In the late afternoon, following the ridge, they came out on a high meadow of grass, with a pond of water. And here, they killed their next to last ox, and made dinner.

Nothing mattered much, she found; nothing mattered except holding Ann close to her, and keeping her feet moving, and finding some water. And food. She thought about food all the time, about thick slices of cheese, how good they tasted, and fresh bread warm from the oven. And cream, the rich thick cream that gathered at the top of the crock.

A day later, Bartleson and his men caught up with them again, leading their mounts, who were too poor to carry riders anymore. Bartleson said nothing, shame-faced, about not taking Bidwell's warning, and nobody had the extra energy to waste on twitting him.

Now, all together again, they set off along the northern bank of the stream, which rapidly led them to another sheer cliff. Ben felt their way along a shelf of a trail. Nancy followed, holding onto Ann with one arm and leading her horse with the other. The trail under her feet was narrowing down to a ribbon of flat rock along the sheer plunge of the cliff. She dislodged a rock with one foot and it bounced away and into the crevasse to her left and it was a long, long while before she heard it land. She was afraid to look back, afraid to do anything but creep along, her shoulder scraping along the stone to her left, her right side hanging over the empty air.

The others inched after her. She heard a horse snort. Through the thin worn soles of her shoes she felt the sharp edges of pebbles, and the narrow rim of the trail. Then, behind her, somebody shouted, dismayed, and something heavy began to drag and slip and fall.

The men wailed, and a mule let out a terrified whinny. Nancy pressed herself flat to the cliff and turned her head to look in time to see one of the mules lose its footing.

It scrabbled desperately at the cliff with its hoofs, as it fell; the animals behind it, panicked, shied back, and then another was sliding and another, and another, and the men were shouting and the animals pitched out into space and plunged screaming and thrashing through the air into the massed treetops below. In Nancy's arms, Ann whined. Nancy shut her eyes. Far below, she heard the crash and thud of heavy bodies.

The mountains seemed endless. Whenever the settlers came to the top of a ridge they looked out westward over mountains in waves like an ocean of rock. The river ran deep, deep in its canyon, out of their reach; they could hear it, even smell it, but they could not reach the precious water.

But they had left the thick dreary pines, at least. Now they were fighting their way through stands of wiry trees, still in leaf, that Bidwell thought were evergreen oaks. The brush between them sometimes so thick a man could only force his way through by hurling his body at the mass of tangled vines and branches. None of it bore any fruit that Nancy could find. They saw no tracks, no sign of any game at all. The country seemed empty, save for the wind and the oaks and the river.

She began to gather acorns from the oak trees. She knew there was a way to eat acorns. That night, they killed their last ox. There was hardly anything on it to eat, just the skin, the lights, and the bones. They gnawed the bones for hours, like dogs.

While they were eating, three Indians approached the camp, talked things over at long range with Bidwell, and finally came in and sat down by the fire. Nancy drew off at once. She was tired anyway; and the Indians made her edgy. They did not seem like Shoshone, although they were friendly enough. One wore a calico shirt. All the men took this for a meaningful sign, as if there had to be a store just around the bend.

In the morning, anyway, the Indians were gone. The settlers' last beef was gone; the men agreed that they had to get better at hunting, or they would all starve. After some discussion they decided that the noise of so many people moving was probably scaring off any game they encountered long before they had a chance of shooting it. Therefore one or two hunters ought to go ahead of all the others, watching for game. Bidwell volunteered, and immediately left the camp. The rest of them gathered themselves for the effort of forcing a path down into the gorge of the river.

They crept single file along the sheer slope, picking a way down along the slippery pathless rock. Nancy's horse clawed for footing; she clung with her free hand to roots, to branches and crevices in the rocks. Ann rode on her hip, her fists locked in Nancy's faded threadbare dress, and her head pressed heavily against her mother's shoulder.

Halfway down they reached the river, Nancy lost one of her shoes, which had worn through so that it simply slipped off her foot and fell, out of reach and useless anyway. She wore the other for another half a day, and then lost that one.

But she reached the river, rushing along through tumbled gray boulders. After she had slaked Ann's thirst and her own she soaked her bare feet in the icy water, glad to numb them. Her mother had told her, long ago, that acorns had to be washed before they could be eaten, like slaking cornmeal. She began to crack open the nuts she had gathered and collect the meat; she used her bonnet to carry the acorn meats down to the river.

At first washing, the water from the acorns was white with some kind of milky dust. Patiently she mashed the acorns and ran water through the soggy mess until the water ran clear. The acorn mash tasted faintly bitter when she touched a tiny bit to her tongue. She washed it some more, until the bitter taste was gone.

That was all there was for them to eat that day: Nancy's acorns. They roasted them in the fire and made mush out of the crumbly meal. Bidwell did not come back, and none of the other men had shot anything. They all sat around eating acorn mush with their fingers, too tired even to argue. The dank smell of the river gorge surrounded them.

Just before dark, the Indians from the night before reappeared.

Bartleson nudged Ben. "Get one of them to guide us," he said. "Get one to guide us on." Ben grunted at him, and pushed him away, but turning to the Indians he made hand signs, as they had all seen Bidwell do, and pointed, and made pictures on the ground. After a while he announced to the rest of them that the old man in the calico shirt would take them on in the morning.

Nancy drew Ann into her arms. She disliked these Indians even more than most. The acorns sat in her belly like gravel. She wondered if she could really make food out of something so strange. Ann was asleep, her head like a stone against her mother's breast. Nancy laid herself down for the night.

In the morning, Ben sent his brother Andy and another man, Jones, out to hunt, and the new Indian guide led the rest of them on. He took them down along a slope that got steadily steeper. Two of the horses were already limping badly; one lay down in the middle of the trail and had to be whipped on. The Indian brought them into a ravine so deep and narrow the sun never reached the bottom; boulders and broken trees clogged it, and here, three horses and two mules refused to go any farther.

The Indian guide was already rushing away, climbing the deadfalls. Bartleson, whose mule had always been the strongest animal they had, was hard on his heels, and the rest of the men straggling after. Nancy's horse balked at first but then suddenly lunged and scrambled up over the broken ground; she followed it, bruising her bare feet on the rocks. She flung a look over her shoulder at the beasts they left behind. They were abandoning five animals, five things to eat. She could not stop; the others were pushing after her. She went grimly on, her legs aching, and the deep grim pain of gnawing hunger in her belly.

They climbed down through the ravine and out onto a wide valley, sprinkled with oaks, where the old Indian made signs that they should camp. Nancy's horse staggered toward the nearest patch of grass. She went to sit down, to rest, her limbs shaking.

Later, she gathered more acorns, cracked them, mashed them, slaked the mash. Andy and Jones did not come back. She saw Ben staring off into the east, watching for his brother in the woods, and took him acorns. She stuffed Ann with acorns. When she lay down to sleep, Andy had not come back, and Ben was still standing there watching for him.

In the morning, the old Indian was gone. Bartleson and the other men went around cursing and kicking the ground and declaring that they had been led into a trap. Their conviction grew as they discovered heaps of bones scattered through the valley: horse bones. Then around midday Bidwell came into the camp.

He had gotten lost, while hunting, and cut back across wild country; he had stories of scaling cliffs, and scurrying around beneath tremendous trees. And he had come on the Indians, on the trail coming here, cutting up and eating the horses that the settlers had abandoned. Clearly this valley was one of the Indians' favorite haunts, and horse was one of their favorite foods.

Ben heard all this with rising anxiety. He turned to Nancy, his eyes burning; she knew he was thinking about his brother.

They walked on, travelling the rest of the day; several times they saw Indians shadowing their trail. Nancy led her horse by the reins and helped the men keep the other horses bunched together. Still there was no sign of Andy. When they stopped, that afternoon, Ben decided to take the other men out and search.

He told Nancy this, and also that she was to stay where she was, and wait. Alone.

A cold terror gripped her. She knew he was right. She said, only, "Leave me a rifle."

They left her with a rifle, her horse, and her baby, and scattered out into the wilderness to look for the missing men. Within moments they were all gone.

Nancy settled herself, the rifle slung in the crook of her arm. Ann was sleeping on the ground, wrapped in the ragged blankets. Ann slept most of the time, now; sometimes Nancy with her heart stopped in her chest laid her fingers against the child's throat, just below the jaw, to feel the pulse there, and be sure she was still alive. There was nothing to eat but acorn mush and water. She stayed close by her horse, leading it from one patch of grass to the next.

None of the men came back. The sun dropped behind the pine trees on the hill above her, and immediately the air turned cold. The night was coming. Dark oozed up out of the canyons, pooled under the trees and spread across the meadow; she began to imagine she heard Indians creeping up on her. Every small sound made her start.

She was alone, a thousand miles from anything she knew, alone. For the first time, she cried for fear.

She could not sit crying and helpless. She would not be afraid. She saddled her horse up; if she were on the horse, when trouble came, she would have a better chance of getting away. She slid the rifle under the stirrup leather, to hold it while she mounted, and with Ann gathered up in her arms climbed awkwardly into the saddle. The horse shifted under her weight and snorted. She held the baby in her lap and the rifle in her arms, and waited.

The horse slept, hip-shot, its head hanging. She watched its ears; the horse would know sooner than she if anything crept up on them. The sweep of the wind through the pine trees on the slope above was like some animal voice, coming from everywhere.

The night wheeled on. Through the pines, she saw the stars glittering; something huge flew suddenly and silently across the meadow past her, and she started, her skin prickling. She decided it was an owl. She dozed. The cool of the night sank into her, waking her, and she bundled Ann more closely and wrapped part of the blanket around her own shoulders.

Ben would come back. And if he didn't—

Her mind balked at that. But she made herself think, if he did not come back, what she would do.

She would go on by herself. She would just keep on going west. If he was not back by noon. She dozed again. Woke in the vast empty blackness of the night, with the wind sobbing in the trees, and the child in her arms stirring and whimpering.

She gave the baby water, and she slept again. When she woke again, the air was turning pale, and up through the trees men were coming.

Her hair stood on end. She gripped the rifle. But they were her men, the gaunt and ragged settlers, and among them, smiling wearily up at her, was Ben. She slid down off the horse and into his arms, laid her head against his shoulder, and sobbed.

They had not found Andy or Jones, although they had seen some tracks, and Ben was sure his brother was alive. They could not afford any more time to look. At noon rain began to fall, steady and cold. Once again, they went through their gear, throwing out whatever they could. Talbot Green, president of the company, took his treasure hoard away into the woods and returned without it.[2] Ben and a few of the others dug a hole, meaning to cache what they could, but stopped when they saw something moving in the underbrush.

"Indians," somebody said. "Don't bother. They'll just dig it up again."

So they merely left it all behind. But Grove Cook hung back. The young Kentuckian, who had hired on to earn his way to California by driving Bartleson's wagon, was hot-tempered, and he took the Indians' predations as a personal insult. As the others led their staggering animals away down the trail, he stayed behind and hid in the brush. Nancy saw him, and turned her head to watch him; Ben called to her to keep up. A few minutes later she heard the

[2]Greene came back for the gold later. He went on to prosper in California for a while; but when he tried to run for public office in San Francisco, his larcenous past was revealed. He announced he was going east to turn himself in, and fled again.

crack of a rifle shot, behind them, and then Cook came running down the path.

"Got him," he announced to Ben. "Soon's we were gone, then Indians come creeping up out of the woods. I nailed the old man square."

A few of the others raised a breathless cheer. Cook swaggered a while, but they were moving along the trail, and soon he was only another one of them, trudging along.

Halfway through the day one of the mules sank down and would not move. They knocked it in the head with a rifle butt and peeled strips of warm raw flesh from its carcass and ate them raw as they walked. That night, they killed the last ox. Its flesh made so poor a meal they killed a mule to eke it out.

The mule meat was even worse than ox, sour and tough as rope. "Most if not all of us," Bidwell wrote, "refused to touch the mule meat for some time. I was always so fond of bread that I could not imagine how any one could live without it. It was bad enough to have poor beef, but when brought to it we longed for fat beef and thought with it we might possibly live without bread. But when poor mule meat stared us in the face, we said if we could only have beef, no matter how poor, we could live."[3] Some of the men ate acorns without Nancy's careful slaking and got sick. Then in the morning Ben was sick.

Nancy woke to find him groaning and gasping next to her, in a sweat of fever. She gave Ann to one of the others to hold and went for water. Ben lay on the ground, his knees to his chest, shivering and shaking. When she tried to give him water, he vomited.

Ann called for her mother, and the man holding her brought her back. The men were milling around together in a restless clump. Bartleson, heedless as ever of anybody else, wanted to go on, and the others were stirring their feet. "We can't wait any more," somebody said.

[3]Bidwell II.

Nancy sat down beside Ben and laid her hand on his shoulder. "I'm not leaving him."

The others muttered and shuffled around for a while. She heard a few words out of their talk and knew they were deciding to go on. Ben seemed steadily worse, his breathing ragged. Nancy tried to give him water again and he could not drink. She laid Ann down carefully on the blankets and tried to cushion Ben's head with her hand.

Bidwell came over toward her, an emissary; the others stood bunched a little distance away. Bidwell said, "Nancy, we have to go on. He's finished."

She flung her head back, staring at him, furious. Frightened. "He's not done. Not yet. I won't leave him while he's alive." She said nothing about how Ben had led them through the mountains. Nothing about how she loved him. Her gaze moved from Bidwell to the other men. She saw how thin they were, how the hunger burned in their eyes, so they seemed like wolves, not men.

Beside her, Ben sweated and moaned; she clenched her hand on his sleeve, trying to hold onto the spirit inside the frame. She faced the other men, angry. "You can't leave him when he's still alive. Remember George Shotwell? You didn't leave him."

Bidwell looked around at the others, and one by one, shoulders slumped, they sank down by the trail to wait. Even Bartleson, grumpy, decided to stay. In spite of their desperation, their complaining, and Bartleson's betrayals, they were committed to each other: the trek had bonded them. They killed one of the mules, and made a fire to cook the meat.

Halfway through the afternoon, Ben asked for water, and kept it down. By nightfall, he was on his feet, although he leaned heavily on Nancy.

She accepted the weight. She could carry Ben, she thought. Somehow, no matter what happened, she knew now she could do what she had to.

The next morning, when they counted their tiny herd of animals, two horses were missing. They knew that the Indians were everywhere around them, waiting to pick off stragglers. Packing up their blankets and waterskins they started off down the mountainside. The way led them through a deep ravine choked with rocks and tree trunks fallen from the high banks; roots hung down through the undersides of the banks like great strands of hair.

The ravine opened on a little valley. Even before they saw the little cluster of huts at the far side of it, they could smell the smoke, and the meat cooking.

The men charged, shouting and setting off their guns. Nancy hurried after them, dragging her horse by the reins. The Indians were racing out of the cluster of huts and off into the woods. She ran up to the edge of the camp; on the cookfires were haunches of meat, and more meat hung on frames by the huts. She knew the quartered carcasses were their horses. The men were already seizing the roasts and tearing off chunks of meat and stuffing them into their mouths. She went to get some for Ann to eat.

Ann could not sit up by herself anymore. As soon as she had eaten she fell asleep, and Nancy sat with the child on her lap, half-asleep herself. She was tired all the time; she wondered how much farther she could go. Her teeth were sore and her belly hurt. Her mouth tasted like copper.

She thought of the baby unborn within her; she felt it moving still, so it lived, but surely it starved also. She shut her eyes, feeling drunken. It took too much effort to worry. Too much effort even to feel bad.

They went on. Ahead of them were more mountains, one especially high one directly before them. Surely California lay beyond those mountains. She put one foot ahead of the other. Held Ann on her hip with a scrap of cloth tied over her shoulder. Her feet hurt so much. That night when they stopped to camp, she lay down on the ground immediately, and slept.

Ben woke her, helped her up onto her feet. He had saved some horse flesh for her. She knew she had to keep moving, but there seemed a huge distance between the knowledge in her mind and the hands and feet that had to obey it. She gathered the child into her arms and tottered away on the trail after her husband.

They were walking down through oak trees; by habit she began looking for acorns, for wild onions, berries, and fruit. She felt numb and somehow separate from all this. She struggled to keep her mind focused on the very center, on Ann, and Ben, and keeping her feet moving; the rest of the world blurred and faded away, inconsequent. That night, they killed her horse to eat, and all she noticed was how thin and poor it was, how little meat.

They moved out of the oak trees, and onto the edge of a wide valley, golden in the haze of the sun. The high mountain loomed on the far side, a rounded double peak, like two horns, but between them lay this wide valley, which they had not even noticed. Astonished, they moved out onto the flat grassland. In the distance a river wound through dark trees. Most of the grass was crisped black by a recent fire; they traveled through a landscape as desolate as the wasteland of the desert. Nancy lifted her head and saw before her a line of men straggling and stumbling along like drunkards; their shadows stretched across the blackened stubble seemed more substantial.

That night all the water they could find was a puddle on the burnt plain. Somebody shot a coyote. Each of them got a mouthful of foul tough meat.

In the morning, they pushed toward the river. The air was warm and dry, full of dust. The air seemed golden with the dust. Nancy staggered along, leaning on Ben, her head so heavy she could barely hold it up. Joseph Chiles followed, carrying Ann. They reached the river around noon, the stream only a trickle through stands of willows and brush. The moist ground along its bed was printed with the forked tracks of hundreds of deer and antelope. On the far side tender young grass covered the valley like a field of wheat in May. Nancy sank down on the grass by the river, too weak to stand. While the men went off to hunt, she lay sleeping, the child in her arms, until their boisterous return woke her.

The hunters were jubilant. By twos and threes they came back laden down with game. They had shot thirteen deer and elk, besides some antelope and wild birds; and they could have shot thousands. As they broke up their game and built fires, they talked excitedly of the bounty of this place. When they tasted the fresh, rich meat, some of the men began to weep.

Immediately Bartleson was making plans to camp here awhile, kill a lot of game, dry the meat to get them over the next stretch of mountains.

Before them lay yet another range, blue and indefinite against the clear western sky. The consensus was that they were still five hundred miles from the Pacific. And winter was on them. Bidwell was keeping track of the date in his journal and told them it was now November 4.

Nancy did not think about what lay ahead. She ate, feeding Ann bite after bite of succulent meat, chewing it up when the child could not. Ann grew happier as her mother watched. With every bite she seemed stronger, her eyes brighter, and her eating more eager. For the rest of the day, they did nothing but eat and rest.

The following day, Bartleson and Bidwell had another quarrel. For once Bartleson wanted to stay where they were, and Bidwell wanted to move out. With the nine men who always sided with him, in spite of the uniformly awful results, Bartleson insisted that they should keep this camp and hunt and dry meat to carry them over the next range of mountains. Bartleson had all the best horses and could hunt far and wide and pack a lot of meat. But even as the others were arguing, Ben and Nancy were stowing their blankets and filling their waterskins and starting off.

Nancy felt stronger, but as she followed Ben along, every step took some of it away. She hooked the blanket around her to carry Ann, afraid her arms might weaken and she might drop the child. The river's bed was a broad wash, tumbled with great trees and heaps of flood-driven brush, with broad stretches of sand and pebbles in between. They climbed down the high bank into it, to go across it, and she had to stop at the bottom of the bank and catch her breath.

She could hear wild birds calling, in the grass above her head. Crossing the river, she saw the tracks of cloven hooves, big and little, by the hundreds.

Before long, Bidwell and the others caught up with them—all but Bartleson and his crew, who had stayed behind to make meat. But there was meat everywhere. As the settlers pushed on, they passed through the middle of a huge herd of elk scattered across the plain; flocks of birds shrieked and flapped along the riverbanks. Among the thickets along the banks of the river Nancy found more wild grapes, and fat purple berries, and seeds.

The giant two-horned mountain loomed over them. That night, they camped by a river, and ate well again, but they all knew hard times lay still ahead of them.

The next day, as they set forth again, they spied Bartleson and his company coming along after them—on foot. The settlers were moving along the flat grassland, heading due west; a long low line of dark trees to the southwest promised a river, and they were discussing sending out scouts when Bartleson and his men caught up with them.

They staggered up, grim-faced and weary. Indians had stolen all their horses during the night; they had nothing left but what they carried in their hands.

This was a disaster. Bartleson's horses and mules were the only sound animals the group had. The few remaining to them now were walking skeletons, although the excellent valley grass was having a reviving effect on them. In any case, Ben got everybody to agree that two of these horses would carry scouts out to see if the dark trees over there marked a river. The rest of them would stop over for a while and let Bartleson and his men rest.

Nancy sank down at once. She knew it was not Bartleson whom Ben Kelsey wanted to rest. Ann was sleeping in her arms, and for a while she merely lay there in the luxury of not having to walk. Then, stronger for it, she got up, and with the baby still asleep went off over the yellow plain, looking for more grapes and berries.

The beauty of the land seduced her. She stood a long while looking around her, feeding her eyes on the teeming richness of this landscape, so gently warmed in the sun. The golden plain stretched away toward the hills to the east, where she had just been; in the middle distance a long dark braid of bodies crept along: some vast herd, elk, probably, or antelope. The hills were darker than the plain, almost purple. In the creases grew thick dark green trees and brush. It was a sweet, serene place; she thought swiftly that she would like to live here.

Behind her somebody yelled her name.

She turned. Ben was running toward her. His face blazed with excitement.

"Nancy! Andy! He's here!" He rushed up to her, seized her by the arm, and beamed into her face. "I mean—he's not here, but Jones is—and we are! Nancy! We're here! We did it! We're in California!"

She laughed. "What? Make sense, will you, Ben Kelsey?" But she understood him. Amazed, she laughed again, and then flung herself into his arms.

And it was true. Thomas Jones, who had vanished in the mountains with Andy Kelsey, had suddenly reappeared, riding into their camp. He and Andy had reached this valley only few days before; Andy was out looking for them too, he would catch up with them in good time. And Jones had brought along an Indian, shy and wide-eyed, wearing a blue cloth coat. Whenever the settlers looked at him, this man said, over and over, "Marsh, Marsh," and pointed to the west. They had found Dr. Marsh, whose letters had brought them across the continent. The trek was over. They had reached California.

CHAPTER

11

Marsh's rancho, Los Pulpunes, later patented for more than 13,000 acres, lay in the shadow of Mount Diablo, the high two-horned mountain the settlers had seen from the foothills of the Sierra. On November fourth, the settlers finally arrived at Marsh's doorstep, after nearly six months of traveling.

What they found there dismayed them.

They had assumed that Marsh was a great man in California. In his letters Marsh had helped them along to this conclusion. And certainly from a Californio point of view, he was a great man, a ranchero. But his mansion was a two-room adobe, with no furniture, no floor except beaten earth covered with rushes, and no fireplace. He slept outside a good deal of the time, with his Indian wife and several children. He had nothing to eat but his stock. To the settlers, this seemed very like the life they had left back in Missouri.

At first, delighted to see them, John Marsh welcomed them wholeheartedly, killed a hog for their dinner, and gave them beef as well, and some tortillas. He explained that a long drought had left the country without wheat for bread. Nancy ate the warm corn flatbread with infinite relish. Like all the settlers she was still giddy with relief and pleasure at coming at last to the end of their journey. Andy appeared, and Nancy and Ben greeted him with hugs and laughter. Ann remembered her uncle, crowed, lifted her arms to him to be picked up. After only a few hours Marsh's place looked like Eden.

Like them all, Nancy tried to find something to give to him, to repay his hospitality. The others were offering him knives, lead, gunpowder; she knew Ben had some gunpowder, and she could sweep and clean his house. She would find a way to honor this generous hospitality.

In the morning, however, Marsh's attitude had curdled. He refused to speak to anybody, turning a cold eye on them all. Bidwell approached him, alarmed, and got out of him only that Marsh now saw them as a burden. They had cost him hundreds, Marsh said, and he would never see it back again, and he wished them all gone.

That shocked them. Ben made his mind up fast: he was not one to stay where he was unwanted. He packed up Nancy and Ann, and with Andy, and most of the rest of the settlers, he headed back out to the great valley they had just left. In the San Joaquin he had seen signs of otter. He could make three dollars apiece for otter pelts. Nancy followed him, as she would follow him her whole life, to build the fire, cook the food, and take care of Ann.

A dozen of the others, however, prised from the now stony-faced Marsh the information that San Jose, a tiny Mexican town, was only a few miles down the road. They set off for San Jose to look for work.

Meanwhile, unknown to any of them, their arrival in California was causing a sensation. The knowledge of their coming spread like a shockwave from the Sacramento and Sonoma to San Jose and Monterey. The news came first to John Sutter's fort, New Helvetia, up on the Sacramento River. Jimmy John, who had left the rest of them behind in the Sierra, had reached the Sacramento Valley days ahead of Ben and Nancy and the others. Starving and half-naked, he stumbled onto an Indian, who took him to Sutter at New Helvetia.

Sutter at once sent word of the impending arrival of thirty Americans to the Commandante of the Armies of Alta California, Don Mariano Guadalupe Vallejo, lord of Sonoma. Sutter told the Commandante that these people were likely to end up at John Marsh's, and General Vallejo went immediately down to San Jose, the pueblo near Marsh's spread, to take personal charge of dealing with these invaders.

Because to the Californios, this was definitely an invasion. In all of California at this time, while there were perhaps two hundred and fifty thousand Indians, there were only about six thousand Mexican citizens. Mexico City maintained almost no military presence in the area, believing that the formidable natural barriers all around her were sufficient to defend California against the world at large. Now suddenly thirty Americans had breached their rear-guard.[1]

In 1841 the Mexican government was viewing all American movements with alarm. Over the previous twenty years they had effectively lost Texas, although they were refusing to admit it, to a slow invasion of American settlers, and now California looked at risk. The United States had for a long while evinced an interest in the territory, had tried to buy it twice. Just before the Bidwell–Bartleson party arrived, the Mexican newspapers had picked up on a rash editorial in an American journal avowing that the United States would take California by force if necessary.

Nor were the Americans the only interested parties. The Englishman George Vancouver, traveling through California some years before this, had remarked on the unique beauty and natural

[1]This had happened before, of course: Jed Smith reached California via the Virgin River, in 1833; the Californio authorities promptly threw him out of the country.

wealth of the country and the ease with which it could be taken by a single British warship. A British vice-consul once announced to Sutter that he expected his country to occupy California at any moment. The Russians, for decades an ominous presence on the coast north of San Francisco Bay, were at last withdrawing, but now the French, who had other colonies in the Pacific, were edging into position, and even the Prussians at one point entertained the notion of taking California and making it the core of a Junker empire.

To the people in Mexico City, the backwater they had ignored for two hundred years was suddenly a fat prize all too vulnerable to passing predators, and here were thirty of the rogues popping in over the Sierra, which everybody had thought impassable.

Therefore, when the dozen-odd American jobseekers turned up in San Jose, Vallejo had them all arrested, and he sent for John Marsh to present himself and explain matters. And had General Vallejo been the obedient tool of Mexico City, he would have either thrown the invaders in jail and let them rot for years, or sent them back into the wilderness.

But as Nancy Kelsey was to learn, General Vallejo was no tool of anybody. From his stronghold in Sonoma he ruled a private estate the size of a small country, and in Alta California he was one of the major bosses. Liberal and strong-minded, he had an open admiration for Americans; he was a friend of the American consul in Monterey, James Larkin, whose pet project was talking prominent Californios into supporting a bid for American statehood.[2]

---

[2]Vallejo was interested in this, although, since he expected to keep all he had, and remain the capo da capos that he was, he would not have volunteered for very long. When he had to, though, he adapted wonderfully; he did lose most of his territory, living out the end of a long life on a "mere" 300 acres, but he served in the Constitutional Convention, was a state senator, founded the city of Benicia, operated in state politics all his life, and by any standards but material (and them too, realistically) he was a flaming success. Compare him to Sutter, or Sam Brannan.

So in 1841 Don Mariano looked on Americans with favor. He talked to some of the settlers in the jail in San Jose, and when Marsh arrived he listened to him report on their good character, and then he issued passports to all of them, including the people like the Kelseys who had gone back to the San Joaquin Valley, so they could legally stay in California.

Marsh signed surety for the newcomers. They all returned to his rancho, and sent into the San Joaquin Valley for the Kelseys and the others. Marsh tried to wring five dollars a head out of them for his help, but nobody had any money, and anyway, they already had their passports. Within a day, the emigrants were scattering off into California.

Several went to Monterey, where American consul Thomas Larkin gave a few of them work and saw others out of the country. Half of them promptly went back to Missouri, one of these being John Bartleson, presumably to dine with his dogs. But Bidwell and the Kelseys and several others linked their fortunes to that other extraordinary emigrant, John Sutter.

Sutter came down to San Jose personally to escort the Kelseys back up to his estate, New Helvetia, on the Sacramento River. The smooth and energetic Swiss must have impressed the Kelseys, especially after their experiences with Marsh. In 1841 Sutter was still young and dashing. The taste for liquor that ruined his later years had not yet begun to thicken his features and his waistline, and he affected gaudy uniforms of a decidedly Napoleonic cast, with gold braid and fancy buttons and helmets with feather plumes. He was already starting to lose his hair. Nonetheless, his address, especially toward women, was superb.

On the trip up San Francisco Bay and then along the great Sacramento River to New Helvetia, he regaled the Kelseys with tales of his life in Europe, where, he said, he had been an officer of artillery of the French King's Swiss Guards. He had, he said, personally put down a Revolution in the Palace, and then, discharged with honors, had returned to his hometown of Baden in Germany, to become rich in trade. At last with this accumulated wealth he had come to California before to found a new colony. He spoke all this with utter conviction, and carried it off with great dash, so most people believed him. His elegant and courtly address left Nancy tongue-tied.

Nevertheless, she and Ben probably reserved judgment on Sutter, at least for a while. Marsh, after all, had talked up his fortunes considerably too.

Then they reached New Helvetia.

The fort itself stood on a low hill, a little above the Sacramento's bank, and downstream from where the American River flowed in from the Sierra to the east. The complex was just beginning to take shape but it was already impressive. Ben and Nancy went in through an opening in a freshly laid adobe wall eighteen feet high and two and a half feet thick; the gates had not yet been hung, but Sutter breezily assured them that all this would be done, all in good time, everything would be done, he had plans.

The fort was huge, twice as big as Fort Laramie. The wall enclosed a piece of ground larger than a football field. Inside were the Casa Grande, which was the big adobe building where Sutter had his office and his quarters, and barracks for his Indian workers, a bakery, a horse mill, a blanket factory, and several workshops. The roofs were all heavy thatch; Sutter explained that his Kanakas did that.

Nancy had thought the big brown men she saw working around the fort were Indians. Now she learned they were from the Sandwich Islands, someplace off in the ocean somewhere. Amazed, impressed, she saw how Sutter drew people to him, into his dreams. Later she would realize that everything was built on debt and promises. But for now, to the Kelseys, New Helvetia looked like a veritable city in the wilderness.

And Sutter had a gift for attaching people. His energy was endless, his faith in his vision steady as the north star. His dreams had the appeal of the new and the power of reality. Where everybody else saw desert, John Sutter saw an empire, just waiting to be summoned into being. From the top of his wall, mounted with cannon, he pointed out over the broad sun-baked grassland and told the Kelseys that someday it would be planted in wheat, as far as they could see, a golden fortune in wheat, and his voice rang with such certainty that Nancy could almost see the nodding heads of the grain.

Ben liked him. Like Ben, Sutter was endlessly bubbling up new ideas. They talked about building a sawmill on one of the rivers, about using the abundant wild grapes to make liquor. Sutter wanted someone to go to Fort Ross,[3] over on the coast, and tear down the buildings there. There were roof shingles at Ross, fenceposts, doors, windows, hinges, and two great threshing floors, which Sutter had in mind to cast into the ocean and float down to San Francisco Bay and hence up to New Helvetia.

Everything was falling into place for Sutter. And now he had settlers. John Sutter must have often smiled across the table at the Kelseys, pleased. He even had a woman settler, now. Of all the people in California, Sutter best understood the import of that. Men came and stayed a while and drifted on, but women made homes. Women made children. Women made worlds. Now here was an American woman, with her baby in her arms, another in her womb,

---

[3]Fort Ross was the Russian establishment on the Sonoma coast. For nearly thirty years, it had served as a port and home for several hundred Russian and Aleut fur trappers. The Russian colonists trapped and processed furs there, built ships, tried to grow buckwheat, wove cloth, played the piano, and grew roses in a glass greenhouse; altogether it was an impressive piece of work. And Sutter had bought it all for thirty thousand dollars. It could as easily have been a million; he never paid them. He himself benefitted endlessly from the deal. He brought much of the furnishings of New Helvetia from Ross, and many Russian tools, including huge awkward Russian plows, which he intended to use to plow the river bottom up, to grow his fortune in wheat, with which he was to pay the Russians, someday.

who had shown the way. More would follow. Out across the Sacramento Valley, little farms would rise. All this, John Sutter saw in the rawboned, half-starved, heavily pregnant nineteen-year-old girl who came to New Helvetia in December of 1841.

The Kelseys stayed at New Helvetia all winter. In February, Nancy bore the baby she had carried in her womb across the desert and over the Sierra. A tiny girl, Sarah Jane Kelsey lived only a few days before she died. For Nancy, the lesson was a bitter one; she had a little grave, now, at each end of her journey. She had come so far, and gotten nowhere.

But Ann throve. The child fed on the cheese and tortillas and beans and beef that stocked Sutter's tables and grew red-cheeked and bright-eyed again, walked and ran, talked and laughed. Nancy herself felt stronger, ready, eager. In the spring, with Sutter's advice and encouragement and some of Sutter's tools, she and Ben and Andy went up to Cache Creek, in the western edge of the Sacramento Valley. The men hunted and Nancy took care of their camp and helped them make boots from the hides and render the fat into tallow.

Nancy enjoyed this life; she raised tents for them to live in, and over the summer they all added a makeshift cabin; she cooked and sewed and took care of Ann and sometimes went hunting with the men. Their camp lay in a little side canyon above Cache Creek, where scrubby trees grew, and deer came down in the morning. There were some Indians living nearby but they bothered nobody. From the door of their tent, Nancy could look out across the broad valley and just see the peaks of the Sierra, and be amazed, again, that she had crossed them.

Whenever the Kelseys had a couple of mule-loads of boots and rendered fat, they packed it all back to New Helvetia. Sutter marked it down in his ledger, gave them coffee, sugar, flour, and beans, and filled them with all the gossip they could hold. Sitting at the big table in his office, Nancy listened to Sutter holding forth to Ben and Andy, and soaked up Californio politics, or at least, Sutter's version.

Sutter loved to rant about the selfish little minds of the Dons, the great landholders in California, and how California would never advance without a government that made people listen to it at least some of the time.[4] Now Mexico City was sending a new governor, with an army, who would bring law and order to the country, and soon everything would go the way John Sutter believed it should.

But from listening to him, Nancy began to suspect that California had always been in a civil uproar. The North, which was Monterey, hated the South, which was Los Angeles; the Dons hated the Pueblos; and everybody hated the governor. Maybe because Sutter tended to make everything grandiose, it was even a little comical. Certainly it had little to do with her.

She talked to Sutter about cloth, and he promised to bring some on his launch, which made regular trips down to the sleepy trading post of Yerba Buena, on San Francisco Bay, and deduct the cost from their profits on the boots and tallow.

They were doing well, too. This was what Ben Kelsey loved best, to hunt and explore and wander the country, and he was good at it. He came back to Nancy with stories of hot springs, of forests of enormous trees, of giant elk, of a snow-capped mountain to the north as symmetrical as two hands tipped together in prayer. Hunting westward up Cache Creek, he and Andy found a magnificent lake beneath a solitary mountain, where heaps of rocks red as bricks broke out on the hills like wrecked chimneys, and hot springs gave up wisps of sulfurous steam like vents from hell. Ben told her how sometimes the ground shook and rumbled, and gave her the teardrops of clear quartz he had bartered from the Indians, a handful of tiny stones like melted diamonds.

The stories were getting wilder and wilder. Their trips were getting longer and longer. Nancy could tell that Ben was restless, even before Salvador Vallejo came.

Zeke Merritt had come up from Sutter's Fort to join them for

[4]An arguable notion even now.

a hunt. Zeke was a former mountain man who had come to California with Joe Walker in 1833. Born in Tennessee, he was nearly forty when he first met the Kelseys, a tall, rawboned man with bloodshot eyes who chewed tobacco so tirelessly that his beard reeked from the leakage. He worked for Sutter as a hunter and helped him round up Indians when Sutter went on one of his slaving runs.[5] Now he and Ben and Andy were getting ready to go out looking for elk, while Nancy did her chores.

She went out to get wood for the fire, and while she was picking up the kindling, she saw a man running toward her up the canyon. She straightened, picking up a big piece of firewood for a weapon. As he came closer she saw that the running man was a Negro, wild-eyed, naked, and out of breath, struggling on the slope up toward their camp.

Then behind him she saw a swarm of horsemen in pursuit. She whirled toward the cabin and Ann. The fleeing man behind her wailed. The pounding of hoofs grew into a thunder; in the doorway of the cabin, she turned and saw, on the slope below, the horsemen catch up with the Negro.

He cried out, and raised his hands, but shots rang out. Nancy gasped. She went a few steps forward, seeing the black man fall. The riders were leaping down from their horses. There were not so many as she had first thought—five or six. They had sabers, long wicked knives, and they plunged them into the body of the Negro.

Nancy screamed. The men with their sabers turned to face her, thin, brown men, dressed in heavy leather riding pants, the blades dripping in their hands. One had not gotten down from his horse. He rode toward her, and she looked up and saw a man dressed all in black, like a renegade priest. He had hard dark eyes; he spoke to her harshly in Spanish.

She shook her head; it was much easier to tell him she spoke no

[5]Sutter engaged in slavery on a wide scale, including selling Indians to other landholders, and stealing children.

Spanish than to try with the tiny amount she had. Her heart was pounding so hard she thought it might leap out of her chest. Then behind her, Zeke Merritt came roaring up.

Zeke was yelling in Spanish. The man in black never bothered to answer; instead, he lifted his sword and whipped Zeke across the head with it.

Zeke fell like a hewn timber. Ben grabbed him and pulled him back out of the way. The man in black rode forward, as if he would trample them all. He kept up a relentless barrage of demands, shouting in Spanish as if they would understand when he got enough volume into it, and he had a crew of armed men at his back who had already killed somebody. Within a few minutes Ben and Andy were handing over their weapons. They got the dazed Zeke onto a horse, and Nancy went and got Ann, and they started south, surrounded by vaqueros.

Ben rode beside her. He said not to worry, they would straighten all this out. But he was tight wound as a spring. He said that the man in black was Salvador Vallejo, which made Nancy even more alarmed. She had heard stories of Don Salvador, back at Sutter's Fort; he came back from raids against the Indians with scalps hanging from his saddle. She got close enough to look, but he had no scalps there now. She cupped her hand over Ann's head, as the child rode before her. Zeke was coming to, slowly, and she could see he was simmering.

Halfway through the day, another rider met them, and after a brief jabber Vallejo with more curt commands in Spanish and pointing and signs sent the Kelseys on to Sonoma, to report there to Don Mariano. Then the Californios all galloped off in another direction.

Nancy was relieved. They were almost as close to Sutter as they were to Sonoma. But Ben was determined to get his rifle back. He spoke to Zeke and Andy a while, and then they left her with Ann, and sneaked after Don Salvador and his vaqueros. Nancy made a camp and waited, her gun in her lap, and Ann asleep on the ground beside her.

Halfway through the night the men came back, in a hurry, but with their rifles. They had crept into Vallejo's camp and thieved their guns back from under the noses of the vaqueros. Without waiting for the sun to come up, they headed down quickly across the valley to Sutter's Fort. Thereafter, they avoided Don Salvador Vallejo.

They all stayed that winter at New Helvetia, putting shingles from Fort Ross onto Sutter's roofs. Sutter's establishment was getting steadily larger. Two of the Kanaka women had borne children, at least one of whom looked suspiciously like Sutter himself. The fort had a blacksmithy now, and outside beehive ovens.

Sutter had a couple of other hands, too, besides Zeke Merritt. Henry Ford, in his early twenties, was a newcomer to the Sacramento Valley, although he had been in California for a couple of years. Born Noah Eastman Ford, he had been in training as a Dragoon, in Pennsylvania, when he heard that his younger brother Henry had died. His commander denied him permission to go home, so he deserted, went west, and assumed his brother's name: Henry Ford. Now he spent his days passing Sutter's orders on to Indians.

John Bidwell was back at New Helvetia too, with tales from his summer at Fort Ross, where he had seen salmon as big as a man and felt an earthquake that made the streams run uphill. He reported that the Russians built Fort Ross so well that it took days sometimes just to separate a single joint. He had brought back shakes for the roof, timbers for walls, gates for the fort, looms and plows and windows, and even cider, made from the Fort Ross apple trees, which Sutter's people drank all winter long.

Bidwell had tried throwing the great Russian threshing floors into the Pacific, so they could be towed down to San Francisco Bay and up the river to Sacramento, but the floors promptly sank. Which didn't matter much, since Sutter's wheat crop had failed as well.

Yet the Swiss was full of endless dreams. In the evenings, playing whist in his quarters with the men while Nancy sat near the firelight and sewed her new cloth into clothes for her family, Sutter talked again of how to get more settlers onto the land. He wanted to send somebody to Fort Hall, to divert any emigrants on their way to Oregon over to California. Bidwell had already written a letter back to the States, encouraging more people to come out along the route they had taken: knowing where to go, surely, forewarned, surely, they would make an easier time of it.

Ben said that he would go to Oregon, and find his brothers and bring them back.

This cannot have surprised Nancy; she knew already that he was restless. It suited Captain Sutter in a variety of ways, since now he could pay the Kelseys what he owed them in cattle, of which he had a superfluity, rather than money, of which he had none. So, in the summer of 1843, with 100 head of cows, and a number of horses, the Kelseys went on north through the Sacramento Valley, to pick up the Siskiyou Trail to Oregon.

Near the head of the great valley, they swam their herds across to the far side of the river. The water was swift and cold and a lot of the animals balked, and tried to double back away from the river, and all the men rode out to drive them. Nancy stayed behind, under a big oak tree, with the wagons and their camp gear.

Standing under the tree, she watched the men struggling to keep the wild, spooky cattle gathered. The hoofs of the stock raised up clouds of dust from the river bar, through which the shapes of riders and beasts fluttered and surged like ghosts. Wild cries reached her faintly through the steady uneven thrumming of hoofs. Slowly the men were forcing the herd across the river; most of them were on the far side now.

A sound behind her brought her attention around. On the far side of the camp stood half a dozen Indians.

She started, her skin tingling. The Indians were stark naked; but they all carried bows and arrows. They were watching her with eyes sharp and keen as knives.

Nancy moved three steps to the side, picked up Ann, who was

asleep, and went back to the tree, where the men had stacked their rifles. The Indians were coming through the camp toward her; they moved silently, looking around at everything.

Nancy had Ann in her arms; she couldn't pick up a gun. She stayed between the Indians and the rifles, and in a loud harsh voice shouted at them to leave. With one hand she waved at them; Ann woke up, now, and began to yell. The Indians paused, unsure, and wary. Then, suddenly, a horseman galloped up.

"Get back! Get moving!"

Nancy jumped so hard she almost dropped her child; it was Bear Dawson, one of Ben's riders. Reining his horse down, he jerked a pistol out of his belt. The Indians recoiled. Distracted by Nancy, they hadn't seen the rider approach, and now, abruptly, one of them jerked up his bow and nocked an arrow.

Dawson let out a bellow, and his gun blasted. The man with the bow drawn collapsed almost at Nancy's feet, and the others bolted away.

Nancy carried Ann quickly away from the dead man; she thought if Dawson had not come, there might have been no killing.

In fact, that death was only the beginning. Ben rounded up some of the Indians, and made them tow Nancy and Ann across the river in a canoe, keeping them under his rifles the whole way. But the Indians were not cowed. A few nights later, near the great white-capped mountain Shasta, they attacked the camp and stole twenty-five horses and shot several more, and in the morning fought a pitched battle with the Kelseys and their hands; Nancy, huddled in the shelter of a tree with Ann, saw twelve Indians go down under the white men's rifles.

Afterward, she heard the men call these Klamath Indians, and even Ben shook his head in reluctant admiration at their courage and strength. They had bows and arrows against rifles, which was the edge; Nancy was glad of that edge. They were not done yet with the Klamaths.

For the moment, however, the Indians let them pass. Driving

the herd ahead of them, the Kelseys followed the Siskiyou Trail through rough, wooded country, scattered with lava bombs like great rock sponges. Once they passed along the foot of a great ledge of lava, all broken and checked into red chunks. For a long while, days and days, they could still see the white cone of Shasta, dropping slowly down under the horizon to the south.

Still the Indians left them alone. Riding along with the train of wagons, Nancy watched the hilltops, and scanned the skies for smokes. Then, one day, she saw dust ahead of them, and knew some large band of people was approaching.

Ben and the other men saw it too, and with shouts and whistles they drove the herds together. Unlimbering their rifles, they rode up around the wagons. Ben stood in his stirrups, craning his neck, trying to see ahead of them. Then he wheeled, and yelled to his brother Andy to go ahead, and see who was coming.

Andy galloped on before them, past the close-gathered cattle and the horses. Nancy shaded her eyes to see. That swarm of people up there, surely those were wagons, up there—they weren't Indians, then. And now Andy was galloping back, shouting, his face red with excitement.

"It's Sam! And Zed, and they say David's come too, back up in Oregon—"

Nancy cried out. "Lucy!" she shouted. She wrenched her horse around, out of the pack around the wagons. Up there, in those other wagons, was a bonneted head she knew, that she had thought never to see again. "Lucy!" she cried, and galloped forward, and in among those wagons, Lucy Kelsey came striding forward to meet her. After thousands of miles of wilderness, and years of travel, the Kelseys had closed the family circle.

CHAPTER

12

The Kelseys fell together again as if they had never been separated. Nancy and Lucy admired each other's children and talked over their treks west. Nancy had forgotten how good it was to have another woman to talk to—Lucy, especially, with whom she shared so much. Ann was delighted to have a sudden flock of cousins to trot after.

Sam was as loud and rowdy as ever, and full of news. In the two summers since 1841, many more Kelseys had come to Oregon; in fact, now that Ben and Nancy had come, there were as many Kelseys in Oregon as there were left in Missouri.

Well, then, Ben must have asked, what was Sam doing leaving again?

Here Sam probably shrugged, and made some remarks about greener pastures. In any case, none of that mattered. All his plans had changed, now that he was reunited with his big brother. They could not separate again, now that they had come together so happily and luckily, and anyhow, Sam told Ben, they ought to go back to Oregon and gather up all the rest of the family. All those people were good recruits for California.

So, when the two settler trains went on, they went on together, heading north and slightly west toward the mouth of the Columbia River, trailing their herds of cattle and horses. At Fort Vancouver, the great headquarters of the Hudsons Bay Company, they found a ready market for the stock, and here also they caught up with the rest of the Kelsey clan.

In fact, they caught up with a lot of other people that they knew. Sam was right: there were a lot of Americans in Oregon, many more than there were in California. Once the first pioneers broke the way, flocks of people had followed them across the plains, including most of those who had chickened out of the first attempt, in 1841. Nancy met some of the Applegates, from Missouri, who were Lucy Kelsey's kin.

Mostly she met Kelseys. Among them were Ben's brother David, with his wife and children, and Ben's five sisters. Suddenly they were surrounded by family again. Going to Oregon was a little like going home.

Ben and his brothers found work at once building a sawmill for John McLoughlin, the factor of the Hudsons Bay Company. The Kelseys built a house in Washington County, near Fort Vancouver, and there, in mid-September, 1843, Nancy bore her fourth child, another little girl, whom she named Margaret.

After the deaths of her son and her second daughter when they were barely out of the womb, she hovered over this new child, anxious and afraid. But Margaret was a big baby. She throve like a wildflower, her skin glowing, her body strong and active. She was going to live. Nancy rejoiced, her spirits soaring.

Margaret seemed like a good omen. The Kelseys were doing very well in Oregon. After years of living in tents and wagons and out in the open, they had a real house. When, in December of 1843, Ben's sister Rebecca was married, she was married in her brother's house. This must have seemed to Nancy like a confirmation. Ben was head of his family now, with Nancy by his side. When his sister Margaret got married, in the spring of 1844, she too was married in her older brother's house.

Presiding over this party, Nancy could see how far they had come. Crossing thousands of miles of wilderness they had built prosperous new lives in a new world. They were bringing forth gardens out of the wilderness, and now that they had proven it could be done, hundreds of other people were coming after them. By the end of the summer of 1844, thousands of Americans would be settled in Oregon.

Which, of course, was forcing a bigger issue.

Oregon in 1844, while Nancy was dancing at her sister-in-law's wedding, was on the verge of a war. Both Britain and the United States had claimed it for years. In the 1820s they had agreed to a joint occupancy while they worked out an acceptable border, a process which was supposed to happen in the course of fixing the boundary between Canada and Maine. In 1842 those treaty negotiations had ended without any settlement of the Oregon border.

There were subplots to this main issue, most of them involving California as well. By 1844 many politicians and newspaper editors were openly saying that America was intended by Providence to extend across the continent, and that both Oregon and California really ought to belong to the United States by will of the Diety.

Around the fires and storefronts of Washington County, people argued up and down and back and forth. Nancy heard a lot of it, around her fire in the evenings, when Ben and his brothers sat back after their day's work, and Nancy did her last chores.

The Kelseys, of course, were American, and they naturally saw things the American way. Up in Fort Vancouver, likely, the situation semed a lot different.

Up in Fort Vancouver, they had a lot of British cannon; in the broad mouth of the Columbia, a lot of British ships.

Ben saw a quick way out of the whole mess. He and his family would go back to California. Nancy would have to give up her house. But there would be another house, in California.

His brother Sam was eager to go. He had never prospered in Oregon, although people there liked him, and he and his wife Lucy had a pack of children. They had been on their way to California when they met Ben and Nancy coming north. Several other relatives or near-relatives agreed to join them: David, with his family, Rebecca and her new husband, a couple of brothers- and cousins-in-law, including one Granville Commodore Perry Swift, of whom more later.

Now they packed what they had into wagons, bought goods to sell in California, and herding along some cattle and horses, went on down the long road through the Siskiyous back to California.

Below Mount Shasta, they camped on the bar of the river. In the middle of the night Nancy woke to the sound of hoofs drumming on the earth. She scrambled out of the blankets. Ben, beside her, roared up, grabbing for his boots and his rifle. By the bright full moon, Nancy could see the other men rushing around, and now she saw the whispering flight of arrows.

"Nancy!" Ben yelled. "Get the kids and run and hide!"

Arrows slithered through the air into the camp. Nancy had Margaret in the curve of her arm; catching up her blanket, she ran across the river bar to the steep short bank, on top of which a dense stand of chaparral grew. Behind her she could hear Lucy, screaming for her children. Wrapping the baby tightly in the blanket, Nancy pushed her in underneath the thick thorny brush, back as far as she could reach.

The moon was bright as a blue lantern; when she wheeled around she could see the whole river bar like an etching in the silvery light, the men scattered here and there shooting, and the Indians running on the far side of the river. She saw the splash of water as a body fell into the river. She dashed back into the camp. Ann was just struggling up out of her bedroll; she saw her mother and cried out, reaching with both arms. Nancy caught her up and ran back to the brushy bank.

"Get in there! Quick! And keep quiet!" Ann burrowed swiftly away into the chaparral.

Crouching down at the foot of the riverbank, her heart thundering, Nancy looked for Ben out there on the river bar; she wondered what was happening, if they were winning or losing, who they were fighting, how many. The uneven crackle of rifle fire went on in bursts. In spite of the cool she was covered with sweat. In the blue moonlight, the great mountain shone white above them; in the darkness she saw now and then the brief streak of a muzzle flash.

The rifles were still firing. Each time a shot rang out she thought she heard a body splash into the river.

After a while, the firing died away. She crawled back under the thorny chaparral and found Margaret, asleep in the blanket. Ann was standing up among the bushes, her face streaked with dirt and her hair snagged. But they were alive. She could hear Ben calling, down on the river bar. They were all alive, although they had lost most of their stock.

She led the little girls back down into their camp; arrows stuck up out of the ground all around the fires. The men were whooping and bragging about how many Indians they had shot. Lucy was trying to quiet and soothe her brood.

Nancy was shaking. Suddenly that snug house in Oregon, and all those proud thoughts of how much they had done, looked like a dream. It looked as if they were back where they started.

They went on down the Sacramento Valley toward New Helvetia. The place had changed dramatically. Halfway down to Sutter's Fort the old path turned into a wide beaten wagon road, and as they came nearer the American River, they passed first one little homestead, and then, only a few miles on, another. Nancy was excited; she craned her neck, looking for the smokes of chimneys, the square edges of roofs and walls. She could hear dogs barking. Once she heard a cock crow.

Before they even came to the fort, they were passing plowed fields, although now overgrown with weeds. It looked as if Sutter's wheat had failed again. But the fort itself was sprawling, huge, stretching far beyond what they remembered. Workshops lined the inside of the square adobe wall. Indians worked on looms and made shoes in the cobbler shop, and a blacksmith was hammering out a plowshare in the forge. Indians in uniforms marched along the walls, carrying ancient muskets, another prize gleaned from Fort Ross.

There were a lot more people here as well. Outside the walls, on the mudflats down nearer the river, were clusters of adobes and tents where Sutter's many guests and hangers-on lived. The hangers on, Nancy quickly learned, were getting to be a problem: ex-fur trappers and drifters and sailors sick of the sea, they congregated in what was getting to be known as Sutterville, and they were a rough and rowdy lot. Sutter did not allow drinking inside the fort but he could not control what happened in Sutterville.

The master of New Helvetia himself was hearty and up-minded as ever. He greeted the Kelseys with a booming welcome. He confirmed that the drought had taken his wheat crop for the third year in a row but this year he knew he was going to get rich: he had about a thousand new ways of doing it. And his settlers were coming. This last year alone more than a score of people had arrived in New Helvetia from the east. They were coming over the Sierra, they were bringing wagons, they were making homesteads here.

And soon there would be more. With great excitement he told them about his important visitor of the previous winter: none other than the son-in-law of Senator Thomas Hart Benton himself.

This son-in-law was an Army cartographer named John Charles Frémont. His influential father-in-law had gotten him the mission of mapping the Oregon Trail, which he had done in 1842. In 1843–44, guided by the redoubtable mountain man Kit Carson, Frémont and a dozen other seasoned hands had mapped Salt Lake, roamed around the northern Great Basin for a while and then climbed the Sierra in the dead of winter, arriving at Sutter's Fort in the beginning of March, looking like skeletons.

The Kelseys would have nodded at this. It sounded as if this Frémont had followed pretty much the same route they had.

Sutter had taken them in, as he took everybody in, and outfitted them again, with horses and mules, harness and supplies, for which Frémont wrote him chits on the U.S. Army. And Frémont had apparently been very entertaining. He liked to talk, and was full of notions, imagining himself someone of great importance; he had paced up and down Sutter's hall orating about how Americans were spilling across the continent like a tide, that they would have Texas next, and soon California, as if he were some great chess player moving pieces on a board. He talked breezily and with no deference of Senator Benton and President Polk—who had been elected, he said, on an explicit promise to take over Texas and California from Mexico. He gave hints that he himself was more than a mere cartographer.

In the end, though, Sutter had fallen out with him. Frémont had a touchy pride, the Swiss told Ben; he took offense at Sutter's authority in Sutter's own country. First he had objected when Sutter tried one of Frémont's men for stealing; then he had objected when Sutter hired men that the Army had turned off. Hard as Sutter had worked at it, he had not made a friend of John C. Frémont.

It never occurred to Sutter, who still then loved Americans, and saw himself always as Swiss, that Frémont considered him a Mexican Don. And Frémont, like the rest of the Americans pushing the Mexican War, had a singular contempt for the Mexican Dons.

But now Frémont was gone, and the glimpse of a vast world stage of grand manuvers had vanished into the usual Californio comic opera. While the Kelseys were in Oregon, the long-awaited governor had arrived from Mexico City, touching off a complicated revolt. Sutter had joined in with enthusiasm, on the side of right and order: the governor's side. But in the end the Dons outwitted him. In the whole business he was the only participant who never double-crossed anybody, and everybody double-crossed him. Finally the new governor was sent packing and Sutter crept back to New Helvetia with his tail between his legs.

The way Sutter told it, of course, he rubbed a little shine onto his part, made it look not so bad, but Nancy could see that he had taken a beating. The more she heard about the Californios, the more she worried about them.

Now the Dons were embroiled in a dispute over whether to move the capital from Monterey to Los Angeles. It seemed to Nancy that they were always fighting.

Fighting without really fighting. In their endless civil wars, no one died. The sole casualty in the entire war between the governor and the Dons had been a mule. The Californios marched and strutted and made proclamations at each other, but they all knew the steps of this dance, the same thing, over and over.

She wondered where the Americans fit into this. Ben liked Don Mariano Vallejo, the master of Sonoma, who was clever and spoke English and had elegant manners like a nobleman, and who had saved them all in San Jose. But when Nancy thought of the Dons she remembered his brother, Don Salvador Vallejo, dressed in black, with the saber dripping in his hand.

In the next spring, 1845, the Kelseys went up into the Napa Valley, a side pocket of the central valley of the Sacramento, and one of the prettiest places on earth. There they built cabins, including one of sawn wood, the first house of sawn wood in that part of the country. Nancy had a real house again, with a door on hinges, and a floor. She planted a garden and got some chickens.

In spite of this appearance of serenity, California was in a steadily increasing state of turmoil. The balance of power was changing, for one thing. In that summer scores of Americans crossed the Sierra, families with children meaning to make homes here. The newcomers were all waving some book, which, it turned out, John Charles Frémont had written, showing the way to California— almost exactly the trail the Kelseys had pioneered. People were even calling Frémont the Pathfinder now, as if he had come first.

Certainly he had made the trip a lot easier. Now Sutter was predicting that a thousand people would come to California in the following year.

And how would this look to the Dons, who thought they owned this land? If there was a war between the United States and Mexico, what would the Dons do then? From the front step of her new house Nancy watched her daughters playing in the sun and worried.

CHAPTER
13

Ann turned six on December 15, 1845. Margaret, the baby, was two, and Nancy was pregnant again, expecting this new child sometime in early spring. They were living in the cabin Ben had built in the upper Napa Valley, a mile south of present-day Calistoga. The place was beautiful, with oaks and meadows of yellow grass, lots of game, and good water, and the Indians were no trouble. In any case, they were all thoroughly terrified of Ben.

The grizzlies and painters were more of a problem. Bears and cats attacked their stock, coming boldly up as close as the pens around their home; once Nancy had to sprint for the cabin when a grizzly startled her while she was out picking berries. But it was a sweet and lovely place. Sam and Lucy with their children lived just a few miles away, down on the Napa River. There was plenty to eat, and the men had reliable work.

The brothers were building a gristmill for Dr. Edward Turner Bale, the Englishman whose ranch lay across the upper Napa Valley.

Bale was married to one of Don Mariano Vallejo's daughters; but he had fallen out with his in-laws after he caught Salvador Vallejo fondling his wife. Losing his head, he took a couple of shots at Don Salvador, who whipped him with his saber and threw him into the jail in Sonoma.

Somebody helped him escape; it might have been Zeke Merritt and the Kelseys, although they were never arrested for it, as several people later swore that Ben and Sam were somewhere else.

In any case, the Kelseys worked for Bale for years, for which he paid them at least partly in land. For the gristmill they brought four great buhr millstones up from the bay, where Zeke Merritt had a little quarry; sometimes they had as many as twenty-five men working in the mill, and Nancy cooked meals for all of them.

Many of the men who worked at the mill were also paid in land. The Hudsons, the Yorks, and several other families now lived within a few hours' ride of the Kelseys. They were not alone anymore.

These families got a jolt when, in November of 1845, General Don Jose Castro came up to Sonoma to visit his cousin Don Mariano Vallejo and talk politics.

From his seat at the lovely oak-shaded mission of San Juan Bautista in the Salinas Valley, General Don Jose Castro controlled the provincial capitol of Monterey and the surrounding country. In the makeshift oligarchy that was Californio politics, he was currently primus inter pares, having masterminded the expulsion of Mexico's governor, back in the war that humiliated Sutter, and then declared himself acting governor.

At Sonoma in November, he and Don Mariano talked over the important matters of Californio politics: namely, how to keep power in Monterey in the face of the determined efforts of the far more populous south to take charge. At the same time, General Castro made a quick review of the Americans in the area.

What he found clearly alarmed him. There were hundreds of American settlers in the Napa and Sacramento Valleys, many of them were heavily armed and planning to stay, and they were expecting more the next summer. This was beginning to look like Texas all over again. Castro interviewed upwards of twenty of these settlers, and he began telling them then that they could not own land, that they did not belong in California, and that eventually they would have to leave.

True to Californio ways, he put no urgency into this: they could wait, he said, until the snow melted in the Sierra. But he was working to slam the back door to California. When he left Don Mariano's casa at Sonoma, he went to New Helvetia, and tried to buy the place from Sutter, whose help was vital to American settlers coming over the Sierra.

Sutter refused to sell. Castro offered him the lands and property of the mission at San Jose, and he still wouldn't give up New Helvetia.

Castro could not linger in the north, could not even pay all that much attention: his main problem, always, was the endemic Californio power struggle between Monterey and Los Angeles. Right now the Abajeños were working diligently to dethrone him as acting governor, clearly a matter of far more moment than the Americans in the north. He went back down to his stronghold at San Juan Bautista near Monterey to hatch a counterplot.

The rumor spread through the American settlements in the valley: the Dons were going to throw them all out.

The women certainly worried about it. Nancy was getting bigger every day with her new baby, and Lucy was adamant against moving again. She was raising a huge brood, including perhaps Andy's children from his early Missouri marriage. She and Sam lived almost under the great mill at Bales' place; Nancy could leave her girls off to stay with Lucy when she went to cook for the mill hands.

Nancy's place, which was blessedly not as close to the racket of the mill as Sam's, lay up the valley a little, toward the hot springs. There her garden was thriving, planted with seed she got from Sutter, and she even had some baby apple trees. Settlers coming in the summer of 1845 had brought seedling fruit trees with them. The road now, it seemed, was broad and straight from Independence to the banks of the Sacramento.

Newcomers told her that in Utah, where she and Ben and the rest had wandered lost for days without water, the way was marked broad and clear as a highway with wagon ruts and castoff junk and dead and wandering stock. You could make a wagon out of the pieces of wagons strewn along the way west. You could capture oxen or mules that had gone wild to draw it, and you could gather a household full of goods as you went.

In the evenings, especially when the winter rains began, Nancy did her mending or sewed while Ben and his brothers and anybody else who happened by sat around in the front room by the fire and told stories about hunting and Indians and fighting and wandering. George Yount, who had lived on the river since 1835, had a house and was building a sawmill; he kept a sort of a store, too, and sometimes Nancy went into his storeroom and poked around and found cloth and needles and ribbon to sew into dresses for her girls.

George was a good source of news, a salty, independent man who got on well with everybody. Yount, like Bale, paid for work with land: Thomas Knight was one of his settlers, with his Mexican wife. Up by the lake, a Californio family, the Berryessas, had a ranch; they spoke only Spanish, but they were friendly, and Ben got on well with them.

Out in the central valley there were new homesteads all over. Most immigrants took to the eastern half; across the great river with its broad sandy wash, water was more reliable. That winter of 1846, a new settler family even put on a quilting bee, inviting everybody for miles and miles. The Kelseys went, danced to fiddle music, and drank and ate of a huge feast, and incidentally, helped piece out and knot several quilts. It was getting, Nancy thought sometimes, a lot like Missouri.

Except it wasn't, of course. Which was more of a problem all the time.

James Clyman, who had come out with the Kelseys in '41, visited them around this time, and admired Nancy for "a fine looking woman." But she was not the same blithe and bonnie girl who had ridden to her wedding back in Missouri eight years before. She was tougher now, quieter, and more cautious, knowing more of the world, and having more of a stake in it, with her two little girls, and the child swelling up under her apron. And that stake was threatened as the year drew to a close by events far beyond the horizon she could see from the front door of her cabin in Napa.

News from the States took a while to reach California: months sometimes. Yet by the end of 1845, everybody knew that the United States Congress had finally accepted Texas' petition to become a state. It looked like a war with Mexico was inevitable.

The outcome was just as inevitable. If the Mexican government couldn't beat Texas, they certainly weren't going to stand very long against the entire United States.[1]

To the Americans in the Sacramento Valley, living under Mexican authority, the prospect of a war made things a lot worse. Castro was already threatening to throw them all out; what would he do if Washington went to war with Mexico City? Nobody really knew, but everybody had detailed and passionate opinions, especially Ben Kelsey. In the evenings by the fire, the talk turned more and more to the possibility of having to fight the Dons for California.

Therefore, when in early December John Charles Frémont showed up again at Sutter's Fort, everybody took notice.

Frémont had only a dozen or so men with him, including his fabled scout Kit Carson. Sutter was away when they arrived, and Bidwell was in charge of the Fort. Frémont told him and anybody else who would listen that he was here to map California, nothing more. After crossing the Sierra, he needed outfitting, and in his usual

---

[1]This clear military advantage made Washington much less inclined to work out a negotiated solution. In Oregon, faced with the powerful British, they did come to peaceful terms.

imperious way he demanded mules, packsaddles, flour, coffee, sugar, in plenty and right now.

Bidwell could give him none of it. The fort was almost without supplies, with winter coming on; there were no mules. Frémont was furious; he suspected Bidwell of Mexican sympathies, and when Sutter came back up river, Frémont treated the Swiss with a cold reserve that was almost hostility. Sutter offered him a salute of seven guns (Sutter always took any excuse to fire off his cannon) and feted his guests at a banquet, but Frémont was barely civil.

During the ten days Frémont stayed at the fort, however, he talked to a lot of the Americans in the Sacramento Valley, including, certainly, Ben Kelsey. Frémont told them all that the United States was on the brink of war with Mexico, if the war had not indeed already started, and he found many of them ready to take on the Dons.

But he could not get the supplies he needed. Sutter confirmed what Bidwell had already told him: New Helvetia had nothing. Frémont left in high dudgeon.

He went down to Monterey, where Thomas Larkin, the American consul, told him, correctly, that the United States at that moment enjoyed a condition of peace with Mexico. Frémont loitered in the beautiful, bountiful Salinas Valley—Don Jose Castro's own bailiwick. Uninhibited by any real information Frémont beheld the situation in California with breathtaking clarity. The Dons, he believed, were cowards and bullies and would not fight, and with all those farms in the Sacramento Valley, California was virtually an American province already.

Understandably, then, given that his men shared this attitude, he had a run-in outside Monterey with some of General Castro's men.

At first, riveted on the immediate, Castro treated Frémont as a mere annoyance. Currently he was embroiled in a dispute with the council of Los Angeles over the provincial treasury, which was supposed to be at Carmel and now suddenly wasn't.

On the other hand, General Castro was certainly aware that the United States and Mexico were jockeying for position along the Nueces River in Texas, and when Frémont finally left the Salinas Valley, he must have been relieved.

Then Frémont came back. And somewhere out in the San Joaquin Valley, he had acquired sixty more Americans, heavily armed.[2] Castro, his full attention secured, reacted with alacrity; he ordered Frémont out of the country.

Frémont took offense at this. It insulted his pride, and his sense of the honor of the United States, to have some backwater strongman give him orders. Besides, he thought Castro was bluffing, and he suspected that the war had indeed begun, and he believed if he could make a stand that a hundred American settlers in the Sacramento Valley would come roaring in to join him in a triumphant conquest of California.

In early March 1846, he led his seventy-odd men up to the top of the highest peak in the range along the eastern edge of the Salinas Valley, and there on Hawk Peak, Mount Gavilan, or Mount Frémont as it is now called, he built a little log fort and raised the American flag.

Frémont was living in a dream. Nobody came rushing to his side; nobody in Sacramento knew about the stand on Hawk Peak until it was well over. But down on the valley floor, clearly visible from Frémont's little fort, General Castro began to assemble an army, and Thomas Larkin, the American consul, wrote Frémont a barely civil letter, informing him once again that the United States was at peace with Mexico, and threatening him with consequences if he did not stand down immediately.

General Castro's army was a shell. He had almost no real soldiers, just half a dozen officers and a few vaqueros with lances; he

[2]Before he ever crossed the Sierra Frémont had divided up his forces, sending these sixty-odd men in by a southern route; they met again on the San Joaquin.

had some cannon but no gunpowder; he would have had considerable difficulty throwing Frémont off Hawk Peak, an excellent defensive position. But Thomas Larkin's letter undercut Frémont's confidence. When a sudden gust of wind blew down the American flag, the Americans sneaked away down the eastern flank of the mountain and out to the San Joaquin Valley again.

Frémont had jumped early by two months. The Mexican War would not officially begin until May. But as he and his men proceeded slowly back up the great central valley, General Castro hurled after him a *bando*, or proclamation, cancelling all passports and ordering all foreigners out of California immediately, including especially the settlers in the Sacramento Valley.

This proclamation reached Sutter's Fort some time in late March, ahead of Frémont himself. Ben heard it immediately; he was rocked back on his heels. The proclamation required the settlers to go immediately and to take nothing with them, not their stock or their crops or any other goods, not even their rifles and wagons. They were being ordered off their homes and into the wilderness; and they were supposed to go on foot and bare-handed, in the winter.

Frémont showed up again a few days after this news broke over the Sacramento Valley. With his full company of nearly eighty men, he avoided Sutter's Fort, camping across the American River, and for once he spoke to almost nobody. As quickly as he could resupply, he made off up the valley toward Oregon, leaving behind him an uproar.

For Nancy Kelsey, Frémont, the war, even the proclamation were only background. Her focus was on something more vital. On April 9, in the cabin in Napa, she bore her fifth child, her second son. She and Ben named the tiny boy Andrew, for his hot-tempered uncle. In childbed, exhausted, she tucked the baby into the curve of her arm and considered that he, like all of them, was being swept up on a roaring current of events going who knew where.

She understood her husband. Ben Kelsey would not meekly put

down his weapons and turn and walk away, just because Don Jose Castro told him to. Whatever he did, Nancy had to be ready to help him, to keep up with him. But now all she had the power to do was lie there, the baby sleeping in the corner of her arm, and the two little girls coming in now to see him and to hug their mother.

Before the day was out, Nancy was up and cooking dinner. This was her world; she would hold it together the best way she could.

Ben went to Sutter's Fort and came back wild with news. Half the people in the valley were talking about moving out to Oregon; the other half were talking about fighting for their farms. Chief among those wanting to fight were men with no farms at all, the rowdy crowd that hung out in Sutterville, the collection of shacks and tents and cabins that sprawled between Sutter's Fort and the river.

These people were steadily becoming a major threat to Sutter himself. Earlier in the year, they had rioted and nearly attacked the fort. In the course of this riot, one of them, Granville Commodore Perry Swift, who had come down with the Kelseys from Oregon in '44, had threatened Sutter himself with a knife.

Sutter, increasingly, was caught in the middle. His boisterous, belligerent American settlers assumed he was on their side; but he was a Mexican citizen. Frémont clearly saw him as the enemy. In late April, General Castro also saw him as the enemy: Castro gave one of his Indian allies the present of a rifle, and suggested he kill Sutter with it. Some of Sutter's men killed the Indian and hung his scalp on the gate of the fort.

Sutter himself couldn't make up his mind whose side he was on. Indecisive, scatter-brained, increasingly drunk, he was losing control of Sacramento, at the worst possible moment.

Into this chaos, once again, came Fortune's Fool, John Charles Frémont.

After the debacle at Hawk Peak, Frémont and his army had gone north toward Oregon. But a few weeks after they left, Sutter sent for Ben Kelsey to come to New Helvetia.

There, Sutter introduced him to a mysterious visitor, Archie Gillespie, who was desperate to find Frémont. Gillespie claimed to be a private citizen traveling for his health, but one of Sutter's men recognized him as an officer of the United States Marines. Ben Kelsey knowing the country better than anybody else at the Fort, Sutter wanted him to take Gillespie north after Frémont.

Ben would not leave his family, not with a war coming, not with Nancy just out of childbed. Somebody else took Gillespie up north. Ben rushed back to Napa, on fire with suspicions.

Surely, he told Nancy, Gillespie was here to give Frémont the news that the war had started. Now Frémont would come down and lead the American defense of the Sacramento Valley. There was going to be fighting for sure. They would have to defend their homes, and Ben was ready and willing.

In mid-May, Frémont, his army, and Archie Gillespie marched back down the Sacramento Valley. This time Frémont didn't even go to Sutter's Fort, but camped up the valley, pointedly at the border of New Helvetia: the Buttes, the little pieces of the Sierra that poke up out of the valley floor near Marysville. Ben and his brothers went up there the next day, along with half the other men on the Sacramento.

Ben expected that Frémont would need only asking to take command of the situation. Gillespie had brought him the signal from Washington. Frémont was an Army officer, and here were all these men with rifles, eager to be led. To Ben, these pieces went together only one way.

To his astonishment, Frémont could not make them fit. After Hawk Peak, the Pathfinder had no spine; and Gillespie had not in fact told him that the war was on. Gillespie[3] had left Washington months before and knew no more than anybody else, which was

[3]Exactly why Archie Gillespie went to California is still a matter of dispute. He figured prominently in later events and was wounded at the Battle of San Pascual, in 1847.

nothing. He believed the war had started, but he had no proof, and that was the threshold over which Frémont stumbled, every time the chance came to take control. In front of the eager settlers, he waffled.

Gillespie, the undercover Marine, was wild to take his place; but nobody followed him. Kit Carson and the other mountainmen who made up Frémont's army had warmed up on the local Indians already. But Frémont stalled.

Instead, he insinuated and hinted and suggested that if, perhaps, some of these stalwart Americans—Ben Kelsey there in front of him—were to go, say, start something themselves, then Frémont would see his way to joining in.

Ben fumed. He was ready to fight, but he was no Army man, and Frémont was. At William Moon's inn on Deer Creek, just a few miles from Frémont's camp, he and several other Americans talked over their options.

Zeke Merritt, who still remembered Salvador Vallejo beating him with his sword, was all for calling out a hundred rifles and shooting up Sonoma. Most of the others were more cautious. And nobody could quite screw himself up to the sticking point of action. Ben went home to Nancy and the mill, but he kept his guns ready and his ears pricked.

Zeke Merritt, for one, was making a lot of noise. The old mountain man took to hanging around Frémont's camp at the Buttes, and several times he begged Frémont to take the war to Monterey, or at least, to Sonoma. Frémont was in an agony of indecision. Everybody was pushing him to act, but his sole attempt at decisive action, at Hawk Peak, had led to a dreadful humiliation. Instead, he repeated his invitation for the settlers to go it alone.

June opened. Nancy had her garden planted, and her daughters were picking thimbleberries. Her son lay in his cradle, growing. The weather was so pretty it was hard to worry about what was going on in Mexico, in Monterey. Ben did not go hunting. He did chores around the cabin, worked on his guns and his horses, his eyes on the eastern approach up the river valley from Sutter's Fort.

Ben had more of a problem than, say, Zeke Merritt. Ben had Nancy. If a war broke out, and he went to fight, he couldn't leave her and his children in an isolated cabin. From childhood he had heard stories of frontier wars; when the fighting started, a man took his family to the fort. But Ben wasn't any too sure how friendly Sutter's Fort was going to be, if a war broke out.

In fact the war was on. In Mexico, an American army equipped with modern weapons and led by trained officers was trampling disorganized Mexican peasants and rancheros armed with lances. Nobody in California would hear any of that for months. But in early June General Castro showed up again in Sonoma.

Once again he told Vallejo that all these Americans were going to have to leave. But he gave no orders to Vallejo to clear them out, and, in any case, Vallejo would not have accepted them. Anyhow, the American settlements were not the main item on Castro's agenda: his major concern was the Los Angeles city council, dominated by his old enemy Pio Pico, which was in the process of passing an unkind resolution stripping Castro of all his power and authority. In the face of that, what choice did Castro have, except to declare martial law? He had to know that Don Mariano understood his position.

Vallejo, who never took part in any of this, offered his cousin Jose Castro sympathy and a glass of brandy, and also agreed to supply him with two hundred horses, so he could defend himself against Los Angeles. He saw no reason to take any other action. Vallejo had the whole great watery moat of San Francisco Bay between him and his rowdy southern compatriots. He knew a lot of his American neighbors were worried but he also knew how powerless Castro really was. He—all of them north of the bay, it seemed to Vallejo—could sit this whole thing out.

Castro went back to Monterey, leaving one of his officers, Lieutenant Arce, to round up and convey the two hundred horses south. Arce assembled this caballado easily enough; the valley teemed with wild horses. The problem was getting the string down past San Francisco Bay. Either Arce could swim the horses across the narrows at Carquinez, or he could trail them around by way of the San Joaquin Valley. He chose to do the roundabout but safer course of herding them around to the San Joaquin. So he started off with his caballado, two vaqueros helping him move them along.

Unfortunately, as he crossed the Napa Valley, Arce stopped by Thomas Knight's cabin, and there he encountered Knight's Mexican wife. Perhaps he thought she would sympathize with the Californio position. Maybe he was just bragging to a pretty woman. But he told her that the two hundred horses would be coming back, each one carrying a Californio soldier, to drive the Americans out of the Sacamento Valley.

Mrs. Knight immediately told her husband this, and Knight told Frémont across the great valley in his camp at the Buttes. Meanwhile, Lieutenant Arce took his caballado on to Sutter's Fort, where he overnighted as Sutter's guest, and went on the next day eastward, to skirt the bay.

Even Knight's news could not bring Frémont to act. But it set off Zeke Merritt. With twelve other men from Sutterville, including Henry Ford, the runaway Dragoon, and Long Bob Semple and Granville Commodore Perry Swift, he took out after Arce. They caught up to him at the Cosumnes River.

Zeke played by Californio rules. There was no bloodshed. He and his riders took the two hundred horses. Lieutenant Arce got to keep his sword, and he and the two vaqueros were sent back to Monterey to carry a taunt to Castro: If you want these horses, come and get them.

When Sutter heard about the horse raid, he was furious. Zeke wisely steered wide of his boss and took the horses up to Frémont's camp. Then he and his band, now swollen to twenty men, went across the Big Valley, spent the night at another ranch, and crossed over the Berryessa Trail to the Napa Valley, to Sam Kelsey's cabin by Bale's Mill.

While Zeke and his men rested up, the Kelseys went into action. Ben and Sam rode all over the Napa Valley, telling the settlers that the fight was on. Everybody who wanted to carry the war to Sonoma should to gather at Bale's Mill in the afternoon of June 13.

Nancy and Lucy went into a fury of preparation. If this move failed, if the Dons won, the families would suffer, too; everybody knew what had happened at Goliad, in Texas, when the Mexican army massacred the settler families. Through that day they packed a wagon full of clothes for their husbands and children, bedding, food and water. Lucy, who was nine months pregnant, would drive the wagon. Nancy put Ann and Margaret into the back, with the swarm of Lucy's children, in among the bundles of clothes.

Toward evening, as men gathered at the mill, Long Bob Semple stood up and started to harangue them. Semple was an educated man, and he put a lot into his oratory. Were they willing to fight? Let those who were afraid stay back, because this could come to fighting. They were going to Sonoma, to take the Vallejos prisoner and commandeer the fort there, and no telling where it would all lead.

From the crowd before him came yells of agreement. The growing mob stirred, charged with the electric energy of the pack.

Nancy saddled her horse. Night had fallen. As she led her mount around toward the wagons, she saw that some people were stealing away from the back of the crowd. Most of the men were cheering Semple, shouting and waving their guns, but here and there a man crept off to the side and quietly left.

She understood that. If this went badly, people would die.

Best that it go well then. And, certainly, best not to run away and let it happen without her.

She was standing there watching the men and listening to Bob Semple rant about the wonders of republicanism when Peter Storm came up to her. Peter was an old salt, a Norwegian sailor who had gotten sick of the sea, jumped ship in San Francisco Bay, and wandered up into Sonoma and Napa long before even the Vallejos arrived. He was tattooed all over, like an island warrior, but Nancy knew he was a gentle, good-natured man who liked to paint pictures and play the flute.

The painting was what brought him to her now. Shyly, he told her that the men needed a flag; did she have any cloth he could paint a flag on?

The idea stirred her. She told him to wait, and went indoors and turned up her skirts and ripped out some pieces of her petticoats—two patches of white and two of red. With her needle and thread she sewed them together into a square, the white on top and the red beneath.

Peter thanked her, delighted, and stretched the cloth across a rock. On the white, he painted a standing grizzly bear, threatening with its paws, and a single star. When he was done, he put it carefully down to dry, and they both went back to listening to Bob Semple.

Around midnight Zeke Merritt gathered his force. He had more than thirty men, each with a rifle and a horse; they were bringing some dogs with them, to chase off bears and painters. While the men were holding a brief conference to discuss possible routes, Nancy climbed onto her horse. Somebody held the baby Andrew up to her. She sat him in front of her on the saddle, his back against her, and wrapped her arm around him, and when her husband started off down the Napa Valley, she followed right behind.

CHAPTER
14

The men led the way south along the river. A brushy ridge ran between the Napa Valley and Sonoma, which got steeper as they went south, but crossing over the easy way would have taken them close to Suscol, Salvador Vallejo's ranch. They all were far more wary of Salvador than they were of Don Mariano. Zeke probably told again the story about being saber-whipped in front of the Kelseys, and people dragged up other dark tales of the evil of the Dons. Some of the men had been arrested during the Isaac Graham Affair, when Americans were shackled and beaten and marched through the desert without water for ninety miles. That had been General Castro, too, they all noticed.

Behind them, the women went along more slowly. Behind Lucy's mule-drawn wagon came half a dozen other families, some with wagons and some riding; like any such train they began to straggle out on their way down the valley. Nancy hung back, to stay with them, rather than hurry on after the men. The June night was cool, almost breezeless, smelling of the ripe bunchgrass. The river, on their left, ran silently along its course.

They turned west, at last, crossing Carneros Creek, and climbed up the steep eastern slope of the ridge; they were passing through Huichica Ranch now, part of the enormous Vallejo hold. On the far side they came down through Lovall Valley. Nancy followed along after the men all through the night, holding the sleeping baby. Even in the dark she could see the men's trail like a crease beaten through the dense thorny manzanita and poison oak. They climbed another low ridge, working a way for the wagons through matted brush.

There on the eastern shoulder of the slope the men had stopped. Nancy stood in her stirrups, trying to see over the hill. She knew Sonoma lay just beyond. The moon was setting; the men were nervously checking their guns and pulling at their hats. In her arms the baby slept without stir or sound. Nancy was tired but it didn't look as if she would be able to sleep for long hours yet. She wouldn't get to sleep until her family was safe.

Up there, in the dark, the men were holding a quick election. Apparently they felt the need for more structure. They had just named Bob Semple, who was clever and literate and whom everybody liked, and newcomer William Ide, who was a Mormon, and who had some ideas about how to set this up, as their Civil Authority. Because Henry Ford had some military training they made him Commander, and Semple, William Fallon, Sam Kelsey, and Zeke Merritt were the Surrender Committee.

To most of them, that was the important work: they had to seize the Vallejos and take control of Sonoma. Very few of them, except Ide, had thought out what to do after that. Ide, on the other hand, was thinking about it a lot.

The other women had caught up with them. Nancy went to look at Ann and little Margaret, asleep in Lucy's wagon with their cousins. The babies looked so soft when they slept, so easily hurt. She and Ben had to do the right thing here, for their babies' sake.

She was remembering again what she had heard about the massacre at Goliad, in Texas, the women and children hacked to death. This was like Texas, a revolution, and now it was starting, that which could not be called back or denied.

She saw no other way than what they were doing. This was her home now; she wasn't going to give it up. Whatever happened, she would go where Ben went. Still, she could not quell the uneasy roiling in her belly; she was utterly weary and she could not sleep. She kept her arms full of the baby, wrapped in his blankets, his miniature lips sucking busily at nothing as he dreamt.

The dawn was breaking. The men slipped down the far side of the ridge and rode off toward Sonoma. The women settled down to wait.

The sprawling mission at Sonoma was unguarded. The gate stood ajar, and there were no sentries. In the first blue light of the morning, the settlers rode across the plaza to the front door of Don Mariano Vallejo's Casa Grande. Zeke Merritt dismounted and, with Long Bob Semple and William Knight behind him, went to the door and knocked. The servant who answered went right to get Don Mariano Guadalupe Vallejo, Commandante of the Armies of the North of the Mexican province of Alta California.

A few moments later, the general appeared. He had taken the time to put on his full dress uniform and he was clearly utterly composed. Zeke stepped forward and loudly, nervously told him that he was under arrest. On the stairs behind him there appeared some others of the household, none as well turned out as Don Mariano.

Zeke recognized one of these sleepy men as Don Salvador. He shouted out to Salvador he had the upper hand now. Once the situation had been reversed, and then the Don had slapped him with his sword. Zeke shifted his rifle in his arms, and then promised not to do the same. But Salvador was in fact also under arrest.

Don Mariano was born to command. He exercised command now. He stilled his brother with a look, and with grave courtesy asked the ragged backcountry men before him their purpose, because if they were here to take California for the United States, he was one of them. And in the meanwhile, would they step into his front room, and have a glass of brandy while they discussed the terms of surrender?

They did. Vallejo had smoothly taken control.

But he wanted what these rough-looking pioneers wanted: American control of California. He was perfectly willing to go along with anything that gained that end. They sat down at the table, and while Vallejo plied them with brandy, Semple began writing down the articles of capitulation.

Outside, Ben, his brothers, and the others were getting restless. A lot of the townspeople, wakening to the new day, had discovered them out there at the edge of the plaza, sitting on their horses with their rifles, and a crowd was collecting to watch and await events. The settlers kept the Sonomans under their guns, and there was no sign of trouble, but the door had shut on Zeke and the others around eight o'clock, and now here it was nine and no further word. They sent in John Grigsby to see what was going on.

Grigsby disappeared behind the doors, and he didn't come back either. Ben and Sam exchanged a look; the other men were stirring in their saddles, alarmed. Quickly, in murmurs, the band talked this over. Ford, the military commander, had to stay where he was and keep watch on the assembled people of Sonoma; but William Ide volunteered to go in next.

Ide, like Grigsby, had arrived with his family in California only that summer. He was a Mormon, therefore both visionary and teetotal, and when he walked into Vallejo's front room and found Zeke Merritt almost passed out, Grigsby pouring another brandy, and Long Bob struggling groggily with the Surrender Terms, he concluded that they were too drunk to carry on, and assumed command himself.

But he too found Vallejo utterly compliant. The Don agreed amiably to everything. He sent out breakfast for the men in the plaza, served by his Indian household, while he and Ide concluded the terms of surrender, a matter of two paragraphs.

In the first, Vallejo and his officers handed themselves over to "a numerous armed force," which they swore henceforth they would not take up arms against. They identified the force no more precisely than that. In the second paragraph, the Surrender Committee accepted them as prisoners, while promising "to establish a government of republican principles."

By eleven, Vallejo, his brother, and his brother-in-law and his French secretary were on their way off to Sutter's Fort. None of them were tied up. Don Mariano was still in possession of his sword. Sonoma had fallen to the Americans; the conquest of California was on.

The women came down immediately from the ridge. Nancy was the first through the dilapidated gate into the Sonoma plaza; Ben met her, and took the baby down, and when she dismounted, her exhausted legs buckled and she sat hard on the ground and for a moment couldn't get up.

Nonetheless, none of them could rest. Thus far the work had been easy. Nobody expected it to stay that way. They had done something they were still struggling to understand, and which would not go unanswered: Castro, or somebody like him, would surely strike back. And Sonoma, as they themselves had just proved, was not a defensible position. Nancy with the others plunged into the job at hand.

The mission San Francisco Solano, at Sonoma, was built in 1823, the last mission, the northernmost, and the only one built after Mexico won its independence from Spain. Within a few years of independence Mexico secularized all the missions and Sonoma passed into the hands of Don Mariano Guadalupe Vallejo, along with almost two hundred thousand acres of land. Don Mariano distributed most of this land in a few grants to his relatives and in-laws; Dr. Bale was one of these. The rest he kept for himself, and he lived in the huge Casa Grande in Sonoma, which faced the broad plaza opposite the gate.

Around the other sides of the plaza stood a thriving small town, with the homes of scores of people, shops, even an inn, called the Blue Wing. Vallejo's sister had a big house on the plaza, and Salvador was in the process of building one nearby for himself; when the Americans took Sonoma, the adobe walls were standing but the roof was only half on. On the south edge of the plaza was the old Mission church, with its high white front pierced with holes for iron bells. Dozens of people lived in the town, including some Americans, and now dozens more were flooding in.

Semple and Zeke Merritt had taken the Vallejos to Sutter's Fort. William Ide, the remaining Civil Authority, was writing a proclamation, which he said he would deliver in the afternoon. Vallejo had issued a *bando* before he left, ordering all within his jurisdiction to lay down their arms and accept the Americans, but nobody knew how much weight that would have. On Ide's orders, some of the Americans had rounded up many of the men of Sonoma and locked them away in the calabozo.

The entire Vallejo family had withdrawn into the Casa Grande, where the Surrender Committee stationed Joseph Chiles to keep watch on the Vallejos and to make sure they went unmolested.

Those local people not rounded up and jailed quietly left and went back into the hills, or hid in their houses with their doors locked and watched out their windows, while the Americans swarmed over the rest of the pueblo like ants. There was no fighting.

Nancy moved her family into rooms in the Blue Wing, which had a kitchen house out in back where she could cook meals. Three American families were already staying there, and Lucy moved in too, so the place was full. Once they all had their children settled, Nancy felt easier, and she went to find Ben.

The plaza was in turmoil. More settlers were arriving in a steady stream. The many Ides had moved into one of the Vallejo houses, across the way from Nancy; already families were having to live out of their wagons parked on the plaza. A crew of settlers was trying to repair the gate, while Henry Ford supervised. Ford was the ex-Dragoon; he looked as if he at least knew what he was doing. Nancy asked around, and finally found Ben in the mission stables.

He and Sam had found several old cannon, obviously unused for years, and were trying to see how to refit them. Nancy remembered somebody telling her that Vallejo had cowed the local Indians with cannon, back when he took control of the mission and the country around it. While the men worked, they told her about arresting Vallejo—about how, afterward, they had looked around at each other, wondering what to do next, and somebody had suggested they loot the Casa Grande and Andy had pulled a gun and threatened to shoot him if he took one stick.

She could see how tired they were. Yet they would not sleep. Some fever of excitement burned in them.

Out there then suddenly, in the plaza, there was a loud cheer.

The Kelseys went out to see what was going on; they joined a crowd gathering around the middle of the plaza. There an old flagpole stood, a white mast. At its foot stood William Ide, reading his proclamation.

"To all persons, citizens of Sonoma, requesting them to remain at peace, and to follow their rightful occupations without fear of molestation."

The crowd listened politely, but after a few more sentences Nancy twitched, restless. Ide was not much of a speaker, and he was full of himself: he was calling himself commander-in-chief now. Behind him, a boy was scooting up the flagpole, something red and white across his shoulder. Ide went babbling on about all their reasons for coming here to Sonoma to overthrow the government.

Somebody nearby murmured, "Did we do that?" In spite of
Ide's pompous, circuitous speech, people were still listening. Had
they really overthrown the government? Then this was a revolution.
At the top of the flagpole, the boy was attaching something to the
mast.

Ide's voice drone on: ". . . to assist us in establishing and per-
petuating a republican government—"

It was a revolution, then, by God. Above Ide's head, the red
and white cloth whipped out and Nancy gave a little yelp. It was
her flag, her and Peter Storm's flag, the red and white stripe, the star
and the standing bear. All around her, a cheer went up. A rising
roar of voices drowned Ide's call to arms. Ben swung his arm around
Nancy and hugged her.

"A republic! We've got a republic!"

"The California Republic!"

"The Bear Flag Republic!"

Now they were all cheering, waving their hats, and above them
the flag fluttered, brave on the wind. Ide was proclaiming amnesty
for all prisoners, ordering the jail thrown open and all the people
within released, but nobody was listening. In the middle of it all,
Nancy looked up and felt the way she did when she'd just had a
baby, as if she could do anything, and live forever.

Nonetheless, the flag came down again by nightfall. Some of the
other people thought the grizzly looked too bellicose. Peter Storm
took it and folded it carefully up and put it away. On the flag that
went up next, the bear was down on all fours, and it looked a lot
like a pig. Which should have been something of an omen.

The word of the Bear Flag Revolt spread across the whole valley;
Americans from all over streamed into Sonoma, the men ready to
fight, the women and children looking for shelter. By June 18, four
days after the raising of the Bear Flag, more than one hundred men
had enlisted in Henry Ford's little army.

It looked as if they would see some fighting. General Castro had issued another of his infamous *bandos*, this one calling for "all good Californians to rise up and wipe out the Bears of Sonoma, and to return later and kill the whelps, too." As yet there had been no real word from John Charles Frémont, except that he had moved down to Sutter's Fort, and taken it over from Sutter.

It looked to some of the Bears as if they might not need him. Young Ford was proving a capable commander. Under his supervision Sonoma was turning into something defensible, with a gate that closed, sentries, and now cannon.

Most of the settlers had rifles, and the Bears had found more rifles in Vallejo's neglected armory—old ones, in pieces, but Ben and Sam cobbled them together into workable arms. Ben had talked Jack Rainsford, an old U.S. Navy sailor, down out of the hills to help re-rig the cannon. Rainsford thought very little of the Bear Flag Republic, but he said that before he died he wanted to see the American flag flying over California. This looked like a step in that direction.

As soon as Rainsford arrived they could all see he knew what he was doing. He helped them make new trucks for the guns, and clean the big brass and iron barrels and load them: they looked fearsome, especially the two big shiny 18-pounders set up by the gate, aiming south down the valley.

Ford didn't dare shoot off practice rounds. They had very little gunpowder, a commodity always in short supply in California; they could not afford to waste any. Ford thought there was more powder at the Fitch Ranch, on the Russian River, and he sent Tom Cowie and George Fowler off to get it, and he sent William Todd and Francis Young to Bodega, to recruit help from the ranchers there.

As for William Ide, he was writing more proclamations. Every few hours he would take a proclamation out and tack it up to the flagpole. At first Nancy went loyally over to read them, but after a while she lost interest. Ford thought Ide was incompetent, and sent a message to Zeke Merritt, back at Sutter's Fort, to come and help him.

Rumors were flying everywhere. Frémont sent word that he had heard Castro was on the move north. A U.S. Navy ship, the *Portsmouth*, had dropped anchor down in San Francisco Bay, nobody knew why. The commander, Montgomery, sent an officer up to Sonoma to see how the Bears were doing. This officer reported back down to Montgomery that everything seemed under control. He let nothing slip to the Bears about the *Portsmouth*'s mission, and he offered no help either.

The whole situation worried Henry Ford, general of the Bear Flag army: Sonoma could hold only so many people, and already they were running out of food, and where the hell were Cowie and Fowler and that gunpowder? On the twentieth, Ford sent out another band of men, under Sam Gibson, to go to Fitch's Ranch for the powder, and find out what had happened to Cowie and Fowler.

Gibson and his men, riding north, ran into a Californio ambush near Santa Rosa. They shot their way out of it, and captured two of the Californios, who led them to the bodies of Cowie and Fowler, still tied to the trees where they had been tortured to death.

The two young men had died at the hands of a band of Californios led by Juan Padilla and Ramon Carrillo, local ranchers; Carrillo was the brother of Señora Vallejo. And, the two Californio prisoners claimed, Padilla's band had also captured Todd and Young.

This news hit the Bears at Sonoma like an electric shock. They had found the enemy, or he had found them, and he was drawing blood.

Padilla and Carrillo, with a number of other Californios, were in fact mounting a vigorous counter-attack to the Bear Flag Revolt. Days before, they had tried to rescue Vallejo, as the Don was being escorted to Sutter's Fort, but Vallejo refused to be helped. Now the band was riding around gathering supporters and attacking any Americans they saw. If Castro with an army came north and connected with Padilla, the Bears would be in serious trouble.

Henry Ford wasted no time. He may have known that Frémont

was on his way to Sonoma at last, but Ford did not wait. Leaving three-quarters of his little army to defend Sonoma, he took eighteen men, including Ben and Sam Kelsey, and went out to rescue Todd and Young from Padilla. Ben had time enough to say good-bye to Nancy, and then he was gone.

Nancy stood at the gate watching them. Behind her, the plaza was in its usual uproar; all around the edges were the wagons and tents of Bear families, and their dozens of children ran and jumped and played war on the broad expanse of the square, shooting at each other with sticks. Cooking fires filled the air with smoke and the smell of bacon and coffee. Somebody had thrown the bones and offal of a slaughtered steer out into the open, where ravenous buzzing flies, ravens, and dogs, and some of the children were scrambling around it. In the middle of it all was the flagstaff, plastered with Ide's dreams and topped by the Bear Flag somebody else had made.

Some of Ford's men were drilling, marching up and down by the line of cannon. Others walked along the walls, watching the country beyond. At the opposite side of the plaza stood the Casa Grande, its doors shut and guards before them. People were going in and out of the church, catercorner from the Casa Grande; some of the Sonoma women were tending the altar there.

The Alamo also had been a mission. Nancy rounded up her daughters, to keep them out of the garbage, and went back to the Blue Wing, where Lucy Kelsey was in childbed.

Lucy lay on her side in the bed, half-asleep; now and then she let out a groan of pain. Nancy found clean rags and good water and a sharp knife, which she laid down on the table by the bed, the edge turned carefully away from the laboring woman. She made Lucy some tea, to ease her pain; if there were hemp available she might have used that. Then, with some of the other women, she sat down to wait.

The women all knew this time, this mystery, its sufferings and its dangers and glories. This for them was the center of the world, a holy and terrible rite. Each time a woman lay down in childbed her life was at stake. Women died all the time bearing babies, died in seconds, or died slow and hard over days. But each time they brought forth the future. Nothing else really mattered.

They sat by Lucy, talking to her when she was awake, and cheering her through the increasing pains. Nancy held her hand. They talked about their husbands, out fighting the new war. Every few moments someone would go, and look out the window, and come back to report: no news. Sometimes, when the pains were hard, Lucy's grip tightened on Nancy's hand until it hurt.

Late in the afternoon some of Ford's men came back, with a herd of cattle and some other provisions. From Sonoma that morning they had ridden west to Petaluma, found Juan Padilla's adobe, and burnt it out; they had gathered all this food and sent it back to the fort. The rest of the Bears had gone on. They had heard that Padilla and his band, still holding Todd and Young captive, were meeting an army from the south, somewhere down near the Indian ranch at Olompali.

Ben and Sam had not come back with the supplies. Lucy wept and sighed and groaned; the women got her up halfway sitting, and held her, and she squeezed out a baby girl, tiny and slick and red and squalling. Nancy wrapped the infant in a blanket and gave her to Lucy, and cleaned up the mess. There was blood enough for a battle, but it was good blood: Lucy had already stopped bleeding, and was sitting up a little, and the baby was sound and strong and would live.

Halfway through the day, the men came roaring home.

They galloped in the gate, cheering and yelling, and the whole of Sonoma, hundreds of people now, poured out to meet them. They had Todd with them, wrapped up in blankets, his bare legs hanging down around the barrel of his horse. Nancy pushed and shoved through the crowd, looking from face to face, and let out a yell—there was Ben! and Sam!

The men looked exhausted but high-spirited. They had caught

Padilla and some fifty or sixty Californio soldiers at Olompali and routed them. They had rescued Todd, although Francis Young had been killed. Todd said that the Californios were ready to kill him, too, and only put it off when he reminded them of the Vallejos, held hostage at Sutter's Fort.

The Bears had won their first battle. Their excitement kept them charged up even though they were tired. Nancy took Ben off and fed him, and Sam went to see Lucy and his new daughter. Out in the plaza, many of the Bears were still whooping and celebrating; that night, there were barbecues all around the plaza.

In the morning, the mood was a little lower. Everybody knew this wasn't over yet. The Californio soldiers run off from Olompali were still somewhere north of the bay; they had no guns, or very few, but their numbers alone made them dangerous. General Castro was supposed to be coming north with a huge army. And now John Charles Frémont made his first appearance at Sonoma.

Frémont had already taken over Sutter's Fort, where he threatened Sutter, made him a prisoner in his own house, commandeered Sutter's favorite horse, and renamed the place Fort Sacramento. Frémont had taken special umbrage at Sutter's dealings with the Californio prisoners, Vallejo and his family, whom Sutter had treated as guests, with sumptuous meals and wine, comfortable quarters, and daily visits. Frémont had given the prisoners then into Bidwell's charge, with orders to treat them properly. Bidwell did, just as Sutter had, and when Frémont protested, quit the job and came to join the Bear Flag.[1]

Now Frémont had come to Sonoma. He sneered at Ide and his proclamations, and treated Ford like a greenling, although Ford had already proven himself more a soldier than Frémont would ever be.

---

[1]Their next jailer was young Ned Kern, who also fell victim to Vallejo's easy charm.

Everybody turned to the next task, finding the Californio force now lurking somewhere the surrounding country.

The mood at Sonoma was on one of its manic upswings. Everybody talked about hunting down the Californios as if it were a pleasure trip, a sport. Frémont made an elaborate pretense of merely going along for the ride, but everybody except Ide looked to him to give the orders, even Ford, who, a trained Dragoon, understood chain of command. With Ford and fifty Bears, and his own eighty riflemen, Frémont set off to find Padilla and finish him off.

For the second time in a few days Nancy watched her husband ride off to the war. Once again the high happy mood faded into worry and fret. Nearly seventy-five men remained behind, to guard the fort, but they were under Ide's command. Nobody had much confidence in Ide, whose proclamations were becoming increasingly egotistical and esoteric. The women went about their work, keeping the garrison fed and the children out of the way, and the men charged the cannon and saw to their rifles and walked the walls, their eyes turned south.

Then somebody noticed something odd about a fish brought in to the kitchen of the Casa Grande, to be prepared for Señora Benicia Vallejo's supper. The mouth of the fish was sewn together. Cut open, it disgorged a message to the Don's wife from her brother, Ramon Carrillo, who was claiming to be with Castro's army. The message suggested that she invite all the Bears to a barbecue in her backyard, the day of June 30, so that Carrillo and the army could fall on them and kill them all.

The news panicked people. Nancy when she heard it immediately went around and gathered up her daughters and Lucy's brood and took them all to the Blue Wing; the other mothers did the same, and the plaza magically emptied of children. The townspeople, most of them Californio, came to Ide and asked permission to leave, which Ide refused. Instead they quietly took refuge, in the Casa Grande, in the church, in the calabozo. Some people were for going after Frémont and Ford and bringing them back.² Doña Benicia, clearly alarmed, begged Ide to let her write to her brother and warn him not to come, that the Americans were heavily armed and fore-warned and would massacre them. Ide ordered the garrison to man the guns and watch the approaches to the fort, which they were already doing.

Night fell. The Bear army had been gone for two days, with no word from Ford or Frémont or any of the other men. In the Blue Wing kitchen Nancy divided up their dwindling supply of food to serve her family and Lucy's. After they had eaten, she went out and took water to the men standing sentry duty and manning the cannon.

The two big brass 18-pounders stood by the gate; the slow matches were lit, glowing red in the dark where their long poles were tipped up carefully against the wall. The guns' flanks caught the reflections like roses under smoky glass. She stood a while and looked south, wondering where Ben was, what he was doing, when he would come home. If.

Her children were asleep at the Blue Wing. She went back there, where she belonged, and tried to sleep herself.

In the middle of the night she woke, hearing people outside calling; out the window, she could see men running across the plaza toward the gate carrying their rifles. Somebody was coming. They

²Which is almost certainly what the Californios wanted. Carrillo was not with Castro's army at all; he and Padilla and the rest of the sixty-odd Californios from Olompali were now trapped north of Sonoma, with Frémont's and Ford's considerably larger and much better armed force between them and escape. The note to Doña Benicia was only one of a flurry of faked notes that appear at this point, all of them aimed at drawing the Bears north, away from San Francisco Bay. The bloodthirsty talk, like General Castro's *bando* ordering the death of all Bears, "even their whelps," was calculated to inflame the Bears to action rather than describe any real intent.

were being attacked. She gathered her sleepy children together, and with Lucy and the other women, she waited, her pistol in her lap.

Outside silence fell. The women looked at each other, wide-eyed; most of the children had gone back to sleep again, but Lucy's boy Joe was eleven, old enough to want to go down and join the men, and Lucy had to grab him a couple of times to make him stay.

Then outside a terrific yell went up. And then, crazily, a cheer and laughter.

Nancy bolted to her feet. In a spate of women and children she raced down out of the Blue Wing and over to the gate, where now a column of horsemen was riding in.

It was Frémont, looking disheveled. Behind him, his men were trading shouts with the garrison, and from their comments Nancy pieced together what had happened. Frémont and his army had approached up the valley, and Ide's men, hearing them coming in the dark, had almost opened fire on them. Riding next to Frémont, Kit Carson had seen the glow of the slow matches, when the cannoneers waved them around to heat them up so they could light the fuses; only the scout's scream of warning had stopped Ide from blowing up Frémont himself.[3]

When she found Ben, he was of the opinion that Ide should have gone through with it.

The trip south had been a disaster. They had gone to San Rafael, the mission on the north shore of San Francisco Bay, with the idea of intercepting Castro and the Californio army as it crossed the water, and found nobody there except a couple of sick and wounded men, victims of Olompali, hiding in the ruined mission. Then, out-

[3]Bidwell reported later an eerie echo of this at Sutter's Fort; Frémont set off a cannon as a salute and the cannon blew up and almost decapitated him.

side the mission, they saw three Californios approaching in a small boat.

Ben looked sharp, and recognized them: old man Berryessa, whose ranch lay close by the Kelseys' homestead, and his two twin grandsons. They were clearly unarmed. One of the boys was carrying a saddle over his shoulder, and the other had a blanket folded under his arm.

Ben rather thought Berryessa would stay out of the trouble, and he said so to Frémont. Likely also they could ask him what he knew, and maybe get some answers.

Frémont said, only, "I don't want any prisoners," and gave him a meaningful look.

Ben said, "What do you mean?" although he knew right away what Frémont meant.

"I mean I don't want the trouble of any prisoners," Frémont said.

Ben exploded. The Kelseys had a gift for colorful language and he used a lot of it on Frémont. Berryessa was a friend of his, a neighbor, and unarmed, and he'd die himself before he shot him. He turned his back on Frémont and walked away. Frémont sent somebody else down, and a few moments later, all the Bears heard the crack of shots and turned to see the three Californios fall.

Ben was still fuming over this. He wasn't a murderer; he could see shooting somebody who was shooting at him, but not an unarmed old man and two boys. All the Bears had been outraged at what Frémont did. In fact, Ben thought Frémont was a fool. The Bears hadn't caught up with the enemy army either. Now Frémont had brought them all back here on a wild goose chase, and nearly got them all shot to pieces by their own guns. Ben was fast losing any interest in following the Pathfinder.

In the morning, though, he was in the saddle again, and once more riding south. Frémont had finally put it all together: he had found yet another planted letter informing him Castro was about to attack Sonoma. Clearly all these letters were decoys. The Bears and Frémont raced back down to San Rafael, and got there in time to see the last of the Californio boats rowing away out of rifle range. The enemy had escaped back into the south.

Frémont and a couple of other men went across the bay themselves, to the presidio on the hill above Yerba Buena, and spiked the guns there. They met no opposition. General Castro's army had faded away. The U.S.S. *Portsmouth* was still anchored in the cove, doing nothing.

The war north of the bay was over, and everybody seemed to sense it. Ide went on writing proclamations. Nancy spent the next few days sewing shirts for Frémont's men, who were in rags after nearly a year in the wilderness. Some of the other women made more Bear Flags, to be sent to other strongholds in the new republic: one went to Bodega, and another to Sutter's Fort. Some people were talking about leaving Sonoma. Those with wheat to harvest in July were especially anxious to get back home.

On July 4, they celebrated Independence Day with speeches, and an officer from the Portsmouth read the Declaration of Independence. Nancy, standing there in the crowd with Andrew in her arms, heard the familiar, beloved words, and felt again the draw of the huge idea, as yet so unrealized, but so compelling, and so essentially American.

"We hold these truths to be self-evident: that all men are created equal . . ."

The Bear Flag Republic was coming to an end. On July 5, Frémont called them all together, and told them that he was taking charge. Nobody except Ide was surprised. Most of them had always expected to be annexed into the United States anyway, and now Frémont wanted to make that a little easier, by rewriting history slightly. He wanted to nullify everything that had happened between June 14, when Nancy's flag went up, and July 5, which was that very moment, and make a new start, with no problems over who had the authority, and what country it was. Frémont wanted to declare that the Bear Flag Republic had never existed.

Some of the men protested, but not many. They all had to get back to their homes, and they were Americans anyway, after all: wasn't that what all this was about? On July 7, the whole issue got stale, when Montgomery of the *Portsmouth*, down in San Francisco Bay, abruptly sent in his men to take Yerba Buena and run up the American flag. On July 8, the U.S. Navy seized Monterey without firing a shot. Castro fled to Mexico; California was an American prize. A day later, the Bear Flag came down the flagpole in Sonoma, and the Stars and Stripes went up.

Ben had had enough. Other men were signing up for Frémont's new army—the Bear Flag Battalion, as they were already calling it, but Ben hated Frémont and he wanted to go home. He packed up his family and left.

They rolled back up the Napa Valley, past the deserted mill, toward Hot Springs. Padilla and Carrillo had ridden through this way, and some of the settlers' places down to the south had been burned, but when they reached their cabin, it was intact, if a little musty. Ben went to put their horses away and bring in some wood for a fire. Nancy moved her belongings back into the house, just as if they had never left, and put on her apron, and set about cooking dinner for her family.

Yet at some point she must have stopped, turned, and seen everything around her with new eyes. It must have thrilled her. Because everything was different now. This was inalterably hers now, hers and Ben's. They had found California, and made it American, she and Ben.

If she suspected already that Frémont would get the credit for this, as he got the credit for blazing the trail across the continent, it probably didn't matter. She was home again, forever, this time. She went back to her work, her hands busy.

• • •

Mainstream historians, starting with Bancroft,[4] tend to disparage the Bear Flag. They brush it aside as an anomaly, which had no real effect on the American taking of California, and often they claim that the Bears were mere thugs out for plunder and blood. This ignores the facts. Some of the Bears, like Zeke Merritt, were pretty rough cut, but most were farmers and had families and were acting out of self-defense.

And they did a good job. Especially contrasted with Frémont's raising of the flag on Hawk Peak, the Bear Flag Revolt stands out as a model piece of filibustering. With Vallejo's inspired help, they took Sonoma without bloodshed and without looting, and maintained good order while they were there, under trying conditions. The abuses of the Bear Flag, the murder of Berryessa and the de Haro twins, and the ransacking of Salvador Vallejo's house at Suscol, were Frémont's doing, not the Bears. On the whole, the Bears showed more skill and foresight than the official conquest, a thoroughgoing piece of incompetence that included the only two battles in the Mexican War that United States lost. But of course the Bears were ordinary people, not government-sanctioned heroes, and therefore, as Frémont himself said, what they did doesn't officially count.

[4]H. H. Bancroft, the historian of pioneer California, is alleged to have told Granville Commodore Perry Swift that he would write him a good biography if Swift paid him two hundred and fifty dollars. Swift declined, and has been vilified ever since.

CHAPTER

15

Well, of course, it wasn't forever. The Kelseys never did settle down. After the war ended, they moved to Sonoma, and Vallejo and Ben built a sawmill on Glen Ellen Creek. Then in early 1848, the word started circulating that somewhere on Sutter's land somebody had found gold.

That got Ben itching, of course. Nancy was heavily pregnant, with three little children; they all went to live at Sutter's Fort, which now people were calling Sacramento, while Ben took off to the high country to see if the rumors were true.

At Sutter's Fort, now a great sprawl of buildings, corrals, and people, Nancy bore another daughter, Mary Ellen. Before long, Ben was back—with a thousand dollars in gold dust, and a strong inclination to go up to the Sierra again and get some more.

Salvador Vallejo had sold Ben a huge tract of land along the southern edge of Clear Lake, including the stock and the Indians living on it. Andy Kelsey and a friend named Charlie Stone were managing it. Ben went to Clear Lake and gathered up all the young Indian men he could, and took them away across the valley and up into the Sierra, to pan gold for him. At the dry diggings named for him, in El Dorado County, he weighed up as much as ten thousand dollars in a matter of a few days.

Ben was shrewd enough also to see that the people making money on the gold strike in the Sierra weren't the miners, but the people supplying them. Rounding up sheep in the lowlands at a dollar a head, he took them to the gold country and sold them for sixteen dollars apiece; when he came back to Sonoma, he had two sacks of gold so heavy that Nancy couldn't even lift them off the kitchen table.

By now everybody knew about the gold in the Sierra. Hundreds of men were streaming into the country, from the East, from South America, from China, all scrambling to get rich. Ben determined to seize the opportunity. He and Nancy opened a trading post in the gold country, to sell food and supplies to the miners.

But Ben's strange intermittent fever caught up with him. Nancy had to bring him down on a litter to Sacramento, to be doctored. It took a long time for him to get well; when they went back up to their trading post, it had been looted and burned.

Ben still had a fortune left. He went back to Sonoma, where he lent money at ruinous interest, and was sometimes repaid. The Indians who had worked for him wound up with nothing. When he fell sick, up in the gold country, his Indians had been left to find their own way home through hostile territory. Few of them ever reached Clear Lake. The Indians had reason to hate and fear the Kelseys.

One day while Ben was sick, Nancy rode into Sonoma to get him medicine (probably laudanum, then a cure for malaria), and on the way encountered an Indian named Augustine, who roped her with his lasso. Augustine was one of the tribe that lost most of its young men to Ben's greed; he intended some revenge.

Trapped in the rope's noose, Nancy refused to panic and run, knowing if she did he would drag her off her horse. Instead she faced him, and put on a good defiant front, her voice high and fierce, threatening to shoot him, although she had left her pistol at home. Finally Augustine let her go. She went on into Sonoma and complained to the alcalde, who had Augustine brought in and sentenced to one hundred lashes. But when Nancy got home and told Ben what had happened he got up out of his sickbed and went into Sonoma and shot the Indian dead.

For the times, this was normal white–Indian relations. Andy Kelsey was managing Ben's great landholding near Clear Lake, including the Indians living on it.[1] Ben had already alienated these people by dragging their young men off to the gold fields, and Andy both overworked and underfed them, and abused some of the girls; possibly they were running a prostitution house. The Indians revolted. The first time this happened Ben and Sam rode up from Sonoma and rescued their brother; but the next time the Indians killed Andy and Charlie Stone.

When news of this reached the Kelseys in Sonoma, they took their guns down, called out their friends, and set forth for revenge. Sam swore an oath to shoot every Indian he saw, and for the better part of a day the band did so, going from ranch to ranch, burning villages, and killing the people or driving them into the hills.

After a while Ben balked. According to contemporary newspaper accounts of the massacres, he even tried to stop Sam and the others, who were blood-mad, and when he couldn't, he put his gun

[1]Most of the big rancheros in California converted the Indians they found on their property into laborers, paying for their work with food, and not much of that. This was basically slavery, and was institutionalized as such in a proclamation by the military governor in 1846, which, sanctimoniously enough, pretended to outlaw Indian slavery, while actually putting it on a legal footing, by making it illegal for an Indian not to have a job.

away and went home again. Sam went on killing Indians and was arrested and jailed. It did no good; within a few months he was out again, still armed, still honoring his oath.

After Andy's death the brothers sold out their Clear Lake holdings, shipped their goods north by sea, and went overland with Nancy, the bitterly protesting Lucy, and their children, to the new settlements in Trinity County. Ben and Sam both joined the new companies founding towns on Humboldt Bay. The brothers broke horses and sold them, and Sam and Lucy opened a tavern. Ben and Sam explored along the south fork of the Eel River, which for a long while was called Kelsey's River, and which still rolls through some of the wildest country in California. Ben forged a new trail north toward Oregon, which to this day shows up on hiking maps as the Kelsey Trail. And in the new town of Union, on the north end of Humboldt Bay, he undertook to build Nancy a beautiful new house, committing the money owed them from the sale of the Clear Lake ranch.

It was to be the most beautiful private house in California. For a while, Nancy must have dreamed about stained-glass windows, and floors with carpets, and shining brass fixtures, and crystal lamps; she planned rooms for each of her children, and a fine parlor for receiving guests; maybe she looked at her growing daughters and imagined them walking down the staircase in their wedding gowns. But the Kelseys' shining times had passed. Ben could ride and shoot and find trails through any wilderness on earth but he was no good with money. He lost the fortune he made in the goldfields, he never collected the bulk of the money owed him for the Clear Lake ranch, and before Nancy's new house could be finished, the workmen were suing him for unpaid bills.

In 1851, Nancy went down by ship to Sonoma with the children, and Ben signed on with Redick McKee, the Indian agent who was going through the northern part of California, meeting with the local peoples, with an idea of coming to a solution of the one-sided and bloody Indian war in California.

It's ironic that Ben Kelsey, who shot Indians like rabbits, should have had any hand in McKee's quixotic and doomed crusade for justice for the first Californians. The slaughter of the California Indians went on unabated for thirty years or more. Many, perhaps most, people deplored it; but nobody stopped it. McKee tried to establish some permanent reservations for the Indians in places where they could actually survive, including some of the most valuable real estate in California. His efforts came to nothing in the face of the immigrants' hunger for land. Rounded up and transported, enslaved and starved, the Indians saw themselves steadily destroyed. They knew it; they were helpless against it. When they fought back, as they did against Andy Kelsey, it only brought them more death.

In 1872, the Ghost Dance swept the northern tribes into a frenzy of belief: a great wind was coming that would blast the whites away, and everything would go back to what it had been before. Many Indians gathered at Clear Lake, to shelter in the caves of Mount Konocti while the terrible winds blew. But the wind never came. Despairing, they crept back to what was left of their homelands. In many areas there was a bounty on their heads, and settlers shot at any Indian they saw, and hunted them for fun. By 1910, the California Indians, a group of human cultures as rich and various as the country they lived in, were all but wiped out.[2]

The Kelseys, too, were on the wane. In 1851, Nancy bore her daughter Nancy Rose in Sonoma, and they were still in Sonoma, apparently, in 1855, when Georgia was born. A year later, Ann, who had crossed the Sierra riding on her mother's hip, was married in Santa Clara County, but by then Ben and Nancy were moving on again.

Sam was drifting too, without Lucy. She divorced him in 1855, unwilling to pack up another wagon or roll another mile; she ran her tavern for a while by herself, and then married a rich man and

---

[2]That they were not totally destroyed, but are in fact now making a comeback, politically and economically, is a testimony to their extraordinary resources, and no thanks to anybody white.

lived happily ever after. Sam was a professional gambler for a while, and also remarried. During the Civil War, he was a Knight of the White Camellia, the forerunner of the Ku Klux Klan. His support of the Confederacy was so outspoken that the merchants of San Bernardino appealed to the nearest U.S. Army post for help in defending themselves against a Sam Kelsey plot to seize the town, loot the stores, and take the proceeds off to join General Lee. The Army went looking for him, but Sam escaped.

John Charles Frémont went on to become the first Republican candidate for President of the United States. John Sutter lost everything in the Gold Rush and died a drunk. John Bidwell got immensely rich and founded Chico and married his childhood sweetheart and ran for President also. Long Bob Semple was buried alive.

Ben Kelsey built a toll bridge over the Kern River near Solitaire in 1856, which, typically, he sold almost at once. In 1859, he got 160 acres of Bounty Land[3] in Tulare County, but in that same year, his health went bad again, and he decided to head down to Texas to improve it.

The Kelseys worked hard, and made their way everywhere they went; but Ben never held onto anything very long. The only constant in his life was Nancy. Over the next several years they went from California to Arizona to Texas to Mexico and back to California, moving almost constantly. Nancy bore her last two children during this trek, William Wallus in 1859 in Arizona, and Samuel, born in 1861, maybe in Mexico. When Sam was born she was thirty-eight; she had been pregnant or nursing for more than twenty years, and for a good deal of it, she had been on the trail.

In that same year, when little Sam was a tiny baby, the family went to Texas, on another of Ben's many moneymaking schemes, this one to buy cattle and herd them back to California. While they

[3]For serving in the Mexican War. Bounty Lands were an established way of rewarding soldiers.

were camped in a dry wash in the desert, the men went out hunting turkeys. Nancy was working around her camp when she looked up and saw Comanches coming.

She loaded her gun, but quickly saw there were too many Indians for a lone woman to handle. Gathering the older children, she told them to run and hide, and with William Wallus and little Sam crawled deep into the mesquite. The Comanches swarmed into her camp, hollering and sporting their horses.

She had forgotten to hide the money they had brought to buy the cattle, and the Comanches took it. Then they found two of the children.

Margaret, who was fifteen, dodged and ducked and escaped them—later, she said she thought some at least of the Comanches were white men painted like Indians—but they caught Mary Ellen, who was only eleven. Nancy heard her screaming, and Margaret heard the blows that struck her down. When the Comanches were gone, and Nancy collected her children together again, nobody could find Mary Ellen.

Nancy searched frantically for her. The dense brush was like a maze, every way looked the same, especially as night fell. When the men came back, they widened the search, looking all through the night, until at last they found her with another band of settlers. This family had come on the little girl wandering in the desert, half out of her mind, sliced with lance wounds, and scalped. Nancy was overwhelmed; she set to nursing her horribly wounded daughter, who was never well again, mentally or physically. Ben and the other men followed the raiding Comanches for days, but never caught up with them.

They went back to California, to Fresno, perhaps, where poor Mary Ellen died in 1866. Margaret had married already by then, in the Owens River Valley in the eastern Sierra, a beautiful green river valley beneath the steep gray scarps of the mountains. Soon Ben and Nancy were living there too, in Lone Pine. Margaret had a little girl, now, named Nellie; Nancy was a grandmother.

In 1869, the Union Pacific and the Union Central Railroads connected at Promontory Point in Utah. Now anybody with a hundred dollars could board the train in Chicago and be in California within three days.

Some years later John Bidwell took the train east. "Swiftly borne along on an observation car amid cliffs and over rushing streams," he recognized Weber Canyon, and remembered what Bill Overton had said, back in 1841, when the emigrants were camped very near this place. It was Overton who had claimed that nothing had ever or would ever surprise him, even to see a steamboat plowing up the mountain stream. "It occurred to me that the reality was almost equal to Bill Overton's extravaganza, and I could but wonder what he would have said had he suddenly come upon this modern scene."[4]

In 1872 a tremendous earthquake shook and cracked and dropped the Owens Valley, and Ben discovered fear. The giant quake had broken his house in half. He sold out, over Nancy's objections; she knew they would get nothing for their property if they sold it so precipitously. But Ben, as always, made up his mind and then did it. He took his family on to Gilroy, near the southern end of San Francisco Bay, where soon Nancy was trying to make a home again.

The children were growing up, marrying, moving away. And Ben was tired. He was sixty, and worn out from sickness and constant hard work. He tried to get a pension from the government, citing his actions during the Bear Flag Revolt, but Frémont remembered Ben's tongue-lashing over the murder of Juan Berryessa and refused to sign for him. Ben was running out of resources. Where once he could have roamed the wilderness, shot an elk or a deer, and brought back meat to his family, now he had to sell his labor for a handful of cash. And Nancy still had no home of her own.

In 1875 she made a good try at getting one. In Lompoc, on the

[4]Bidwell III.

coast near Santa Barbara, she beguiled a wide-eyed young newspaper reporter with tales of her pioneer days until the bedazzled writer went off to the Lompoc Valley Company and suggested they donate a piece of land to these wonderful old pioneers, now reduced to poverty. The Company, getting Nancy Kelsey only secondhand, ignored him.

The Kelseys went south, to the land-boom community of Puente, and then to Los Angeles. A major terminus of the Southern Pacific Railroad, Los Angeles was a rowdy city of brawlers and vigilantes, cockfights, orange groves, beanfields, and grazing cattle. Ben and Nancy rented a house there, and there, in 1887, Ben died.

He was rough and wild, and he could not settle down, but he worked hard all his life, and he went, very often, where no one else had gone. His name is everywhere in California, Kelseyville on Clear Lake, the forgotten hamlet of Kelsey in El Dorado County, the Kelsey Trail, the Kelsey River, Kelsey Canyon, Kelsey Creek. With his hands he made sawmills and cabins, boots and tallow and heaps of gold, bringing forth a new country from the wilderness. Some of his faults were unforgivable, especially his treatment of the Indians. His works were indispensable. Ben, and men like him and women like Nancy, midwived California out of isolation, and set it on course to be the world leader that it is today. Whether that was a good thing or not is irrelevant. It happened, and it happened because of these people.

After he died, Nancy could have stayed where she was; or she could have gone to live with one of her children. Of course she did neither.

She was in her mid sixties, by this time, but she was still strong and hale, and she went back to the life she loved: the tough, challenging life of the pioneer. She went up to the dry wilderness country of the Cuyama, at the south end of the San Joaquin Valley, and built a homestead there.

Now, at last, she had a home of her own, even if it was only a tiny cabin. She raised chickens, planted her garden, roamed the surrounding hills on her paint horse looking for herbs and berries. The people in the area began to realize that if someone fell sick, or broke a bone, or had a baby coming, they could depend on Nancy Kelsey's patient, resourceful help, exhaustive knowledge of herbal remedy, and sense of humor.

She rode down into Cuyama, every now and then, and sold some of her eggs; she was so thin that some of the people there, particularly Addison Powell, a prominent local farmer, got worried about her health. Powell sent his son to lead a cow over to her homestead. After that, she had milk and cheese.

She was happy there, serene as only an old person can be who has seen and done it all. When an old bruise on her face[5] developed into cancer, she accepted it with her customary courage. Powell and other friends in Cuyama took her to see a doctor in Santa Maria, who told them there was nothing to be done. Nancy took this calmly. She had left her fear of death somewhere up in the Sierra, sitting her horse in the dark, her baby in her arms, and a rifle across her saddlebows. She went back into the hills, kept on with her garden, her chickens, her herbs, her help to sick and injured neighbors.

Minnie Heath, a young woman who had come to teach school in Cuyama, took to walking over the hill to talk to Nancy, three or four times a week, and to hear the old woman's stories of pioneer times. Nancy told good stories. Like the Lompoc reporter, Minnie Heath was enthralled. Sometimes Nancy embroidered a little on her tales to see the lights dancing in her listener's eyes. She was especially proud of being the first American woman to cross the Sierra, and was not above fudging a little on her dates to pad her claim.

Everybody loved her. As she grew weaker, her friend Addison Powell took her away to a house closer to town, where she could rest comfortably and die in peace. Nancy told him the story of her

---

[5]She was traveling in a stagecoach when it struck something in the road and threw her violently against the side. Her straw bonnet was crushed against the side of her face. In this complicated lesion the cancer began.

life, and he wrote it down in her own words. Looking back, she saw that she had lived a great adventure, had accepted every challenge, had tasted everything that life could offer. On August 10, 1896, content and full of years, Nancy Kelsey died, proud of who she was, and rightly so.

She crossed the continent when more than half of it was track-less wilderness. She climbed the Sierra and walked barefoot into California, carrying her baby in her arms. She saw the great valleys of California before the plows broke a single clod. She hefted pounds of gold during the Gold Rush and she starved in poverty. She shot deer and elk and saw the Bear Flag go up and down its flagpole and met at least three men who would run for President of the United States. Above all, she went wherever Ben Kelsey went, and made a life there. Great- and simple-hearted, she was an ordinary woman, and ordinary people, doing what they have to do, make the world.

SELECT BIBLIOGRAPHY

Bailyn, Bernard. *Voyagers West.* New York: Knopf, 1989.

Bancroft, H. H. *History of California.* 11 vols. San Francisco: The History Company, 1884–1890.

Blevins, Winfred. *Give Your Heart to the Hawks.* New York: Avon, 1973.

Dillon, Richard H. *Captain John Sutter: Sacramento Valley's Sainted Sinner.* Santa Cruz, Calif.: Western Tanager Press, 1989.

Egan, Ferol, and Richard Dillon. *Frémont: Pathfinder to a Restless Nation.* Reno, Nev.: University of Nevada Press, 1985.

Evans, Peter A. *The First Hundred Years: A Descriptive Bibliography of California Historical Society Publications, 1871–1971.*

Fischer, David Hacket. *Albion's Seed.* New York: Oxford University Press, 1989.

Gudde, Erin G. *Sutter's Own Story.* New York: Putnam's Sons, 1936.

Hafen, Leroy. *Broken Hand.* Denver, Colo.: Old West Publishing Company, 1931.

Hamilton, Dr. Alexander. *Gentleman's Progress.* Edited by Carl Bridenbaugh. Chapel Hill, N.C.: University of North Carolina Press, 1948.

Heath, Minnie. "The First Woman to Cross the Sierra." *The Grizzly Bear*, 1936. (This article reprints Nancy's deathbed narrative, as recorded by her Cuyama friend Addison Powell, which was originally published in *The San Francisco Examiner* just after her death in 1896.)

Holmes, Kenneth, ed. *Covered Wagon Women: Diaries and Letters.* 2 vols. Glendale, Calif.: A. H. Clark, 1983.

Ide, Simeon. *Who Conquered California?* Glorieta, N. M.: Rio Grande Press, 1967.

Jackson, Donald, and Mary Lee Spence, eds. *The Expeditions of John Charles Frémont: Travels from 1838 to 1844.* 2 vols. Urbana, Ill.: University of Illinois Press, 1970.

Levitin, Sonia. *The No-Return Trail*. New York: Atheneum, 1978.

"A Pioneer's Story." *The Lompoc Record*, August 1872.

McKittrick, Myrtle Mason. *Salvador Vallejo: The Last of the Conquistadores*. Arcata, Calif.: self-published, 1949.

———. *Vallejo: Son of California*. Portland: Bunfords & Mort, 1944.

McLaurin, Melton A. *Celia: A Slave*. Athens, Ga.: University of Georgia Press, 1991.

Nunis, Doyce. *The Bidwell-Bartleson Party: 1841 California Emigrant Adventure*. Santa Cruz, Calif.: Western Tanager Press, 1991. (This book reprints all journals and recollections of the Party, complete with notes, including the journal of Joseph Williams and the journals and letters of the Jesuit priests, as well as some sketches by one of the Fathers.)

Ruxton, George Frederick. *Life in the Far West*. Edited by Leroy Hafen. Norman, Okla.: University of Oklahoma Press, 1951.

Unruh, John D., Jr. *The Plains Across: The Overland Emigrants and the Trans-Mississippi West, 1840–60*. Urbana, Ill.: University of Illinois Press, 1979.

de Voto, Bernard. *Year of Decision*. Boston: Houghton Mifflin, 1950.

Warner, Barbara. *The Men of the California Bear Flag Revolt and Their Heritage*. Spokane, Wash: Arthur H. Clark Publishing Company for the Sonoma Valley Historical Society, 1996.

UNPUBLISHED

Kelsey, Nancy. "Her Story." (This is a corrupted samizdat version of the Addison Powell narrative, with a curious and suspicious provenance.)

———. Letter to Helen Weber, 4/11/1872. Bancroft Library, University of California at Berkeley, Oakland, California.

———. Letter to Helen Weber, 10/9/1872.

————. Letter to Helen Weber, 2/7/1873.

Fountain, Suzy Baker (Mrs. Eugene F.). Papers. Humboldt
    Rooms of the Humboldt State University Library and the
    Humboldt County Public Library, Humboldt, California.

Goldrup, Tom. "The Children of Ben and Nancy Kelsey."

Hall, Phil. "Jacob Castle."

OTHER SOURCES

The Family Archive of The Church of Jesus Christ of Latter-
    day Saints, Eureka, California.

www.edddy.media.utah.edu/medsol/UCME/b/Bartelson.html
    (article by David Bigler)

www.nanospace.com/home/marsh

www.monterey.edu/history/johncfremont.html

The
FUNNY
THING
About
NORMAN
FOREMAN